THE
UMBRELLA
LADY

V.C. Andrews® Books

**The Dollanganger
Family**
Flowers in the Attic
Petals on the Wind
If There Be Thorns
Seeds of Yesterday
Garden of Shadows
Christopher's Diary:
   Secrets of Foxworth
Christopher's Diary:
   Echoes of Dollanganger
Secret Brother
Beneath the Attic
Out of the Attic
Shadows of Foxworth

The Audrina Series
My Sweet Audrina
Whitefern

The Casteel Family
Heaven
Dark Angel
Fallen Hearts
Gates of Paradise
Web of Dreams

The Cutler Family
Dawn
Secrets of the Morning
Twilight's Child
Midnight Whispers
Darkest Hour

The Landry Family
Ruby
Pearl in the Mist
All That Glitters
Hidden Jewel
Tarnished Gold

The Logan Family
Melody
Heart Song
Unfinished Symphony
Music in the Night
Olivia

The Orphans Series
Butterfly
Crystal
Brooke
Raven
Runaways

**The Wildflowers
Series**
Misty
Star
Jade
Cat
Into the Garden

The Hudson Family
Rain
Lightning Strikes
Eye of the Storm
The End of the
   Rainbow

The Shooting Stars
Cinnamon
Ice
Rose
Honey
Falling Stars

The De Beers Family
"Dark Seed"
Willow
Wicked Forest
Twisted Roots
Into the Woods
Hidden Leaves

**The Broken Wings
Series**
Broken Wings
Midnight Flight

The Gemini Series
Celeste
Black Cat
Child of Darkness

The Shadows Series
April Shadows
Girl in the Shadows

**The Early Spring
Series**
Broken Flower
Scattered Leaves

The Secrets Series
Secrets in the Attic
Secrets in the Shadows

The Delia Series
Delia's Crossing
Delia's Heart
Delia's Gift

**The Heavenstone
Series**
The Heavenstone Secrets
Secret Whispers

The March Family
Family Storms
Cloudburst

The Kindred Series
Daughter of Darkness
Daughter of Light

The Forbidden Series
The Forbidden Sister
"The Forbidden Heart"
Roxy's Story

The Mirror Sisters
The Mirror Sisters
Broken Glass
Shattered Memories

**The House of Secrets
Series**
House of Secrets
Echoes in the Walls

The Umbrella Series
The Umbrella Lady
Out of the Rain

The Girls of Spindrift
Bittersweet Dreams
"Corliss"
"Donna"
"Mayfair"
"Spindrift"

Stand-alone Novels
Gods of Green
   Mountain
Into the Darkness
Capturing Angels
The Unwelcomed Child
Sage's Eyes
The Silhouette Girl
Whispering Hearts
Becoming My Sister

V.C. ANDREWS®

THE UMBRELLA LADY

Pocket Books

New York   London   Toronto   Sydney   New Delhi

Pocket Books
An Imprint of Simon & Schuster, Inc.
1230 Avenue of the Americas
New York, NY 10020

Following the death of Virginia Andrews, the Andrews family worked with a carefully selected writer to organize and complete Virginia Andrews's stories and to create additional novels, of which this is one, inspired by her storytelling genius.

This book is a work of fiction. Any references to historical events, real people, or real places are used fictitiously. Other names, characters, places, and events are products of the author's imagination, and any resemblance to actual events or places or persons, living or dead, is entirely coincidental.

This Pocket Books paperback edition May 2022

V.C. ANDREWS® and VIRGINIA ANDREWS® are registered trademarks of Vanda Productions, LLC

POCKET and colophon are registered trademarks of Simon & Schuster, Inc.

For information about special discounts for bulk purchases, please contact Simon & Schuster Special Sales at 1-866-506-1949 or business@simonandschuster.com.

Interior design by Erika R. Genova

Manufactured in the United States of America

10 9 8 7 6 5 4 3 2 1

ISBN 978-1-9821-5842-2
ISBN 978-1-9821-1449-7 (ebook)

THE
UMBRELLA
LADY

PROLOGUE

The dream begins and stops the same way always: Daddy starts up the stairs.

CHAPTER ONE

We had gotten off the train because we were supposed to wait for another, which Daddy said would come soon.

"I promise," he had said, which made me wince.

I remembered how much Mama hated promises. She told me that promises are only good for things people will or won't do. It's not necessary to promise it will rain or snow or the sun will come up in the morning. She said, "It's not even necessary for your mother or father to say, 'I promise if you keep doing that, you will get hurt.' In your heart you know you will, so you stop. Why promise that something that has to happen will happen? A promise is a cousin to a lie. It's just a way to get someone to stop asking for something or believe in something that very well might be untrue. Your father's an expert when it comes to that. Don't believe in his promises."

When the Umbrella Lady appeared, I was already sitting on

the bench with my new blue and white carry-on bag beside me. Daddy had bought it for me yesterday. I had been totally absorbed by the new coloring book he had bought me, but I had paused to take a rest. My wrist actually ached, I had completed so many pages.

I didn't know Daddy had gotten me a new coloring book before we had left. Because we had departed so quickly and he had so much on his mind, I imagined he had forgotten. He had kept it in his black leather briefcase with his three initials in raised bold silver on the outside, *DFA*, Derick Francis Anders. Besides saving me, it was the only other important thing he was able to rescue, because, as usual, he had left it in the entryway when he had come home that day, and all he had to do when we rushed down the stairs was scoop it up while still balancing me in his arms, avoiding the flames, and charge through the front door.

After we had stepped off the train and he had led me to the bench, he had snapped open the briefcase and taken out the new coloring book and a box of new crayons.

When he had handed them to me, he had said, "Work on this until I come back from getting a few things."

"What about all the other things we'll need, Daddy?"

After all, I thought, we had to fill a new house.

"Don't worry. I'm getting us everything essential soon after we get there."

"We'll be shopping and shopping," I had said. "And without Mama to help us get the right things."

It was more of a warning, because I knew he didn't like shopping. He was always hurrying Mama and me along when we went to malls, even if he was with us at the grocery store. If Mama ever forgot anything, she'd blame it on his rushing us, and they'd argue about it. Sometimes, mumbling under his breath, he'd have to go back to get what we had forgotten. I wanted to feel sorry for him, but Mama wouldn't let me. "Don't pity him," she would say. "It's his own fault."

He had pulled the collar of his dark-blue cashmere overcoat up around his neck and stared at me a moment before replying to my concern about our new home. Shadows were washing over him so that he looked like a man without a face, just like the man in my dream.

"What you'll need, you'll have. Stop worrying. You're too young to worry."

"I'm almost nine. How old do you have to be to worry?" I had asked.

Just like always when I asked a question he didn't want to answer, he had looked away, shaken his head, taken a breath, and talked about something else.

"I'm off just to get some things we absolutely must have before we get on another train. I want a newspaper, and I'll get you something fun to read, among other small things like toothpaste. I don't want to go shopping as soon as we get there. It'll be late, and you'll be tired. I'll be tired, too. Stay busy, and don't move," he had said, jabbing his right forefinger at me. Mama often called him a "tank commander" when he spoke like that. After he had left the house, she would imitate him and, with her finger jabbing, say, "You *will* do this; you *will* do that."

I thought she was joking, even though she didn't laugh.

I had watched him walk off the train platform.

He had started away slowly, pausing and almost turning back. Other departing passengers bumped into him because he had stopped so suddenly. I saw that some excused themselves, but most did not. Some looked angry at him. He didn't turn to look back at me. He made sure his collar was up and continued, picking up his pace until he was close to running, weaving in and out around other people. He went around the platform corner and disappeared.

Daddy had looked so frantic and confused when we had left in the morning. He had still looked that way when we had stepped off the train. He had been gazing everywhere as if he was expecting to see someone and had forgotten to take my hand. I had hesitated on the last step, and he had turned around to help me off as if he had just remembered I was with him. The last step was high up, and I was small for my age.

During our train ride here, he had sat with his eyes squeezed closed, not like someone sleeping but more like someone who didn't want to see where he was going or like someone expecting to feel a pain. I often did that with my eyelids when I didn't want to see something, especially in our house. I hoped that when I opened them again, what I didn't want to see would be gone. Sometimes it was, but more often than not, it wasn't.

"Temporary blindness cures nothing," Mama had said when she saw me doing it once. Mama could stop herself from seeing without closing her eyes. At least, Daddy said so.

After a while, I had fallen asleep on the train and hadn't woken until I felt it coming to a stop at this station. Daddy still had his eyes closed. The fire in our house and Mama's funeral seemed like a long, bad, never-ending dream, and dreams could make you very tired. Many times during the past days, I had closed my eyes and wished and wished it had all just been in my imagination, but what I saw and heard when I opened them reminded me it was real and it wouldn't go away. No matter where we were, I couldn't get the smell of smoke out of my nose. I thought Daddy's plan for us to run as far as we could from all that was a good idea.

For a little while after he had left me at the bench, I simply sat there and stared at the corner of the train station to see if he would suddenly reappear and come rushing back to me. I had no idea how long he would be gone. He didn't say. Thinking about time and how much had passed was like watching an icicle melting off a corner of our roof. Staring at it too long would make me nauseous, because after a while I could feel the drips falling into my stomach.

When he hadn't reappeared quickly, I opened my new coloring book and then opened the box of crayons. I always liked to inhale the scent of them. Once, I mentioned that to my mother. I said, "They smell good enough to eat," and she said, "Chew up a coloring book first."

She didn't smile. She simply said it and walked away. This was when she started to say things like "Falling is a wonderful feeling. For a few seconds, nothing holds you or traps you. The higher up you are when you fall, the longer the wonderful feeling lasts."

Everything she had said recently would make me think and think until I had packed her words of cloudy thoughts into an imaginary trunk decorated with wooden forget-me-nots. Sometimes they slipped out and fluttered around me like confused butterflies.

I dove into my coloring with the same enthusiasm my mother had when she washed the kitchen floor, even though she had washed it only an hour earlier and no one had walked on it. But coloring was never a chore or just a way to pass time for me. It was part of my art class she conducted. Mama said I had artistic talent. It was always fascinating to bring something more to life. From the moment I could hold a crayon until now, I was very good at keeping within the lines and choosing interesting or just proper colors for the object I was coloring. I never painted black canaries or yellow crows or purple monkeys. My project before the tragedy was to create my own coloring book. Mama had actually suggested it.

At one point while I was sitting at the station, I looked up and realized that while I had been coloring, many people had walked past me in both directions, and although I had barely noticed, a few trains had gone by, some stopping and then going. I wasn't worried about that. None of them could be the right one, because Daddy hadn't returned yet, and he knew the train schedules. He had them in the top pocket of his coat.

However, I also became aware that it had grown colder, and the light-blue cotton jacket I was wearing was not very warm. Daddy should have bought me a heavier coat before we left. Mama would have insisted, but he was in too much of a rush, and it wasn't as cold that day when we did what he called "survival shopping." I really didn't know what that meant. I mean, I knew what the word *survival* meant, but how did you shop for it?

Of course, he'd had to buy me something else to wear under my jacket. What I had been wearing reeked of smoke, and washing it at the motel didn't matter. I helped him pick out the two-piece top and pants set I was wearing now, another blouse, and some socks and underwear. I had something similar to this top and pants in my dresser drawer, washed, neatly folded, and ready to wear, but Daddy had said that everything we had, everything we all owned, in closets and drawers and rooms, had gone up in smoke. It was as if the Magician of Fire had said, "Poof," and it was all gone. He had told me that there was no point in ever going back to look for anything. When he had rushed into my room that night, he was already dressed and had scooped up some clothes for me to wear. I hadn't heard him dashing about my room until he had shaken me awake.

"Hold this tightly, embrace it," he had said, and put everything in my arms before he had lifted me into his. "There's no time to dress. You'll put it on over your pajamas to keep warm as soon as we're outside."

"Outside?" I knew it was the middle of the night. No wonder it seemed like a dream for so long afterward. "I can walk," I had said.

"No time. There's only one way out. We can't afford a second or a mistake."

He didn't say anything more. It had been some time since he had carried me, even on his shoulders. With me in his arms, he hurried down the stairs. There was already so much smoke. I started coughing, and he told me to keep my mouth shut tight and stop breathing. The flames were coming out of the kitchen, but they looked like they were in the living room, too. He was probably right. There wasn't much time, and I would surely have been confused about which way to go.

"Mama," I had said, looking back up the stairs. Why wasn't she right behind us?

"I couldn't wake her," he had said. "It was either carry her or carry you, and I had to get you before it was too late. The fire's been going too long."

I really hadn't understood what that meant. Why couldn't he wake her? Why would he have to carry her, anyway? Surely, she would know how to go or just follow us.

"Mama!" I had screamed, but the smoke was burning my eyes.

I couldn't think or remember much more detail about the fire while we were fleeing. The flames had looked overwhelming, and there was so much smoke that I had to bury my face against my father's chest. All that would come later, but as soon as we had shot through the front door, I wondered if Mama was already outside. Maybe she had told Daddy to get me and then left, confident he would.

When we had rushed from the house, he had brought me to the street before he set me and his briefcase down. I had looked everywhere but didn't see her. People on our street were coming out of their houses, and a fire engine could be heard rushing toward us with police cars ahead of and behind it.

"Get your clothes on," Daddy had said, and I had started to dress. I remembered being hypnotized by the flames leaping out of the windows and now the front door. I hadn't even felt cold. I knew which windows were in Mama and Daddy's bedroom. I had heard the glass explode and seen the curtains turning into blazing shapes dancing gleefully.

"Mama," I had said again. "Where's Mama? Why didn't she wake up?"

He had put his hand on my shoulder. "Don't think about anything but tomorrow."

How could I think about tomorrow? What about Mama? I had wondered, and turned around looking for her. There wasn't a tomorrow without Mama. Someone out here must have been helping her, I thought.

Daddy had stared at the fire, the flames lighting his face, making his eyes look like blue stars. Then he had started to button his shirt calmly as people rushed in around us. Everyone had stepped back away from us when the fire engine arrived. They seemed more frightened of us than they were of the fire. No one spoke to us or asked questions.

I had turned to press my face against my father. I didn't want to look at our house on fire, my room in flames, and think about Mama still sleeping inside.

He had put his hand on my shoulder again.

I was sure I had heard him whisper, "Tomorrow," but I think he was talking more to himself. Later, I had to go with him to a police station to answer questions about the fire and especially about Mama. I was so tired that I kept falling asleep, even when someone was talking to me. I didn't want to think about Mama sleeping in the fire, much less talk about her, anyway. Everyone had been nice about it. No one had wanted to speak loudly in front of me, but I heard a policeman say something about the gas stove being left on. "These older houses have no sprinkler systems," he had added. The house had been burned to the ground. There was nothing retrievable. Raking through the ashes had produced nothing, not even any of Mama's or Daddy's jewelry in any decent condition, since they weren't kept in a safe. Nothing was worth the effort, I heard Daddy say. It was going to be easier to bulldoze it all away and put the land up for sale.

Later, while Daddy was talking in an office, I had sat with

a young woman who had short black hair and dimples in both her cheeks. She looked like she was going to start crying but sandwiched my hand in hers and kept telling me I'd be all right. I hadn't cried then and wasn't crying now. Someone had told my father in a hallway that I was still in shock and would need more tender loving care.

"Don't we all," I had heard my father say and then promise he would take care of me. Right now, that seemed a long time ago; it was like looking back through a tunnel and hoping you don't see what was at the start of your journey through the darkness.

After coloring an elephant dark gray, I looked up and down the train platform, but I still didn't see him. I wondered if I should go look for him or stay where I was, because if he returned and I wasn't here, he might go off looking for me, and we'd never find each other. How would I even know the right direction to take once I went around the corner, anyway? The sign on the station read "Hurley," but I had no idea where we were. I could barely see past the lighted area, and to my right there were trees and no houses, and to my left it was the same.

These trees had lost most of their leaves, just like the trees back home. Trees without leaves always looked sad to me. "Leaves fall like crisp tears until the trees are cried naked," Mama once said. "That's why they call autumn the fall. They're not friendly."

We were talking about nature. It was part of my home-schooling.

I didn't understand how trees without eyes could cry and not be friendly, but I knew that the younger trees had sharp branches that could catch on your clothes. I had been scratched a few times running through woods full of leafless trees in our backyard. Leaves were softer, especially when they were green, and made the branches behave. It didn't surprise my mother when I asked her if trees were unfriendly because they were angry that they had lost their leaves.

"You're so poetic for someone your age," she said. "Actually, children are more poetic than adults. Their imaginations aren't cluttered with reality."

After thinking a moment more, she added, "Yes, yes, I believe trees can be angry, and rightly so."

"People are unhappy when they lose their hair," I said. I thought she might think that clever and tell me how brilliant I was. She used to when I said something she thought was characteristic of someone years older than I was, sometimes adding a kiss on my cheek. Her kisses were my gold stars for excellence.

But to me, what I thought and said was simple. I had seen bald men in television commercials looking grouchy until something was shown to them that would help them grow back their hair. That made me think of the trees and the leaves. Maybe whatever it was could be sprayed on the branches and speed up the return of leaves.

My father was losing his hair. He never stopped complaining

about it, because he said it was premature and came from stress. I had no idea what all that meant, but I told him, "It'll grow back in the spring. With the leaves."

Mama laughed, but back then, I didn't mean it to be funny. I thought it might happen.

He didn't think it was funny, either. He looked at me without smiling and then turned to my mother and said, "She's your daughter. You had most to do with making her this way. You handle it."

I looked at my mother. What was there to handle? And what did he mean by "making her this way"? What way was I?

Memories like that flowed through my mind as I sat there waiting and coloring. Occasionally, I would look up in antici- pation of him coming back around the corner, and although I was still quite tempted to go look for him, I didn't. Later, the Umbrella Lady would tell me that not rushing off to find my father was very good logic for an eight-year-old girl.

"Your mother was a good teacher," she would say. "Good teachers don't simply fill their students with facts; they teach them how to think correctly."

My mother insisted on homeschooling me even though my father had thought I belonged with other children my age. He said he was even willing to spend the money on a private school. But Mama, who had her teaching certificate and until the time I was born had worked as a substitute grade-school teacher often, believed she could prepare me better for what was to come. She also claimed that teaching me gave her something important to do.

"I'm not saying you can't do it, Lindsey," he told her. "I'm saying she needs to be with other children her age, although sometimes you act as if you are one of them."

She ignored him, which made him angrier.

His face reddened. "You're keeping her here to amuse you because you won't return phone calls from our friends and do something with other wives. You think you're punishing me, but you're punishing us all."

I didn't know what that meant, but after a while, he stopped arguing with her about it. But because of what I had seen on television and what I heard other children my age say to each other, I knew they had made friends in school and went to birthday parties and went to friends' houses to play or had friends come to theirs. I had no friends. I never had anyone to my birthday party. I wished Mama had agreed with Daddy about it.

Only a week or so before the fire, Mama had stopped to look at me while I was sitting on the floor watching a television show that had children my age doing things together. I could feel her gazing at me and turned to her, my eyes surely full of question marks. It wasn't unusual to see her stop and stare at me and then move on when I looked back at her, wondering if I had made a mistake, like putting on two different socks, something I had often done because I was in a rush to get dressed. What was it now? What had I done wrong?

"You'll have friends, too, when you go to school. It won't be that much longer now. Don't be sad."

Was I sad? Why didn't I realize I was sad? Didn't sad people cry? I wondered. I couldn't remember when I had cried last. Even Daddy had thought about that. He had looked at me at dinner one night and said, "This kid never whines." He had said it as if that was a terrible thing. I had looked at my mother, who did seem to think hard about it for a moment and then nodded and said, "She's precocious. She already realizes the futility."

I didn't know what any of that meant, but I could see it wasn't an answer Daddy liked. He had put his head down and eaten faster, after which he abruptly rose and left us.

I had turned back to the television show. I didn't agree or deny I was sad. I really wasn't sure. She had left the room. I had listened to her going up the stairs with those very slow, ponderous footsteps, sounding as if she was climbing up forever. She might go into her bedroom, sit on the bed, and just stare at the wall as if it was a television screen. Soon after, her eyes, like melting icicles, would drip tears down her cheeks.

Daddy had been right. She had no friends, either. No one invited her to a birthday party. Maybe she should return to teaching in a public school, I had thought. The memory of all that floated through my mind like a passing bruised cloud dragging in a storm. Just like leafless trees, the sky could look angry, too. Maybe the clouds were mad at the wind for pushing them roughly about. Sometimes I thought we were surrounded by unhappiness, and if we left the door or window open, it would spill in.

A chill brought me back to today and this train station.

I had no idea how much time had passed while I was sitting on the bench and coloring. I didn't have a watch, and there was no clock on the platform. The station looked small and old, more like one in some cowboy movie I had seen watching television with Daddy. The wood of its walls was a fading gray, and there weren't any windows on the side where I sat, just some old posters, practically unreadable, some lopsided, and a rusty-looking wheelbarrow overturned. I could see spiderwebs in it.

Now that I was paying more attention to where I was, I realized that darkness had crept in everywhere and challenged the rim of illumination the station platform lights had created. It looked like shadows were constantly trying to invade the lit space but were bouncing off. I put my nearly finished coloring book inside my closed coat, pulled up and embraced my legs, and rocked because it seemed to keep me warmer. It was so quiet that I could hear the hum of the lights above the platform.

I was a little tired again, so I shut my eyes and tried to think of nice things and nice times, like when Daddy and I flew a kite in our backyard and when Mama could still pluck laughter out of the air like someone picking the blueberries that grew on bushes in the woods behind our house. I could feel my face soften into a smile from the memories and lowered my head to my knees.

That was when I heard someone say, "My, my, my. Look at what I've found here."

When I opened my eyes, there she was, standing right in front of me, a lady holding a closed black umbrella with a silver handle. I didn't know from where she had come. No train had pulled in. She was suddenly there, as if she had taken shape from a shadow.

"Are you waiting for a train, missy?" she asked.

There were little brown dots over the crests of the Umbrella Lady's cheeks and on both sides of her chin. They weren't freckles. They looked like someone with a sharply pointed brown Magic Marker had dabbed her face when she was asleep and she couldn't wash it off. There was even a very small one at the tip of her nose.

Her eyes reminded me of large purple-blue marbles like the ones in a flowerpot Mama had kept on a shelf by the dining-room window. The marbles went around the inside rim. There hadn't been a flower in it for a long time. Daddy had called it "a potted gravesite" and said, "It's just dirt, not very attractive, even with those silly marbles you've placed in it so carefully. What's the point of a pot of decorated dirt, Lindsey?"

Mama had seemed not to notice or care. Maybe she was always expecting a new flower would just appear, because she would often pause to look at it. She did that so often that I grew into the habit of looking at it first thing in the morning, too, hoping the flower would be there.

"Yes, I am waiting for a train," I said now. "Thank you for asking. I'm waiting for my father to return first, and then we'll board."

I did that quite perfectly, I thought. *I'm a little lady.* Mama would flash one of her recently infrequent smiles if she had heard me. Part of homeschooling was something she called social graces. She would show me how to walk and sit and greet people. If I did it right, she'd clap and hug me. I knew I wouldn't get that from a teacher in public or even private school.

Lately, however, whenever she had smiled, she looked like she had just risen and was surprised it was daytime, even if she had been up for hours and hours. And then her smile would float off and evaporate. She would return to what Daddy had called "her face drenched in sleepwalking." She had cut back on my homeschooling, too. Sometimes it barely lasted an hour before she would get that far-off look in her eyes. I had to do a lot more to amuse myself.

The Umbrella Lady glanced behind her and then down toward the other end of the station platform before she looked longer and with more interest at me. She was tall, with shoulders that seemed as wide as Daddy's. In the dim light, her face and neck were yellowish white.

"Where did he go? The station is closed."

She sounded angry, and I wondered if she was some sort of train-station clerk. She wasn't wearing any sort of uniform, nor did she have a badge. The hem of her gray dress stuck out from under her heavy wool black coat. Her black shoes had thick, wide heels, and she had black socks that went up under her skirt.

"I don't know exactly," I said. "He wanted to buy us things we need right now."

"What things?"

I shrugged. I didn't want to list anything. "Things. We don't have very much with us. I know he wanted a newspaper, and he was getting me some books."

She started to smile but abruptly stopped and looked quite upset.

"When is he supposed to come for you? There are no more trains tonight. And why wouldn't he take you to buy things, if that's what he's doing?" She asked her questions with her head tilted a little, as if she was testing me to see how I would answer, if I knew the answer.

"I don't know," I said. I had begun to wonder that myself. Mama would never, ever leave me alone like this, and she would surely be very angry at him for doing so now. But I couldn't tell her. I couldn't tell her anything, ever again, and I certainly wasn't going to tell the Umbrella Lady.

"Did he say anything else?" she asked. "Well?" She sounded like someone who had run out of patience and would soon be stamping her feet.

I looked again for him. I didn't want to say anything that would get him in trouble. Maybe this lady really was some sort of policewoman in a disguise. I recalled Daddy accusing Mama of being one when she had confronted him with something on our credit-card bill, but I had no idea what it was or why she was so angry.

"My father said, 'Work on this until I come back,'" I said, and took out my coloring book to show her. Maybe that would stop her from asking all these questions, I thought.

She plucked it out of my fingers and looked at it, turning it around to look at the back and then the front again.

"Is this brand-new?" She brought it to her face and closed her eyes. "It smells brand-new and still has the sticker that tells its price on the cover." She looked very suspicious.

Did she think Daddy had stolen it?

"Yes. He bought it for me today or yesterday, and a new box of crayons, but he didn't give them to me until we were here and I was sitting on this bench."

"Why didn't he give them to you on the train?" she asked. She looked even more upset now. "You'd think he'd know enough to do that. For children, it's boring just sitting on a train. Well?" she followed again when I didn't answer instantly. She scowled and looked quite disapproving.

I shrugged. It wasn't a mystery and certainly nothing to get as upset over as she was. "He forgot and fell asleep. Then I fell asleep, too. He wouldn't wake me up just to give them to me."

She paused, her scowl slowly disappearing. Then she took a deep breath that lifted her bosom up against her coat. She tilted her head back, as if she wanted to look down at me from a great height.

"Sleep is the best way to travel," she said, nodding. "Most children will if they have to travel long."

She started to smile again but stopped.

"But giving you things to do is just as good. He should know that. Even my father knew that, and he wasn't fond of children. But fathers and mothers were children once, too. They should remember all that when they have children of their own. Some people turn their childhood memories off like a faucet because they can't stand remembering, and some people should shut them off because they never stop babbling about how much better things were then. They can rupture your ears."

She paused and looked harder at me.

"Which one are you? Someone who can't stop remembering or someone who should?"

I shrugged. I didn't want to tell her I had memories I wanted to stuff in a hole in the ground. It would surely make me cry, and she would have many more questions.

"I don't know. I turn my faucet off and on, but I'm too young to remember much yet."

"Very clever," she said, nodding. "You know how to avoid an answer, and yet you are very honest. I like a little girl who is honest and clever at the same time."

She flipped through the coloring book and continued nodding, with a look that was now full of approval and delighted surprise.

"The colors you chose are perfect for each and every thing you've colored in, and not a color out of the lines. It's all very good," she said. "If I were going to give it a grade, I'd give it an A plus, plus."

She paused and squinted at me.

"It's almost all done. You must have been working on it carefully for hours and hours. Has it been hours?" she asked suspiciously.

"I think so," I said. "I don't have a watch."

"Oh, you don't need a watch to know you've been here long. We all have a built-in tick-tock. You know just when it's morning. You know just when you're hungry, and you know just when you're tired enough to go to sleep. What else would a little girl like you need to know?"

"I need to know when my father will return," I said. I almost added, *thank you very much*, but didn't because it would surely make her feel foolish.

She smiled. I guess I was making her happy, and she looked like someone who needed to be happier. Maybe that was why she stopped to talk to me. She couldn't be pleased about her graying light-brown hair. I thought she had it cut too short. It was so thin that I could see the little bumps on her scalp because of how the station-platform lights shone on and behind her head.

"You're such a smart little girl. Some parents can't handle their children when they are so smart. They ask too many questions. For them, it's like too much rain. You can't ask for no rain, can you? That's a drought, and nothing will grow, just like if children don't ask questions, they won't grow."

I didn't know what to say. She sounded right, but I had never thought of questions that way, and for a moment I worried that I hadn't asked enough and I wouldn't grow. I looked anxiously at her, expecting her to tell me more. She seemed very wise.

"Did your parents ever tell you to stop asking questions?"

"No," I said quickly. I almost added, *but often they would act like I hadn't asked anything*.

"I see," she said.

"Are you waiting for a train, too?" I asked. Maybe she was hoping she could ride with Daddy and me.

"What?" She smiled softly. "Is that what you think? I told you there are no more trains tonight."

I shrugged. "Maybe you're waiting for someone who's coming on a train. Are you?"

"There are no trains leaving, and there are no trains coming tonight. But you are inquisitive. See? You are full of questions. That's good. You're bound to grow up fast," she said, and then paused. "Maybe too fast. That kind of little girl gets into big trouble if she is not guided correctly."

I didn't know what she meant. How do you grow up too fast? And how could she say there would be no more trains? Daddy told me we were getting off to get on another one. *She just doesn't know*, I thought. Daddy had the train schedule in his pocket, didn't he?

She handed my coloring book back to me and stood straighter, pulling her shoulders back but keeping both palms down on the handle of her umbrella. She looked left and right again. We were still alone on the train platform, and the only thing I heard was a car horn far off to my right, sounding mournful and sad, like a lost goose. We often heard them over the lake near our house.

"There's probably nothing sadder in the world than a bird losing its sense of direction," Mama once told me when we were both sitting outside and listening. "A panicked bird will fly in circles until it dies."

We couldn't see the birds, so I wondered how she knew any had lost their sense of direction. I sort of felt like that right now. I knew Mama had felt like that often.

There wasn't anything nice about where I was right now. There was nothing pretty to look at or interesting to hear. The bench was feeling hard and uncomfortable, and I was tired of talking. I didn't like what I smelled around me, either. It made my stomach growl. I thought the Umbrella Lady would realize all that and would leave if she wasn't waiting for someone and there was no train for her to catch, but she leaned toward me, both her hands still on the handle of her umbrella, looking like someone I had seen on television who was about to do a dance with an umbrella.

With her face so close, I could see tiny pimples under both her eyes, which were really that purple-gray color like some of the flowerpot marbles. Her eyebrows had little gray strands in them, too. I sat back a little more, because she was close enough to kiss me. Also, it took her longer than it would take most people to speak again. She was staring hard at me and thinking too much, I thought. Maybe I was thinking too much. Daddy accused Mama of that all the time.

"The long silences in this house are unhealthy," he had told her. He had looked at me and then added, "The kid hardly speaks. I wonder why?"

When Daddy spoke to Mama like that, the silences only got longer and deeper.

"What's your name?" the Umbrella Lady asked finally, like someone who just remembered it was an important question to ask.

"Saffron," I said.

She nodded and said, "Good," as if that was the right name. Most people when they heard my name would smile and say, "How unusual, but fitting." They were thinking about the color of my hair.

"Saffron Faith Anders," I said.

"Well, you are the first Saffron I have ever met. Do you like your name?"

No one had ever asked me that. The Umbrella Lady asked as if she could change it if I wanted it changed.

"Yes," I said.

"Well, Saffron Faith Anders, I think you should come home with me. You probably haven't eaten, and you are probably a little cold. Maybe more than a little, huh?" She pinched the collar of her coat closer together to emphasize how cold it was. "Brrr," she said, shaking her head. "Yes, you'll come with me, okay?"

"But if I go with you, Daddy won't know where I am," I said, a little annoyed that I had to tell her something any grown-up would know.

She thought a moment and then raised her right hand, her forefinger up. She shoved it into her dark-blue overcoat pocket and came out with a pencil that looked like it had been sharpened down to the size of a thumb. There was some fuzz around it that had come out on her fingers. She blew it off like someone blowing out birthday candles.

"We'll need something to write on," she said, taking back my coloring book. She opened it and found some blank space, which she carefully tore out.

"Don't worry. I'm not ruining any of the pictures. I'm leaving your name, my address, and my phone number for him to find," she said as she wrote on the paper. "I think it would be a good idea to put this under the corner of the coloring book so the coloring book keeps it from blowing off the bench when we leave, because there is quite a breeze, and a breeze can become wind. Okay?"

"I don't know. He bought it for me so I would have something fun to do."

"When he comes for you, he'll bring the coloring book, won't he? And then you can finish it when you continue on to wherever you're going with him," she said rapidly, like someone who had lost all her patience. Mama could get that way, and the words would burst out of her mouth in an explosion that would hurt my ears. Daddy had a way of shutting his off on the inside. At least, Mama said he did.

I thought about what the Umbrella Lady was saying. She obviously wanted me to think hard about it. It was like one of those logical things Mama told me she wished wasn't true. I wished this wasn't true, but it was cold, and I was hungry.

"Well?"

"I suppose so," I said.

She smiled. Her face could change so quickly, including the shapes of her eyes and her chin, as quickly as someone taking off one mask and putting on another.

"You really are a smart little girl. I just knew the moment I set eyes on you that you would be," she added, and picked up my bag so I would stand up. I started to, but it was as if Mama had her hand on my head pushing me down, so I stopped.

"Oh, you mustn't be afraid of coming with me, Saffron. I'm as full of good things as a jar of mixed jelly beans."

She smeared her friendly smile over her face again. If I had a grandmother like the ones I saw on television, she probably would look like the Umbrella Lady looked right now, I thought. I shouldn't be afraid. Maybe she was someone's grandmother. Maybe her granddaughter or grandson was waiting for her at home and she wanted me to meet her or him.

Out of the corner of my eye, I saw a rat scamper across the train platform and disappear off the far corner. Just as the Umbrella Lady had predicted, a stronger breeze lifted the strands of hair off her forehead, where the wrinkles deepened and spread to her temples, making it look like her face was cracking.

My stomach churned, not only from the ugly odors but probably because I hadn't eaten for some time. Mama used to say, "Someone inside is complaining that she's starving." Then she would laugh, and we'd have lunch. The Umbrella Lady would probably say, "There. Your clock has told you."

When I looked up, I realized that because of the station lights, I couldn't see any stars. Stars were always comforting. With the darkness on both sides and across the tracks, it felt as if I had slid into a large black box. I shivered. Where was Daddy? I wondered. Why was he taking so long? Why didn't he think I'd be cold and hungry? I didn't want to stay here and wait any longer, and her idea was logical and seemed okay. Even though I wished I could, there was no way I could say no.

I rose again, and she put the note and the coloring book on the bench carefully, just the way she had said she would.

"There. He's sure to find it. He'll look and find it because this is where he left you, right?"

I nodded. She took my hand, and we started away. Her palm felt rough, and her fingers were thin and long like wires clamped tightly around my hand. When we stepped away from the station lights, I finally could see some stars in between gray-black clouds that puffed up proudly as they floated over them. She looked up, too.

"I always carry an umbrella," she said. "Just in case. Weather commentators don't get it right too often. Despite their science, I call them fortune-tellers. And besides, more things can fall out of the sky than just rain, snow, and hail. We just don't see them, but they're falling all over us. Believe me."

I had no idea what that meant. I turned and looked back when we reached the corner of the platform. What if Daddy was angry at me for leaving? I remembered how his face could get so ugly and scary that I thought he could wear it on Halloween.

I stopped walking.

"Now, now," she said. "You don't want to change your mind, do you? You can't sit in the cold much longer without getting sick, and how would your father like that? He'd blame himself, and everyone would be upset. That's not a way to travel, now, is it, sniffling and coughing?"

I shook my head, but I looked back again.

The coloring book would be the last thing he had given me, and I wouldn't have it.

CHAPTER TWO

When you're older, time seems so much more important. At home, I would go almost all day without looking at a clock or caring what time it was. Mama would tell me when I had to do my schoolwork and when I could play. It was only lately that even she would forget or not care what time it was. She didn't check my schoolwork and often didn't give me anything new to do. My father didn't know because he was still angry about her not sending me to public or private school.

"You'll be responsible for what happens," he had told her.

It became just like the Umbrella Lady later described. My stomach would tell me I was hungry, and I would go looking for lunch. Mama might be just sitting in the old maple wood rocking chair with the cushioned seat and staring at the picture in the ruby wood frame over the fieldstone fireplace, a picture of a sailboat heading for the horizon. A woman was seated, and a man was standing and pulling on a rope running up the mast. I used to think it was heading toward the edge of the world, and if the sailboat continued, it would fall over and tumble down into nothingness. Maybe Mama had given me that idea when she said, "I hope he gets it turned around before it's too late."

Whenever she saw me standing there, she would realize it was lunchtime and get up. More and more, she forgot and I had to remind her.

Anyway, I rarely thought about the actual time. However, I always believed most adults looked at a clock at least a dozen times, if not more, every day. They certainly looked at their watches that much. Daddy usually did, so I thought everyone did, except Mama.

She had a watch in a jewelry case. It was a watch that Daddy had bought her when they first were married. It was gold, not with a round face but shaped more like a triangle. It had a tiny diamond next to each number. On the back was inscribed *Love, D.* There was a tiny scratch next to his initial. I always wondered if it had been there when he had first given it to her. He had said it was custom-made for her, but one day she decided that she didn't like anything on her wrist or her fingers. She wouldn't even wear her wedding ring anymore, and she never wore a bracelet or a necklace. I remembered Daddy complaining about that, asking her why she let him buy her all those beautiful things if she wasn't going to wear them, and her saying, "I'm not a Christmas tree. Stop trying to decorate me. It won't change anything."

I had waited for him to say something else, say at least that he knew she wasn't a Christmas tree, and what was supposed to be changed? He had merely shaken his head and walked away with his shoulders slumped. Then he had stopped, turned around, nodded at me, and said, "When she finally goes to school, give her the watch."

Before Mama could say anything, he had added, "Time is what staples us to reality, Lindsey. Otherwise, we're like astronauts untethered in outer space." He had waited a moment and then went "Ah," waved his hand as if he was chasing a fly away, and walked on to his home office to, as Mama said, dive into and swim in his computer to either get ahead on or finish his work at the insurance company.

I was thinking about time while we were walking to the Umbrella Lady's house, because the streets were so quiet. It had to be very, very late, or as Daddy might tell Mama when he realized she wasn't getting me ready for bed, "It's a day past her bedtime."

No children were playing outside, and there were no cars going up and down. There were no stores on this street. We had passed a few on the way from the train station, one that was by a gas station, so I stopped to see if Daddy was in there.

"Wait. Daddy," I had said, but I didn't see him.

"Satisfied?" the Umbrella Lady said when it was clear there

weren't even any other customers in there. She tugged me by my hand.

We continued until we turned on a street with more houses and no stores. The lights I could see through some windows were dim, if they were lit at all. Some looked lighted only with candles, like when the electricity was broken. It seemed like everyone was asleep. I wished now that Daddy had saved Mama's watch from the fire. He could have given it to me before we had left for the train. If I had a watch, I would have known that it was much later than I had imagined it to be while I was sitting at the station. Now it was probably so late that even parents had put themselves to bed.

I couldn't tell if the Umbrella Lady wore a watch, because her thick black wool coat sleeves reached her hands. The sleeves looked too long for her. Maybe she had shrunk since she had bought this coat. Mama told me people could shrink, but mostly inside. I didn't understand and I had stopped asking Daddy about the strange things Mama often said, because he would simply shake his head or close his eyes and put his hand on his throat as if he was going to choke himself.

If I had seen the time and added up all the hours that had passed after Daddy had left me, I would have been more worried, and probably, I would have cried out my concern immediately to someone who was rushing to a train or coming off one before the Umbrella Lady had approached me. Seeing how late it was now, I was tempted to pull my hand free of the Umbrella Lady's hand and run all the way back to the bench on the train-station platform.

I nearly did, but she said she was going to make us a pizza, and afterward we would have ice cream. I stopped thinking about how late it was and how much past my bedtime. She said I could choose vanilla or chocolate. I thought only about that and wondered if I could ask for a little of both. Daddy did that once, and Mama accused him of not being able to make a decision.

"I did make a decision," he had said. "I decided to choose both."

He had looked at me and smiled. She had left the kitchen without having any dessert.

"She leaps on me every chance she gets," Daddy had said. I didn't think he was talking to me. He had looked like he was talking to himself, just like Mama often did. "There is no forgiveness in that woman. Every day she drives in another nail."

"In where, Daddy?" I had asked him, and he had looked at me, surprised, as if I had heard his thoughts and not his words. He had simply shaken his head and eaten more ice cream, both flavors. I had, too.

"I think you're going to be very happy soon," the Umbrella Lady said now. "One thing's for sure, you'll be happier than you were back at the train station. Maybe happier than back where you lived, too," she added. "There's my house," she said.

It was a real gingerbread house, orange-brown with a white

roof. The house was on the end of a street like our house was. I knew it was called a cul-de-sac, which meant the street didn't go anywhere, and at the end it circled. People who didn't pay attention to the sign that read *No Through Street* would have to turn around in front of our house to get out. Mama said she hated all that traffic. That was why she had insisted on keeping the curtains closed in the front windows, but Daddy had said it made our house more valuable for us to be on a cul-de-sac, and closing the curtains all day made it dreary.

"It's not 'all that traffic,' either, Lindsey. You exaggerate everything."

"Not everything," she had replied. "Some things exaggerate themselves."

He had shaken his head, glanced at me, and walked away.

Our house was a two-story house, and so was the Umbrella Lady's, but ours was bigger. Hers had more land around it, so the nearest house was what Daddy called "too far away to hear an elephant scream." Mama didn't care about having neighbors. She said they asked too many questions and lived to make senseless chitchat. If I was with her and we saw someone come out of his or her house, she would rush us over the pebble-stone sidewalk that led to our front door, telling me not to look back at him or her.

"You'll turn into stone," she would say. I had no idea what that meant, but I would walk as fast as she did over the sidewalk.

There was a short but wide walkway of silvery square stones

that looked more like metal plates in front of the Umbrella Lady's house. They went from the gate to the three cement front steps. Bushes almost as tall as me were on both sides. The patches of lawn had grass the color of straw. Her porch went only a few feet to the right or left of the front door, and it had nothing on it, not even a chair. One of the spindles under the railing was split. The lights were on in the house, so I wondered if my suspicions back at the train station were right. Maybe there was someone else living with her, someone who was waiting for her to come home and would be surprised she was bringing me, like that grandchild I had imagined, actually hoped, was there.

"There's no one else but me," she said, as if she really could hear my thoughts. "I'm a widow. Do you know what a widow is?"

Before I could answer, she said, "Widows are women who were married but whose husbands have gone on to heaven first to get everything prepared for them. At least," she said, leaning toward me a little, "you *hope* they went to heaven."

She laughed, and then she opened the gate and led me to the steps. I looked behind and down the dark street to see if Daddy might be hurrying after us after he had read her note, but there was no one there. Shadows looked thicker and wider, because some of the houses I had seen dimly lit had no lights on at all now. Her hand tightened a little more around mine, and I looked up at her, surprised. It was as if she was afraid I would run off.

"You must watch your step," she said, shaking my arm for emphasis. "You must look where you're going. Most accidents happen at home. Did you know that? People fall when they don't pay attention or they are thinking too many things at once. People are careless mostly at home. That's how most fires happen. Someone might smoke in bed or leave the gas on in the kitchen stove."

I felt my heart begin to beat faster.

Who had told her what Daddy said Mama had done?

She smiled. "You won't have any accidents here. Don't worry," she said, softening her grip. "I'll make sure of that. I'll be like your guardian angel. Who else but a guardian angel would have rescued you from a closed train station on a cold, dark night when who knows what was scampering about you?"

She paused, put down my bag, and opened her door. She stepped back to urge me in. The short entryway had a full-length oval mirror in a maple wood frame on one side and a maple wood coatrack on the other. There was a bench made from the same wood beneath it with a pair of shoes and a pair of furry boots on it. The floor looked like it was the same stone as the walkway.

"Let's take off our coats," she said, and helped me take off mine. She hung it on the rack and then took off hers. She didn't have a watch. Her dress had long sleeves buttoned at the wrist. "We take off our shoes, too," she said, "and leave them under this bench when we come in. Did you have to do that at home? It keeps your house cleaner."

I shook my head. I didn't want to tell her how clean Mama kept our house, probably cleaner than hers, even though we didn't take off our shoes. She removed her black shoes and then sat me on the bench so she could slip off my shoes.

"Don't worry. Your feet won't be cold. I left the heat on seventy-five so it would be warm and cozy when I returned," she said. "Take your bag. We can't leave it in the entry." I wasn't going to part with it anyway, but what she said reminded me of Daddy leaving his briefcase in our entryway.

I picked it up, and she put her hand on my back and directed me to the kitchen, which was on the right.

She had me sit at a small wood table that had four chairs of the same wood as in the entryway. Her floor was light brown like the tile floor in our kitchen. Everything else about her kitchen looked older. The paint was chipped, peeling, and scratched on the white cabinets. The counters were darker stone than the floor and cluttered with canisters, old newspapers whose paper had turned yellow, pill bottles, and a few different shakers, more than salt and pepper and sugar. She had a window over her single sink. It looked dirty on the outside, and I could see where it needed to be cleaned around the edges of the windowpane. Mama would use a cotton swab. Daddy had said she didn't just clean dirt but pounced on it.

"Just sit here and watch me work on our pizza," the Umbrella Lady said. "I have them in the freezer, but I put lots of extra good things on them before I bake them. Any little girl who eats my food will grow quickly, like a magic tree, even if she doesn't ask questions."

She laughed at what she had said as if someone else had said it.

I sat and pulled my carry-on bag closer to me. Although there was nothing cooking or baking in her kitchen, it smelled like there was. Mama had told me that the aromas of thousands and thousands of meals were in the walls of old houses, even a house like ours, and when the wind blew through, it would bring back something made as far back as twenty years ago. The wind was blowing harder now, so I thought that might be happening. It also made me worry a little about my coloring book and the Umbrella Lady's note back at the train station.

Suddenly, a snow-white cat came into the kitchen and paused to stare at me suspiciously. It had eyes as green as new spring grass.

"Oh, look who's come to say hello," the Umbrella Lady said. "Mr. Pebbles. Just hold your hand out, and he'll rub his head against it," she said.

I did, and the cat did just what she had predicted. Then he curled up at my feet and looked at the Umbrella Lady expectantly, as if he had done something worth a treat.

"I'm glad Mr. Pebbles came down. He lives upstairs in my bedroom. I like to talk to someone when I work in the house, and if there is no one here, which is most of the time, I'll talk to Mr. Pebbles. The first Mr. Pebbles died years and years ago," she said. "I have that picture of him." She nodded at the wall on my right, where a black-framed picture hung of a white cat sitting and looking like it was posing for the camera.

"It looks just like this Mr. Pebbles," I said.

"Oh, yes. Like identical twins."

I had always wanted a cat, I thought, but Mama had said we'd be eating cat hair no matter how much she cleaned. The hair could float up the stairs and into our noses while we slept. "Dogs bark harder at people who've swallowed lots of cat hair," she had told me.

"People who have dogs or cats usually get another one after their dog or cat dies," the Umbrella Lady said now. "Some people can't do that, but this is a way I kept the original Mr. Pebbles alive, you know, by having another cat that is identical. I feed him the same as I fed the first Mr. Pebbles and the second, and he sleeps in the same cat bed."

"Second?"

"Oh, yes, there was a second. The second Mr. Pebbles was hit by a car full of teenagers who drove up on the sidewalk out there. In the summer, he used to sleep on the sidewalk. The first and the second are buried in the backyard. I'm the only one who knows exactly where. If you looked in the spring, though, you would see some pretty wildflowers coming up, and you would know, I bet. Wouldn't you?"

I nodded, even though I didn't know why I should especially be able to know there were cats under the flowers, and why would I be here looking in the spring?

"I don't think it's right to forget something or someone who died just because they're buried and out of sight. Which brings me to the big question. What happened to your mother? Why are you with only your father?"

I didn't answer. It was something she hadn't seemed very concerned about knowing. I was glad of that, because it made me sad to think about it and actually horrified at the idea of explaining what had happened to Mama. It was still much better to think of it as a bad dream, but suddenly, she pulled her question out of a hat, as my father would say. I could almost see her reach up over her head and pluck it off a question tree to toss quickly at me.

She stopped working and looked at me when I didn't answer. She had a hopeful expression on her face, the sort of expression where eyes are smiling and there is the start of a little laugh at the corners of one's lips.

"Is your mother still alive? Did your father and mother divorce? Most of the time, children stay with their mother when there is a divorce, especially children as young as you. Were you visiting your father and returning home to your mother? What have you been told or, rather, told to tell other people about your father and your mother? Divorced couples have so many secrets buried in their heads that they have to look away from other people's inquisitive eyes, and they tell their children basically to tell lies. But divorces born out of lies give birth to lies. Is that what's happened? Is that what's going on? You should tell me what you know. What do you know?"

Her questions came one after the other, with just a tiny pause in between during which she could tell I wasn't rushing to answer.

Finally, she stopped working on our dinner and turned completely toward me. She had her hands on her hips. The dark-green apron she was wearing was embroidered with red and white threads. I didn't understand what the words meant. It read: *Chefs help those who help themselves.* If they helped themselves, why would they need the chef's help, anyway?

"So?" she asked. "Let's start slowly and see what you know. First question, maybe the most important question. Is your mother still alive?" She said each word slowly, as slowly as she might if she was asking someone nearly deaf.

I still didn't want to answer, but she stood firmly, her lips pressed so hard together that her mouth looked more like a pale pink gash across her face. She wasn't going to move until I told her something about my mother. I could see that.

I shook my head.

"Ah, so there was no divorce. How sad," she said. "Any child would rather have a divorced mother than a dead mother."

She stood there thinking. Then she reached into a cabinet and took out a jar almost full of pennies.

"I put a penny in this jar every time something sad happens to me or to someone I like."

She opened her purse and found a penny. I watched her drop it through a slot in the lid of the jar.

"There. That takes care of that," she said, and smiled. "Now we'll only think about something happy, like our pizza and ice cream. Okay?"

I nodded, now wondering if she really meant it. Would she never mention it again?

Because of all the pennies already in the jar, I thought she had gone through quite a few sad thoughts. Maybe that was why she wanted to change the subject very quickly, which was really another sad thought itself.

"That's good," she said. "People who stay sad too long, especially people like me, in middle age, grow old too fast. Sadness makes you wither like a grape never picked. But you're safe if you use the jar. After you drop the penny in, you don't have to think about it anymore, and if you do, you get another penny quickly. The jar will keep your sad thoughts so you don't have to keep them."

That sounded like a fairy tale, but she looked so serious that I had to believe she believed it was true. I had once asked Mama if adults believed in fairy tales and she had said, "The only fairy tale I know is my marriage. No," she had added.

Now I glanced at the door, wondering if my father had found my coloring book and her note by now. I heard nothing, no footsteps, no knock.

"Think about only something happy," she sang. She continued to work and then paused. "Later, in between happy things, if you want, we can squeeze in something sad. But always remember we have to drop in another penny as soon as we do," she added, smiling.

She looked at me, hoping I would smile, too, at her fairy tale, but I didn't. And why would I want to think about anything sad, anyway, unless she meant thinking about my daddy still not here?

"I suppose it's time you knew my name since I know yours. I'm Maisie. My father used to call me Maisie-Daisy. And do you know why?"

I shook my head. Another question for me to ask? Around her, I could grow quickly if what she had said about children asking questions was true.

"That's my real surname, only it's spelled a little differently. Daisy is spelled D-A-Z-Y. It's almost Lazy, but I always worked hard just so it could never be. Then one day, because I couldn't stand being kidded about it, you know what I did?"

I shook my head. Another question?

"I changed the spelling of my first name to Mazy, M-A-Z-Y. Isn't that smart? I made fun of myself so no one cared to do it anymore. Mazy Dazy. I have a friend who works in the government and helped me change my name legally and very quickly, too. I have the papers in a locked drawer upstairs in the closet in my room.

"Everyone thought my father was too old and far gone, but he understood why I had changed the spelling, and he laughed when I brought him the document to show him what I had done. He was in a home for the elderly by then. When you're ninety and you can still laugh, you're lucky. But you don't have to think about that for a long, long time. And neither do I. Right? Thinking about getting old can make you old."

Why doesn't she talk about her mother, too? I wondered, but didn't ask because I thought she would ask more questions about mine, and I didn't want to think about her right now, especially without my father. I was afraid I might start crying, and I didn't want to cry in front of someone I barely knew.

Instead, I just nodded and looked at the door again. She turned to it, too, and then turned back to me.

"If your father doesn't come today, maybe he'll come tomorrow, but you shouldn't worry. Your room is ready for you to use as long as you need to use it. I certainly wouldn't take you back to the train station, would I? Now, back to our pizza," she said, as if we were making it together.

My room? What room?

I watched her work, remembering how Mama would concentrate so hard on what she was preparing for breakfast, lunch, or dinner that she didn't hear either my father or me talk to her. She'd turn and look at us with a puzzled expression and say, "What? Did you say something, Derick?"

"A month ago," he would reply, and she would smirk, bite down on her lower lip, and turn back to what she was doing. Daddy would look at me and shake his head.

Eventually, I had realized Daddy wanted me to help him with

Mama. More often than not, when I spoke to her, she would listen. If I asked a question, she would answer, so I would, at his request, ask a question he had just asked. He wouldn't request it in so many words. He would give me a certain look of expectation, sometimes turning up his palms, and I would pick up on what he had said and repeat it.

Recently, he had told me I was more like a translator at the United Nations.

"Why is that, Daddy?" I had asked.

"Because it's a place where many people speak in foreign languages and need translators, people who change their words to English or from English to their languages."

"Mama speaks English," I had said.

"I guess I don't speak English," he had muttered. "Lucky you do." He had said everything loudly enough for Mama to hear, even though she had closed her ears.

I know Mama wasn't always like she was right before the fire. Daddy had often remarked about that, too, stressing that Mama had become different and that my original mother wasn't "the woman she is today." I wasn't sure why, but I knew that something Daddy had done had upset her and changed her smiles to frowns and her frowns to tears. They rarely yelled at each other, but I remembered hearing them arguing. It was all muffled in the walls between my bedroom and theirs. In the morning, I would think it had been some dream. But that was when the silences grew deeper. They both grew sadder, and Daddy started to sleep in our guest bedroom.

Not long afterward, whenever Daddy sat by my bed to put me to sleep because Mama already was asleep in hers, he would describe Mama the way a mother or father would tell their child a bedtime story. He would talk about her as if she was already no longer with us.

"Once upon a time, your mother was quite beautiful. That was the way she was when I first fell in love with her. She was always very shy, but I thought that made her even more beautiful. She had that smile that would melt a block of ice. And she wanted to do everything she could with me back then, too. She'd go anywhere with me. Right before and after we were married, I felt ten feet taller when she was at my side. I'd worry I'd bump my head going through a door."

"You did not," I had said, and he'd laughed. "Tell me more, Daddy," I'd said. "I'm not tired enough yet."

He'd sit there, remembering, his face brightening as he recalled one thing after another, especially describing how Mama would take great care of herself and spend lots of time fixing her hair and doing her makeup. He'd describe how she would shop for pretty clothes and shoes. And then he would stop, and the light in his eyes would dim. He would stand up, and, looking down at me, he would sigh and end with, "Well, that was then; now it's now."

Was that something that was true for everyone? I wondered. Daddy would have a now's now, too? Would I? Did everyone change into a different person? I had asked Mama about it recently, and instead of acting like she hadn't heard me, she had turned and said, "When someone you trusted disappoints you, something inside you dies, and you change. My best advice for you is, don't trust anyone, and you won't change."

I was thinking so hard about that and Daddy's bedtime stories that I didn't hear the Umbrella Lady ask, "Do you want to see where you could sleep if your father doesn't come until tomorrow? We have to wait a little while for the pizza."

She took some steps toward me and was standing by the table.

"What?" I asked. It was funny, because I could remember her question even though I didn't hear it. It was still in my ears. I was acting just like Mama.

"You have to listen if you want to hear," the Umbrella Lady said, her voice sharp and her eyes turning steel-gray. "My mother told me that when I was your age. If you don't listen and words go in your ears, they'll bounce right back out and bump right into all the new words coming, and then everything will sound all jumbled up."

I didn't say anything. That sounded as silly as putting pennies in a jar to stop sadness. She continued to look at me hard, with her eyes small, swimming in a little pool of anger. I think she wanted me to say I was sorry that I had ignored her, but I really wasn't. I was still thinking about Daddy, and that was more important. Anyway, I hadn't asked her to bring me here; she had asked me to come. I tottered on getting up and running out, but I was hungry, and the aroma of the pizza baking was circling around me.

Suddenly, as if shocked with another thought, she widened her eyes the way someone who was surprised might. "What is your age?"

"I'm eight," I said.

"Eight. Didn't they feed you? You look like five, maybe six. What grade are you in?"

"I think third. Mama was my teacher."

She smiled. "Of course. You were homeschooled. Your mother was using books children in the third grade would use. Did she tell you that?"

"I don't remember, but I'm going to start school when we're in our new home," I said.

"Um." She looked thoughtful. "You're quite bright, but I don't know as your mother challenged you enough, and your father dropped the ball."

"What ball?"

"Never mind. Just know that you can't always use your age as an excuse for disappointing other people, like not paying attention to what you're asked or told. I'll let you do that this once since we just met, but when you're with me for a while, whether you like it or not, as I said, you will grow older quickly. There's no baby time for you anymore, no baby time for someone left at a train station."

"Why would I be with you for a while? Daddy's coming to get me," I said.

She smirked and acted as if I hadn't spoken. "There was no baby time for me when I was your age, and I had problems just as big, if not bigger. I never went to kindergarten. I had house chores to do. We didn't have preschool, either, and there were no iPads and smartphones like the cell phones now so I could go lock myself in a closet and secretly talk about things to other girls that would shock and even frighten my parents. I don't even own a cell phone now. I never owned one. There is no one I just have to talk to and can't wait until I get home to do so, anyway."

"My mother stopped using hers," I said. From the way she was talking, I thought she would be happy to hear that. "She always forgot to charge it, which upset my father. But I want to have my own cell phone someday."

"Of course you do," she said. "You're the 'look at me' generation. You dream of doing selfies, don't you?" She pressed her lips together so hard it created crevices that ran up her cheeks.

"I don't know. I don't remember a dream about that."

"Doesn't matter what you dream. You won't do them. You'll be different. You won't grow up like most of the other children your age, and you'll be a better person for it."

How did she know all that?

"Did your mother have a computer?" she asked.

"She did, but she didn't use it very much."

"She didn't use it very much?"

She put her hands on her hips and looked at the wall. Her

face seemed to be in constant movement, her tongue licking at her lips, her cheeks going in and out, and her eyes blinking rapidly. The lines in her forehead seemed to ripple. I couldn't help but be fascinated. Then she spun on me.

"Well, didn't she teach you how to use it?"

"She did and then stopped," I said.

"Stopped?"

She had stopped doing a lot with me, but I didn't want to talk about Mama. Daddy never told me not to talk about her now. I simply felt that if I did, it would bring back all the sadness and relight the fire. When that happened, I would cry and, sometimes, fight back a scream.

"So what did your mother tell people she was doing?"

"She used to teach in a public school, but then she became a housewife and mother," I said, remembering how Mama would answer the same question if anyone had asked while we were all out doing something together. It had been a long time since we had been.

"Well, lucky you. You had your mother always there when you needed her." The Umbrella Lady wagged her head, but it didn't sound like she really meant I was lucky. "My mother left us when I was just a little older than you. Matter of fact, she got on a train at the station where I found you and never returned. My father was a lot older than she was, so maybe that was the reason. Never marry a man a lot older than you are. Your husband won't keep up with you. He'll be cranky and full of aches and pains, while you want to go dancing. Or even just for a walk down the street!"

She closed her eyes and took a deep breath, as if she had to fight off the attack of bad memories. Then she burst into a smile again. It came like a small explosion on her face, widening her eyes and deepening the corners of her mouth.

"You'll be happy to hear that I had to grow up quickly, just like you will. I had to become the little lady of the house and take care of my father. Later, mainly because he had suggested it, I became an elementary-school teacher and worked right here for twenty-five years. He was hoping I would remain a spinster so I would have no one else but him. But I fooled him."

I stared at her, because her face changed from happy to angry and back to happy so quickly.

"Hello. Do you know what a spinster is?"

I shook my head.

"So many good words are rotting away like unpicked apples. A spinster is an unmarried woman who probably won't marry. But I fooled my father."

I was just looking at her. It didn't seem interesting, and I didn't want to stop thinking about Daddy.

"Don't you want to know how I fooled him? Aren't you full of curiosity, like Mr. Pebbles?"

I really wasn't, at least about her right now. Right now, I was tired and wanted my father to come take me away, but I nodded because I knew she wanted me to.

"I met a widower who was happy to find a woman like me to marry. My father was so unhappy about it that he had a stroke, but he survived and then ended up in the old-age home, clinging to life like a spider to a web. By then I had to retire. That's what I got for getting married to an older man. I could have gone on teaching right up to today, but I had to take care of my husband, who was an accountant who suddenly could no longer remember numbers."

She stared at me a moment. I was sure I was gawking at her now. No one I had met with Mama or Daddy ever told me so much about himself or herself as quickly.

"Maybe it was my own fault," she said, thinking aloud. She looked up, as if she could see those thoughts in a cloud, just the way they appeared in the newspaper cartoons Daddy read. "You can't always blame the choices you make on someone else, or fate."

She looked at me again.

"I didn't marry until I was thirty. My husband was forty-six. He divorced his first wife when he was thirty-one. He didn't have any children with her, and what happened to him up here," she said, pointing to her temple, "was considered premature."

She waited a moment, probably to see what I would say. I was thinking about Daddy telling me his losing his hair was premature. When I said nothing, she thought I didn't know the meaning of the word and quickly added, "Another apple rotting. That means it shouldn't have happened yet. My father outlived my husband. Can you imagine that? My husband just forgot what he was doing one day and took too many sleeping pills. I didn't know."

Then, more firmly, she said, "Don't think I knew. I wasn't trying to escape."

I didn't understand. Escape? Escape from what?

She pressed her lips together quickly, as if she had said something wrong or terrible. After a moment, she continued in a softer tone.

"Anyway, I was all alone in this house again. Except for Mr. Pebbles and Mr. Pebbles and Mr. Pebbles," she said. She paused, and then suddenly, she slapped herself so hard on the right side of her head that I jumped in the seat.

"Stupid, stupid me, talking about my dead husband when we should be talking only about you. Here I am, going on and on about sad things, too. I don't have enough pennies for all that I've told you already. If I keep up like this, I'll have to go to the bank first thing in the morning and get rolls and rolls of pennies."

I stared up at her, astonished at how hard she had slapped herself. The side of her face was so red I thought she was bleeding. Then, just as suddenly, her face softened into a smile again.

"Come, let me show you the room," she said, plucking my hand off the table. I rose quickly so that she didn't tug me. I had no doubt she would have nearly pulled my arm out of my shoulder.

She saw me glance with concern at my carry-on bag.

"No one is going to steal your things, Saffron. This is not a train station. It's my house," she said. "And Mr. Pebbles doesn't steal."

Mr. Pebbles rose to follow us.

I walked with her past the small living room on the left, with furniture that looked, as Mama might say, because she often had said it about some of ours, "exhausted." She wouldn't know where to begin to clean in this living room, I thought. There were magazines on the table in front of the dark-brown sofa with torn skirts. Some of the bottom of the sofa appeared to be touching the floor where the springs had dropped through. I could see the thick dust on the dark wood coffee table and side tables, and the gray carpet looked like it hadn't been vacuumed since it had first been installed. There were stains as big as coffee cups on it, and the ends were frayed. Crumpled pieces of paper were on a side table, and bread crumbs were in a small light-blue dish. Another dish contained the browning core of an apple.

"I'm not as neat as could be when I'm all by myself," she said, seeing how my eyes were scanning the room. She smiled. "You can help me clean it up properly. I bought all that furniture in there when I first got married. After my husband died, I planned to buy new furniture. But then I thought, what for? Everything has been broken in and fits me. Why get a new horse when the old one still takes you wherever you want to go?"

Horse? I thought. *What horse?*

"I was right, wasn't I?"

When most adults ask if they're right, they are really not asking you a question. It's usually something they want you to do or believe. But the Umbrella Lady really was waiting for me to respond, as if my opinion was important. I didn't want to nod, but I thought I had better, even though I didn't understand what a horse had to do with furniture.

Satisfied, she smiled, and we continued down the hallway, past the short stairway on the left, to a door on the right. I could see there was a door to the outside at the end of the hallway. It had a frosted paneled window and a silver doorknob. She knocked on the door on our right and said, "Hello in there. Are you decent?"

Then she laughed.

"There's no one there, but I like to do that. It's fun to imagine people here sometimes. I'm sure you'll do it, too. There's nothing wrong with having imaginary friends. I bet you have one already. I had one at your age. I still remember her name, Pookie. Do you still have an imaginary friend?"

I shook my head. "I never had an imaginary friend."

She didn't look pleased. "Well, you should have had one. Imaginary friends keep you from being lonely. Did you have any real friends, a neighbor?"

"Mama was my best friend," I said, and she smirked with a twisted smile.

"Did she tell you to say that?"

"No."

"Not in so many words, you mean."

She opened the door and reached in to flip a switch that turned on a fixture that looked like a big bowl in the center of the ceiling. It was so bright I couldn't look at it long.

"I'm going to replace that soon with something softer and more fitting for a child's bedroom. I just needed the extra light right now. I'm not that old, but my vision's not what it used to be." She thought a moment and then added, "But nothing is what it used to be. Sometimes that's good." She smiled at me. "It will be for you."

What did that mean? The more she said confusing things, the more I longed for Daddy to come to her house and take me off to our new home.

"It's a beautiful room, though, isn't it?" she asked.

The bedroom was the strangest I think I had ever seen, not that I had seen all that many bedrooms in other people's houses. The furniture was nice, but the walls had streaks of blue and gold, pink and green, going haphazardly in all directions.

"What color do you like the best?" she asked before we took another step.

"I like blue," I said quickly. I always had. Daddy liked blue, too, but Mama liked green.

"Oh, so do I. This is called robin's-egg blue," she said, placing the palm of her right hand on the streak. "I knew any little girl who could color as well as you do would see how perfectly it goes with the princess white furniture. Don't you love this bedroom? Can you just imagine how perfect it will be? It makes me wish I was a little girl again, but then, lots of things make me wish that.

"Don't worry. It'll be a while before you have such a wish. There's not much you can do about that, anyway. When you're older, you'll realize that life is simply a list of important documents: your birth certificate, your diplomas, maybe a marriage certificate, your AARP card, and your death certificate."

Now she was really confusing me.

"I'm not being sad," she quickly added. "No pennies necessary. I'm just stating facts. But let's think about the room. Don't you love it?"

I gazed at the poster bed. The top of each post had a sparkling crystal ball. The curved headboard and footboard had embossed ribbons and bows. There was a white comforter and a very large white pillow. On the right of the bed was a matching desk and chair, and on the left was a dresser with an oval mirror framed in the same wood. There was only one side table with a lamp. The shade was a darker white. A pinkish area rug was rolled up and off to the left side. The floor had narrow dark-brown wood slats and right now was covered here and there with what looked like brown wrapping paper, probably to keep dripping paint off it.

Above the headboard was a picture of a little girl in a light-pink dress with a blue bow tie.

Had this been that little girl's room? Where was she?

"Is that the girl who lives here?" I asked.

"Oh, no, no. That's not anyone. I bought the frame, and it had that picture in it. Actually, that's why I was attracted to the frame. She is, I'll admit, the granddaughter I wish I had."

It's not her room? Why, I wondered, was there a little girl's room in her house, then? The furniture looked too new for it to have been her little girl's room when she was my age. And why was she painting it? Was there someone else she was expecting?

I was going to ask, but she clapped her hands together.

"I just had a wonderful thought." She paused, thinking and nodding to herself. "We should have another jar, one for wonderful thoughts. We'll put nickels in that one, because nice thoughts are worth more than triple what sad ones are worth.

"Anyway, this is my thought. If you stayed here for a while, you could help me paint the room blue. You're probably better at that than I am. I could never color perfectly within the lines. I'm sure you'll be much neater than I am, too. I'm always in a rush, but a girl who can color like you do must have great patience, and to do anything right, you have to have great patience. Worth a nickel, my idea?"

I looked up at her, puzzled. I didn't have a nickel. "Daddy's coming for me," I said. "We have to catch another train. I can't stay here and paint a room."

"Of course, of course. I was just dreaming. When you get to be my age and you're alone, you spend more of your time dreaming and talking to cats."

Mr. Pebbles was right behind us.

"Whose room was this?" I asked. Did she have a niece? It was definitely a girl's room. "Whose is it going to be? Maybe she will want a different color."

"Oops," she said, instead of answering. "The pizza!"

She turned, taking my hand, and hurried us back to the kitchen. Mr. Pebbles stayed right behind us.

"You set the table," she said. "The dishes are in the first cupboard on the right, and silverware is in the drawer beneath it. Napkins are right there on the counter. Glasses are in the second cupboard on the right. We'll get bowls for ice cream after."

She went to the stove.

I wasn't afraid to do it. Often, when Mama stayed in bed longer, I would set the table, but it seemed to make Daddy angrier, so I stopped doing it. Either he would do it, or Mama would finally get up and come down to start breakfast or dinner. To get to the Umbrella Lady's dishes, I had to step on the small stool she had in the corner of the kitchen.

"Should I get a plate and a glass and silverware for Daddy, too?" I asked.

"Oh, what a good idea. If he showed up now, he'd surely be as hungry as we are. How sweet of you to think of him."

Why wouldn't I think of him? I thought.

"Careful," she said. "We don't want you breaking a bone and going to the hospital. I'd have to call an ambulance. I don't have a car anymore. I walk to the grocery and the drugstore. Why do

I want a car?" she asked, as if I had complained. "No, we'd have to take you in a screaming ambulance to an emergency room with sick and injured people, blood everywhere, splattered on floors and walls."

The very thought of that made my hands tremble and my insides tighten as if something was inside me squeezing, but I was as careful as could be. When I had it all on the table, I stood looking toward the front door and listening.

"You go look for your daddy while I get the pizza. Maybe he doesn't know this is the house and he's walking all over the street," she said. "It's not easy to read the numbers when it gets dark."

I went to the front door, opened it, and stepped out on the porch. She was right about the house number. It was faded so badly and now in some shadows. Anyone would have to stand right in front of it to read it. The dimly lit street was still very quiet. There was no one in sight, and no cars were being driven in either direction. The air was suddenly much colder, too. The wind had picked up, and some dust danced over the macadam right in front of me and landed on the Umbrella Lady's lawn. I looked up. Most of the stars were under a dark purple blanket now. That gave me a cold shiver. For a moment, I felt like crying, but I sucked back my tears. I knew that once they had started, I would have a hard time stopping them.

"It's ready!" I heard her cry.

I stood on the porch for a few more moments. I was tempted

to shout for Daddy. Where was he? Should I just run up the road screaming for him?

"Do you want lemonade or Coke?" she asked.

I entered the house and closed the door. The aroma of the pizza was stronger now.

"Lemonade," I said, and walked into the kitchen.

She paused and looked at me. "Daddy still not there?" she asked, smiling.

I shook my head. Why was she smiling?

"I must tell you. All the stores are closed by now. We're going to have to talk about this," she said, and put the pizza at the center of the table.

She stood up with her hands on her hips and pulled her shoulders back. I hadn't known her very long, but already I realized that when she did that, her voice would deepen, and she would say something very serious or important.

"Talk about what?" I asked.

"We're going to have to talk about what to do. But let's eat first. We can think better if we're not starving," she said. "Oh," she added, "you need to wash your hands first." She nodded to my right. "The powder room is right there. Go on. Hurry up, before it gets cold, not that cold pizza isn't good, too. I've eaten plenty of that. You can't eat if you don't wash your hands, Saffron."

I hesitated, not because I wasn't hungry. I kept thinking it was wrong to start without Daddy.

"I'm very hungry," she said. Then, with a sharp tone, she added, "And I'm going to start eating any minute. It won't be the first time I've eaten alone."

I trembled at the anger in her voice. Then she smiled.

"Of course, Mr. Pebbles was always here. He's waiting for you, too."

I looked at the cat, who was looking at me as if he had understood every word she said.

I felt like I had fallen down a well, like Alice who fell into Wonderland.

Only I was still falling.

CHAPTER THREE

When I came back, she was at the table, waiting.

I sat across from her. Mr. Pebbles moved to sit near me.

"This is very nice," the Umbrella Lady said. "How serendipitous that I decided earlier to walk to the train station. I don't usually. It holds both good and bad memories for me."

She stared at me a moment and then nodded to herself.

"You don't know what that means, 'serendipitous'?"

I shook my head. She looked at Mr. Pebbles.

"Dying words, Mr. Pebbles. Her generation will have to use sign language eventually. They will be that illiterate. Books will end up in museums."

I was only eight, and I had yet to go to an actual school, and I never had heard that word, I wanted to say, but didn't because I didn't want her to get angrier than she already looked to be. She took a deep breath.

"Okay, okay. Don't worry. It means something nice happens by accident or coincidence. I had no reason to walk to the train station. Something made me turn in its direction, and I kept walking. I wasn't even thinking about it. But when something wonderful happens spontaneously, something without any planning, you can call it serendipitous. Can you think of something serendipitous that happened to you?"

I shook my head.

"Nothing, ever?"

I shook my head.

"Well, now something has," she said. "Something joyful for the both of us. Fewer pennies in the jar . . . Let's eat. It should be cool enough to sink your teeth into it."

I did start on my piece, and it was very good. She watched me eat and smiled.

"It's good, isn't it?"

I nodded. It was.

"I knew you were very hungry as soon as I saw you," she said. "Did your father get you anything to eat on the train?"

"No, because I was sleeping," I said, and kept eating.

"Just don't eat too fast, or you'll get a tummy ache. Little girls need to eat well, even better than little boys."

She started to eat her piece.

"Why?"

"Didn't your mother ever say that and then explain it?"

I shook my head.

"Girls do more than boys do. Girls, when they grow old enough, become mothers. Can you imagine men walking around with someone else inside them? They may have more muscles, but inside, they are fragile china moaning about every little pain." She laughed. "I told my husband once that if men had to give birth, the world would have no people."

She laughed again.

I don't know why I decided to ask the question that Mama would tell me was very personal. She taught me that you had to know people better to ask them personal questions. But I couldn't stop thinking about the little girl in the picture above the bed in the bedroom I had been shown.

"Did you ever have someone inside you?"

The strange woman stopped chewing. "Yes," she said slowly. "But it was sad."

Then her eyes widened, and she practically leaped out of her chair to open her purse. She took out a penny, showed it to me, and dropped it in the jar before sitting again quickly.

"Sorry. I promised less sadness, but sometimes it just sneaks in like a snake. When I was married and wanted someone inside me, I was too old to have a baby, but I didn't listen to my doctor. My husband, Arthur, did not want us to have children anyway, so he was actually happy about it."

"I saw a towel with an *A* on it in the bathroom, so I didn't use it."

She smiled. "You could have used it. That was Arthur's towel. He liked his initials on everything he owned, including me."

I widened my eyes.

"That's a joke," she said. "A sick one, but still a joke. Anyway, you are smart. You ask the right questions." She leaned forward. "That's how old the towels are, too, by the way. But they're washed and ironed and kept in a nice-smelling closet. On Saturdays I do the house laundry, Saturday morning. You can help with that tomorrow."

"Tomorrow?"

Tomorrow still seemed like ages away, and I was still very confident Daddy would soon arrive and we'd leave.

"I bet your mother didn't let you iron," she said quickly. "She was probably afraid you'd burn yourself, but my mother made me iron even before I was your age. At first, it was heavy in my hand, but as time went by, I got stronger and stronger, and my mother gave me more to do, like wash the kitchen floor every night. And I'd do a very good job of it, too. I can remember that my mother was happy about that, not because she was proud of me but because she had less to do. My mother was lazy, a lazy Dazy. When I think about her now, my blood starts to boil. She made me into more like an old lady than a little girl. I don't think I was ever a little girl, and . . . Oh."

The way she stopped made me realize that I had paused chewing my second piece of pizza and had closed my eyes for a few seconds. Her voice was making me sleepy, I realized.

I forced my eyes open.

Had I done something wrong, something impolite?

"Of course, you're tired, and here I am going on and on about my mother and house chores," she said. "Just hearing about them can exhaust someone as young as you. Maybe you should lie down and rest. We can warm up the rest of the pizza when we want it, and we can have the ice cream later, too."

"What about Daddy?" I said, looking toward the door again. "You said the stores were closed."

"Oh, yes, a while ago." She thought a moment. "But he certainly should have been here by now."

"Where is he? Where could he go if the stores are closed?"

"Sometimes men stop in bars to get a quick refresher."

"What's that?"

"A little alcohol to give them courage," she said. "Courage to live," she added, sounding bitter. "My husband, Arthur, did until his ankles got too swollen. Drinking at home never did enough for him. He was a very unhappy man. He drank himself silly sometimes. Most people don't have a magic jar for pennies, and the sadness makes them weak and small. But don't worry. As soon as your father comes here looking for you, I'll come get you."

She stood up and came around the table, holding her hand out.

I didn't like what she had said. Why would Daddy leave me at the station while he had a refresher?

"Guess what I have in the bathroom next to what will become the blue bedroom."

"I don't know," I said sharply.

I was getting more annoyed about Daddy. Who cared about what was in the bathroom? I looked at the front door again. Lately, Daddy hadn't come home for dinner, but Mama always put his plate and silverware and napkin on the table. It still would be there in the morning when he had his breakfast. The plate I had left for him here at the Umbrella Lady's house stared me in the face.

Suddenly, I realized the Umbrella Lady was shaking her hand in front of my eyes, urging me to take it.

I stood up quickly. "Maybe we should go to see if Daddy's having a refresher," I said, stepping back. If she said no, I could run out and down the street. "You don't have to come, too," I said, even though I didn't know where a refresher place might be.

"Oh, children can't go to places like that, and there are simply too many of them for us to visit. We'd be out all night going from one to another—and what if your daddy came here and there was no one home? He might leave."

"No, he wouldn't."

"Now, don't be stubborn. You're just being difficult because you're tired. A tired child usually gets herself in trouble."

"Daddy should have been here by now," I insisted.

"Shoulda, coulda, woulda. Balloons without air."

She shook her hand at me again, the anger dripping from her face. I took it, and she closed hers tightly around mine. Maybe she was afraid I would run out anyway. Was she going to reach for my hand every time I walked through her house and was close to one of the doors?

She was smiling again.

"In the bathroom, you have a brand-new toothbrush with brand-new delicious-tasting toothpaste," she said, and took me directly to the bathroom to open the cabinet above the sink to show me. "And guess what else I had in the dresser in the bedroom that has to be painted," she said, handing me the toothbrush.

I shook my head. "I don't know," I said quickly.

I really meant, *I don't care. I want my father. That's all I want.* I know I sounded cranky, but I was too tired and upset.

"Of course you don't know, nor can you think of anything. You can't stop thinking about your daddy. I know that, but I'm going to help you stop enough to get some good rest. On the bed are beautiful, soft pajamas. Brand-new, too, with nice blue slippers. You change into them and lie down. I'll come back and put out the lights," she said. "I bet you fall asleep as quick as a sparrow at sundown."

"When did you put the pajamas there?" I asked. "They weren't there when you showed me the room."

She stared at me with a look of annoyance, and then she suddenly smiled.

"You're not shy. That's good," she said. "It will keep me on my toes, and goodness knows, when a woman like me lives alone, she needs someone to keep her on her toes. I forget what

I'm doing or why sometimes, but not as long as you're here. That's for sure. I ran to the room and set out the pajamas while you were washing your hands, Miss Marple."

"Who's that?"

"A famous woman detective. Go on, do your business and brush your teeth," she said, and walked out, closing the door behind her.

After she left, I gazed at myself in the mirror. I looked as tired as Mama often did. I thought I looked more like her than I did Daddy anyway, tired or not, even though she had light-brown hair and mine was closer to the color of a dark melon. Daddy's hair was really more chestnut brown, which everyone who ever saw him said made his brown eyes with green specks more striking. Mama had eyes closer to the color of mine. Hers were soft blue. Mine were a darker blue, "blueberry blue," Daddy said. Mama's lips were slightly more orange than mine, but Daddy used to say, "You'll never need lipstick, either." My complexion was what Mama once called light olive. She often complained that her own was too pale.

"Once it was attractive for women to look like this, especially wealthy women, but now . . . now I look like I have poor circulation. I should spend more time outside, but I've become too agoraphobic."

"What's that?" I asked, but she didn't answer. When she talked about herself, she often seemed to be talking to herself and not to me, because she said so many things I didn't understand with words I never had heard, just like some of the Umbrella Lady's words, and Mama often didn't look at me when she spoke like that. Sometimes I felt as if I shouldn't be listening. I was hearing secrets.

But no matter what terrible thing she said about herself, I thought Mama was beautiful, and surely Daddy had, too, just like he had told me sometimes when he came into my room to get me to sleep. Like her, I had what Daddy called a "button nose." Mama was thin, very thin, before the fire, so her face looked like the skin had been stretched over it and zipped up at the back of her head. She wore her hair up most of the time and cut it herself when she thought it was too long. She trimmed mine, too, and used to spend more time brushing it than she did hers. She brushed it so long sometimes that I would fall asleep, and when I woke up, she was often still brushing it and didn't stop until I spoke.

Tonight my hair looked raggedy, the strands curled. I hadn't washed it for days since I had taken a bath in the hotel room after the fire and really hadn't washed it well, anyway. Daddy hadn't helped me like Mama often would. I thought I still smelled like smoke and remembered that I had thought Daddy did, too. Even now, in the Umbrella Lady's house, I still smelled it, especially coming from my hair. For the past few days, instead of brushing it, I just pushed it away from my face. I wished I could push the bad memories out just as easily.

There was a blue-handled brush on one of the shelves on the

right side of the sink. I picked it up and turned it over; it looked brand-new. There were no one's hairs in it. I tried running it through my hair, but it kept getting stuck in the small knots, so I gave up.

I used the toothbrush and toothpaste she had given me. I did like the taste, but even though I was very tired, I wasn't eager to change into pajamas and lie down. What if Daddy came in a few minutes? I'd have to change back into my clothes. *No*, I thought. *I won't do that. Maybe I'll go back and wait in the kitchen.*

But the Umbrella Lady was right out there waiting for me when I opened the bathroom door, her arms folded under her breasts. She stood blocking the hall, as if she thought I might come out of the bathroom and run off. I glanced at the side door. She saw where my eyes had gone and stepped to her right.

"Ready?" she asked.

"I don't want to change into pajamas. What if Daddy comes?"

"Oh, my goodness," she said, smiling and unfolding her arms. "Don't you think your father would want you to rest first anyway? And what about him? He needs a little rest, too, doesn't he? Don't be selfish. Little girls are mostly selfish by nature, and some never lose that characteristic and become selfish women. Their prized possession is a mirror. Come along, now."

"I don't know if I should," I insisted, but not strongly. I hadn't thought of Daddy being that tired. Certainly, it made sense that he would be. Maybe I didn't want to think of it. I was becoming more and more like Mama, hating logic. She used to say she wished one and one didn't equal two, because the truth more often than not could be ugly.

"Well, I do know," the Umbrella Lady said sharply. "We're not going to let him rush right out this time of night. What kind of people would we be?"

Would we be? She made it sound as if we had been together a long time.

"Come along," she said, seizing my hand roughly. "I can see you need lessons on how to behave."

"No, I don't," I said. "I want my father."

"Want, want, want, the call of a buzzard," she muttered.

She practically dragged me into the bedroom, where I saw the new pajamas on the bed. They were blue but had little moons on them, too.

She picked the pajama top up off the bed and held it up in front of her.

"Now. Isn't it pretty? Won't you be happy wearing it? Aren't you ashamed of yourself for being so recalcitrant?"

She glared at me, waiting for my answer.

"I don't know that word."

"Surprise, surprise. I guess your mother wasn't as good a teacher as she thought she was," she said. "It means defiant, un-cooperative. Resistant! Understand?"

I didn't answer. I didn't like what she had said about Mama.

"My mother was a very good teacher."

"Oh, Lord, give me strength," she said. She lunged forward

and began to help me take off my clothes, a little roughly, I thought.

"These clothes . . . need to be washed," she said. She brought my two-piece top and pants to her face and sniffed. Then she leaned forward and sniffed my hair. "I don't know what's wrong with me," she said. "I should have had you take a hot bath first and tried to wash your hair. We'll do that first thing when you wake up, and then I'll have to change the sheets and the pillowcase and wash the comforter, because everything will stink."

"Stink?"

"Of course it will. You were on a train and sitting at a station so long. Little girls have to always smell fresh, like a new day," she said, and started to put the pajamas on me. I was too tired to do anything but let her.

She pulled back the comforter. I hesitated and looked at the doorway.

"Oh, for God's sake," she said. "I promise. I'll wake you up if your father arrives. I'll bring him right to this room so he can see that you're doing fine."

She patted the pillow and waited.

Still a little reluctant, I got into the bed. Then she rushed at it, tucked me in, and touched my forehead with the ends of her fingers. She moved them up to my hair and shook her head.

"What is wrong with me? I don't know why I didn't think you would need to be washed first. I'm simply out of practice when it comes to caring for someone other than myself, especially someone so young. We'll both have to learn a lot about each other, and quickly, too. Do you say prayers before you go to sleep?"

"No," I said.

"Why doesn't that surprise me? But you don't have to ask God to help you if you're a good person. Good people make God proud of creating Adam and Eve, even though they were a big disappointment to him. Do you at least know that story?"

"A little," I said.

"Oh, I have so much work to do. I can see God's a bit of a stranger to you."

"God's like a chef," I said, to show her he wasn't.

"What?"

"He helps those who help themselves. Like it says on your apron," I told her, even though that didn't make any sense to me, either.

I closed my eyes, tired of the day, and when I opened them again, she was smiling.

"You are a wonder," she said. "Why anyone would leave you at a train station . . ."

I vaguely heard her going on about it.

"Precious, pretty . . . someone to be proud of . . ."

I had to explain it logically; otherwise, I'd be more frightened than I was. "Daddy had to buy things quickly," I said drowsily.

From the moment I had taken her hand at the station until

now, there was a very slight but clear trembling inside me. It never had stopped rumbling. But exhaustion hit me hard and quick, and keeping my eyes open was becoming more and more difficult.

She shook her head and clicked her lips. Then she went to the door, flipped off the light, and walked out, closing the door behind her. I wanted to stay awake to hear Daddy come in, but almost as soon as I closed my eyes, I fell asleep.

I didn't wake up until morning light started to move across the bedroom, washing over the bed and making me squint. For a few moments, I forgot where I was. I rubbed my eyes and sat up. As if she was waiting outside the door for the sound of my awakening, the Umbrella Lady entered.

"See?" she said, gesturing toward the window. "A new day always brings hope. How do you feel after a good night's sleep, Saffron?"

"Where's my daddy?" I asked.

"Oh, he's not here, my sweet little princess, but don't worry about it right now. First, get up, and we'll get you washed up properly," she said, moving to the dresser and opening the top drawer. "Afterward, you can put on this nice blouse."

She showed me the blue blouse and opened the second drawer.

"I have a blouse in my carry-on."

"Not like this. And besides, I had to take everything unimportant out of it and put it in the garbage. I put the bag there, too."

"What? Why?"

"It smelled, just like sadness. If we kept it, you'd look at it and remember sad things. We'd be putting pennies in the jar forever. Now, here's fresh underwear," she said, plucking a pair of pink panties out of the drawer.

"I had new underwear in my carry-on bag."

"Stop saying that. I just told you. We don't want anything from a smelly bag when we could have fresh things, now, do we?"

"My bag wasn't smelly. It was brand-new."

"Of course it was stinky. It was with you, and it was on the train for hours. Trains stink inside because of all the people sitting and sweating. Okay?" she said, moving to the closet and opening the door. "Now, here is a brand-new skirt that should fit you well."

She took it off the rack, where there were other clothes, and held it up.

"See how nicely it matches the light-blue blouse. Oh, there's a nice creamy white light sweater that you can wear over the blouse, too."

She moved quickly to the dresser and opened the bottom drawer to pluck it out to show me.

"I'm sure your things in your smelly carry-on bag were not as pretty."

"Whose clothes are these?" I looked up at the picture above the bed. "Are they hers?"

"Of course not. She's not real. I told you. She's a picture in a frame. They're your clothes, of course, and they're all clean and fresh. I'll run that bath for you," she said. "Remember we said we would do that? It won't be enough to wash your face and hands."

She turned to hurry out before I could say a word.

"But Daddy . . ." I said when she was already gone. I heard her start the water in the tub.

"You'll wash your hair, too!" she cried from the bathroom. "Let's see if we can get you smelling sweetly."

I got out of bed but sat there, still feeling dazed and confused. Why had I come here? How long had I been here? She returned and stood in the doorway, staring at me.

"Why do I have to wash my hair now?"

"You know very well why your hair doesn't smell good, Saffron, and I don't simply mean your riding on a train for hours and hours and sitting on a dirty train-station bench where bums probably sleep."

I hadn't told her about the fire. Could she smell it on me? Did she mean the fire or something else?

"Well, let's hope we do a good job on you," she added. She smiled. "I'm going to make you a wonderful late breakfast, too," she said. "You had to sleep, so I let you sleep late, but we don't sleep late here. You don't waste any of the day. That's sinful," she said, and smiled. "Come on, get yourself into the tub."

She stepped back, and I walked slowly out of the bedroom

and to the bathroom. At the door, I stopped and looked up at her.

"What about Daddy?"

"One thing at a time," she said. "First, you have to clean up. What would your father think of me if he found you still smelly and dirty?"

She put her hand on my back and practically pushed me into the bathroom. After I took off the pajamas, she held my hand until I was safely sitting in the large tub. It had claw feet, and there was rust around the drain.

"I'll watch to see how you clean yourself first," she said, and stood back with her arms folded under her heavy bosom. She was wearing what Mama called a duster. Mama had one the same color, an aqua cloud floral with a zipper front. She watched me scrub myself for a while but then suddenly cried, "Oh, dear, dear!" and rushed at the tub, ripped the washcloth from my hand, and rubbed the soap hard against it.

I thought I was going to cry, so I pressed my lips together hard.

"You have to scrub," she said, and started on my back and shoulders. "Dirt gets into you and not just on you. Remember that. If my mother could, she'd use sandpaper on me. You're lucky I don't use it on you, because the dirt is so deep in you that it will become a memory if we don't get it out immediately."

She reached in and scrubbed my legs and between them. She had me stand up to do more and then decided we had to wash my hair to see how that would be. She scrubbed and scrubbed it and then sat me down and dipped me under the water before I had a chance to protest. I nearly gagged. When I sat up, she scrubbed again. She stopped and leaned over me to sniff my head.

"Ugh. No good," she said. "No good. We'll have to do something else."

I didn't know what she meant until she opened the cabinet and took out a pair of scissors. The blades looked so big.

I started to get out of the tub, but she put her hand on my shoulder and pressed me back into the water.

"It will grow back," she said. "Clean-smelling, too."

She began to chop at my hair, dropping the large clumps into the trash can under the sink. I cried out, but she didn't seem to notice or care. I tried to get out of the tub, but a strong hand kept pushing my shoulder down between cuts at my hair.

"You'll thank me," she said. "Weeks and weeks from now, you'll thank me."

Weeks and weeks? What did she mean? Wasn't Daddy coming today?

I tried to pull away, but she kept holding my head firmly. I was crying heavily now, not just sobbing, and the ache hurt in my stomach and my chest.

"Daddy!" I said. I was really calling for help, not asking where he was.

She didn't say anything until she was finished, and then she said, "There. Get up, and let's get you dry and dressed for breakfast. Every morning is special, but this is an extra-special one. C'mon, step out."

She seized my arm, pressing so hard that it hurt. I stood up and stepped out of the tub. I was shivering more from fear than from being cold. She wiped me vigorously and then got me dressed, moving me around as if I was a doll, tugging at this and that roughly, until she was satisfied with how the clothes were fitting me.

"You're so perfect that you could be in a storefront window," she said. "Put these on for now." She handed me the slippers. "We'll think about new shoes for you today, maybe. I didn't want to put any on you that weren't fitted perfectly to your feet. No blisters live in Mazy Dazy's house."

I watched her emptying and washing the tub, sucking in my tears, as she worked to scrub it clean.

"Next time, you'll do this yourself," she said. "I'm sure of it. Little girls should not turn their mothers into maids."

What did she mean?

She wasn't my mother.

When she was done, she washed her hands and then, like every time before, took my hand and led me through the hallway to the kitchen. When we got there, I stopped instantly. I was so surprised I almost couldn't breathe.

"My coloring book," I said. There it was on the kitchen table. Surely this meant Daddy was here.

"Yes, yes. I didn't want you to lose it."

"But . . ." I looked around. "Where's my daddy?"

"I don't know," she said.

"Well, who brought my coloring book here?"

"Late last night, Miss Marple, when I realized he still hadn't come here, I returned to the train station and saw your coloring book and my note still there. If I didn't get it, the early train people would see it, and some other little girl would probably have taken it. But don't worry. I wrote out another note and put it on the train-station door. If your daddy comes looking for you today, he'll see it for sure. Okay?"

I shook my head. It wasn't okay. What did she mean, *If your daddy comes looking for you today*? Why wouldn't he be looking for me?

"Well, after a good breakfast, everything will look better and better to you. You'll see. We all do better on a full stomach," she said. "Sit. I'm making you scrambled eggs with cheese and a slice of whole-wheat toast. I have nice strawberry jam. There's your orange juice. Drink that first."

I *was* thirsty. Very thirsty. My skin was still hot from the bath.

She watched me drink. She was looking at me, poised to rush to the left as if she wanted to be sure I wasn't going to get up and run off, which was exactly what I was thinking I might do. If I ran through the streets screaming for my father, someone would hear. Maybe he was at the wrong house and would hear.

"Okay," she said, and went to the stove to make the scrambled eggs and toast. Mr. Pebbles returned and, as before, curled up at my feet. She noticed and nodded.

"He'll be hoping you drop something, even though I give him plenty of cat food."

I reached up to feel my hair, or really just my head. There wasn't any hair, just bristles. I was afraid to look at myself. Mama would cry and cry. She was so proud of my hair.

"It will grow back," the Umbrella Lady muttered, like someone who had eyes in the back of her head. "What doesn't grow back is youth, so cherish it. Don't be in a rush to grow up. Every young person is in a rush. If I could, I'd freeze you."

I felt my eyes widen in fear and my heart thump. My warm skin became cold instantly. *Freeze me?*

She smiled. "Stop looking so frightened. Of course I won't *freeze* you. You'll never be warmer or more comfortable than you will be here."

After she brought the eggs and toast to the table, she sat across from me to watch me eat. I couldn't help being hungry, even though I was still crying inside from what she had done to my hair and how roughly she had washed me.

"Do you know if you have any aunts or uncles?" she asked.

I shook my head.

"Your father never mentioned anyone?"

"No."

"Then you haven't met any cousins," she said. "What about your mother's parents? Did you meet them?"

"No."

"Did she tell you that they had died?"

"Yes."

She sat back with a little smile on her face. Why was she smiling? It was sad.

"How did they die?"

"It was a car accident when she was in college."

She nodded. "And she already had met your father? Was that the story she told you?"

I nodded.

"Love conquers all," she said. "What did your father tell you about his parents?"

"His father didn't like him after his mother died from a disease."

She nodded as if she had expected that answer, too.

"There's truth buried in all that. Families fall apart because each one thinks he or she is the most important."

I didn't understand. Who was more important? What truth?

"The main thing is that you shouldn't be without someone who cares more for you than she or he does for themselves in this life. Every little girl especially needs someone like that, more than every little boy. Boys have less trouble being alone. That's what I learned."

I kept eating, but I saw she was looking at me and thinking hard about me.

"I'm sorry you didn't have any grandparents. Grandparents

can be very important." She paused and then said, "I have a suspicion about you."

I drank some more juice as I rattled around the word *suspicion* in my mind. I didn't think it meant something good, not the way I remembered hearing it.

"You know what I think?" she asked. She waited, as if she really wanted me to say, *What?* But I didn't. She leaned forward, clutching her hands. "I suspect you weren't loved as much as you should have been until now. Your parents were too into themselves, their own problems, and more often than not, they forgot you even existed. You spent a lot of time alone, too much time alone for a girl your age. And I don't mean without other little girls and boys. You need someone to be teaching you and telling you important things all the time. You need to be loved. A little girl without love will fade like a flower without water. As long as you're with me, that's not going to happen."

She stared at me a moment and then sat back.

I shook my head. "My mother taught me important things and loved me."

"Yes, maybe, but I have so much more to teach you." She smiled. "I'm a witch when it comes to seeing the truth and predicting."

"I *was* loved," I insisted. "My daddy still loves me."

"Truth can be like stubborn weeds. It just keeps coming no matter how you prune and spray."

I had no idea what she meant, but I didn't really care. I didn't like her smile now.

"When will my daddy come for me?" I asked, practically demanded.

"We'll see, but don't worry if it's quite a while. I'm really a professional teacher like your mother, only better, and this is a nice house, and you will have everything you need. Believe me, I know exactly what you need. When my mother left us, my father looked at me as if he had hoped she would have taken me, too. We didn't have this nice a house, and I had no one to look after me like I will look after you."

What she was saying fell like stones into my stomach.

She clapped her hands together. "We have a lot to do. After we clean up the kitchen, we'll start to paint your room. And soon we'll go shopping for your new pair of shoes, maybe two pairs. After a while, we'll buy you more clothes and more coloring books. I have all the other books you'll need. We'll never be sad," she said. "You'll see. The jar will starve."

She laughed so hard and loud I widened my eyes.

"Isn't that funny? The jar will starve?"

I nodded. It was funny, in a way. How could a jar starve? But she had a strange laugh, as if she was laughing at someone who wasn't here, so I didn't laugh, too.

"Finish your food," she said, losing her smile quickly. "We have a lot to do. We're going to build a world around you. Isn't that right, Mr. Pebbles?"

I looked at the cat, who was staring at her.

"You can't tell," she said, "but Mr. Pebbles is very happy

that you're staying. Why, he'll probably end up sleeping in your room most of the time."

"Staying? How long will I stay?"

"Well, you can't exactly leave until . . . until it's safe to leave."

"I don't understand," I said. "Daddy must be very frightened because he didn't find me."

"It wasn't exactly brain surgery to find you."

"What? I don't understand. What does that mean?"

"Stop saying that," she snapped. Then she smiled again. "It's not important that you understand everything right now. Right, Mr. Pebbles? Right now, we have to do what's important for right now. People who live entirely on hope pop like bubbles. Look how happy Mr. Pebbles is. I haven't seen him this happy for years, and it's all because of you."

I looked at the cat again. He turned to me as if he really did understand what she was saying.

Even though everything the Umbrella Lady was saying made sense, Mama wouldn't like this, I thought. She wouldn't like any of it.

"Shouldn't we go look for Daddy instead of painting the room?" I asked.

"Where would we look?" She raised her arms. "I've been to the train station, and I left the message for him. Why don't you think it should be the other way around, that he should be looking for you?" she asked angrily. "Why do *we* have to walk our ankles off?"

"Maybe he didn't see the note . . ."

"Oh . . ." She rolled her eyes. "How convenient an excuse for him. I'm sure that's exactly what he'll say."

"Why don't you want to find him?" I asked. I knew I was raising my voice and that was impolite, but I couldn't help it. "Maybe he got lost. He doesn't live here."

She shook her head. "The optimism of innocence."

"I don't know what you mean."

"I mean," she said, looking angry now, "you're warm and safe where you will be well fed. Be grateful. Your daddy can't miss the note. He has to go into the station to ask if anyone has seen you, right? It's right at the center of the station door, and the stationmaster said he wouldn't take it down for a long time. So let's not worry about that. Let's think of good things now, okay? We want those nickels in the other jar."

She stared at me, waiting, but I wasn't going to say okay.

Suddenly, she went to a drawer and took out something and slammed it on the table so hard that it made me jump in the seat.

"Here," she growled. "This is your own roll of pennies. You know where the jar is. If you continue to have sad thoughts, we'll need *two* jars." She stared a moment and then looked softer. "Anyway, it's here. It will help you."

I looked at the small roll. How would this help me find Daddy or Daddy find me?

Seeing that I didn't think pennies to put in jars were important, she tried even harder to soften her expression.

"You *have* to believe," she said. "Nothing comes true if you don't first believe in it. Oh, there is so much to teach you. Obviously, your parents didn't do a good job until now. Just a little of the Bible, a little about daily life and taking care of yourself, and a little, if anything, about planning for the future. Not much education at all."

"Yes, they did," I said, tears burning my eyes. "Mama taught me how to read and add and how to be a little lady."

"That's just a very basic, simple part of life," she said. "There is so much more, it would fill up this house and pour out of the chimney."

She clapped.

"Now, I want you to get up, take your dish and glass to the sink. Scrape off the dish, and then rinse both the dish and the glass before you put them into my dishwasher. Let's see how you do."

She stepped back, folding her arms over her breasts, and watched me. Did she think this was hard? I did what she wanted and then turned to her.

"Okay. Now we know you can clean up after we eat," she said. "That will be one of your chores. Right now, we'll go to your room and see how good you are at taking off your bedsheets and pillowcase. Remember? We have to wash all that and the comforter first. See? We're going to be so busy that you won't have much time to think and worry about your daddy. Leave all the worrying to him."

She waved her hand toward what she was calling the "blue bedroom."

I looked at the front door.

"If you run away," she said, "you'll freeze to death. We'll have to put you in hot soup to soften you up so we can bury you."

The image was terrifying. She waved toward the bedroom again, and I turned and started toward it. As I walked, she sang behind me.

"Bye, baby Bunting, Daddy's gone a-hunting, gone to get a rabbit skin to wrap the baby Bunting in."

I stopped and folded my arms across my chest just the way she did hers.

I could feel her close behind me. "What are you doing?"

"I'm not going back to the room until we go to the station and see if the note is on the door," I said. I said it as firmly as I could. I could feel her breathing on my neck.

"You are very stubborn, a very stubborn little girl. Sometimes that's good, but right now, it's not."

I started to cry. "Maybe the note fell off! Or maybe someone took it off! Daddy won't know where I am!" I wailed.

She put her hand on my shoulder. I spun around and ran back to the front door, but I couldn't open it. It was locked. She walked up slowly behind me.

"Okay, okay," she said. "Stop crying. I always lock the door at night to be safe. We'll go back to the station. Maybe that's a good idea. It's always better to look truth in the eye."

I watched her suspiciously as she stepped forward, took my jacket off the rack, and handed it to me.

"Put on your shoes," she said.

I sat on the bench and did so as she put on her coat. I didn't trust her even if we walked out of the house. I thought she would do something to stop us from returning to the station.

She grabbed her umbrella and opened the door.

"Back to the scene of the crime with Miss Marple," she said, and laughed. She reached for my hand, and we stepped out into the partly sunny but cool morning. At the gate, she stopped. I was afraid this was as far as she would go. "If anyone sees us and asks who you are . . ."

"What?"

"You tell them you're my granddaughter," she said. "Otherwise, the police might come and take you away, and your daddy will never find you—ever—because they'll put you in a home with orphans no one cares about."

I had been thinking that I might run to a policeman, but what if she was right? What if he asked where my father could be or where he had said he had gone? I had no answer, so he might not believe me and do just what she had said.

What if no one in this town had seen him?

We continued on, my heart racing.

CHAPTER FOUR

People saw us, some pausing to watch us walking, but no one called to the Umbrella Lady or stopped us to ask who I was. I was glad, because I wasn't sure I could lie and say I was her granddaughter. I didn't feel like I was, and Mama had taught me to always tell the truth. She said lies became little scars on your heart. I remembered her telling me that at dinner and looking more at Daddy when she said it. He had kept eating and didn't look at either of us.

Much later, when we were alone, I had asked him about it, and he had said, "Lies are tools. Just like a hammer and a saw. If you use them right, use them to help someone or maintain peace and happiness, fine. Unfortunately, if your intentions are not recognized, you're in danger." He had looked at the door-way. "Someone will slice you up."

I didn't understand what he had meant. Even though he

had said it would bring peace and happiness, it sounded wrong to use lies.

I wanted to ask the Umbrella Lady if she was using lies like a tool. Was she doing that now, lying to keep me happy?

She held my hand firmly and marched ahead, still facing forward, never looking to her right or left. I practically had to skip to keep up with her, and she squeezed my hand so hard when she made turns that it hurt. I was afraid to ask her to slow down or to complain. After all, she was taking me back to the station and, hopefully, Daddy. I imagined him sitting on the bench looking so sad, but the moment we appeared, his face would explode in happiness. I wondered if the Umbrella Lady was hoping that, too. Maybe, despite what she had said about how wonderful it was finding me, surely she really wanted to get rid of me now. That way, she wouldn't have to take care of me anymore.

At the same time, there was no question that she was angry that I was making her walk to the station. I was very confused.

Even though we were going faster, it seemed longer walking back to the station than it had walking to her house last night. Of course, now there was traffic, so we had to pause to cross the street. The few stores located close to the station were open. I watched the customers going in and out, just in case Daddy had come back and had stopped in one to ask about me.

As we continued, I saw that more people were looking at us, but again, no one called out to say hello to the Umbrella Lady.

Didn't she have any friends who wanted to greet her or wave to her? She didn't seem at all upset about it. In a way, she reminded me of Mama avoiding our neighbors.

I pushed the thought aside; that wasn't the most important thing right now. Right now, my attention was fixed on the station the moment it came into view. Maybe Daddy hadn't read the note she had put on the station door yet. Perhaps he didn't see it and, as I imagined, had gone right to the bench to wait for me, expecting that wherever I had gone, I'd want to come back or someone would bring me back to the very spot where he had left me. He'd be shocked about my hair and my new clothes, but the Umbrella Lady would explain it. She'd talk about how she couldn't get it to smell fresh, no matter what. He'd thank her. "Sure," he'd say. "It will grow back," and we'd get onto the train just as he had said we would.

The Umbrella Lady was right about one thing: a new day brought hope.

We turned the last corner and walked onto the street leading right to the station. In the bright morning light, the station, the platform, and everything around it looked older and more run-down. The platform floor was dirtier and had all sorts of papers, cans, and bottles thrown across it and around the tracks. I hadn't been able to see any of that in the darkness.

A group of about a half dozen men were waiting for the next train. Some were reading the paper, or struggling to because the strong breeze made it difficult. Two women who looked about the age of the Umbrella Lady sat on my bench, talking and laughing. I was disappointed, but I was happy now that she had returned to the station late last night and retrieved my coloring book.

As we headed directly for the entrance and the ticket booth, people glanced at us curiously, probably more at me, because my hair was cut almost down to my scalp.

When we reached the door, the Umbrella Lady stopped.

"There," she said, releasing me. She gave me a little nudge toward the entrance. "See for yourself, thank you."

I stepped closer, saw the note taped to the door, and read it. *If you're looking for Saffron, please call 555-2332. Or come to 351 Wildwood Drive.*

"Well?" she said. "I think I deserve an apology for your thinking I was lying to you."

"I didn't think you were lying to me."

"Yes, you did," she said firmly.

She stood there, staring and waiting.

I was so confused I didn't even know if I thought for sure she was lying. Not knowing what to do, I said, "I'm sorry," then quickly added, "We should go right back. Maybe he saw it this morning and he's on his way there."

"If he wants to find you and he went to the house, don't you think he'd wait?"

"I don't know." I really didn't. I was too confused.

"Well, I do. I'm a little older than you. I think I know what's best. You are really a nervous Nellie."

A nervous Nellie? My father had not come back for me. Why shouldn't I be nervous? He wasn't here waiting on the bench right now, either.

I felt like bursting into tears but swallowed the urge. I know my eyes were tearing up.

I looked at the people waiting and then heard the train coming.

"Where's Daddy?" I moaned.

"Where, indeed?" she said. She thought a moment and lost her grouchy face. "All right. C'mon. Since you got me out, there is no point in just standing here wasting time. I wasn't planning on going out this early, but we'll start by getting you those new shoes. And after that, since we're close by, we'll go to the grocery store and get a few things we need. You can pick out some cookies."

I glanced at the note again. It loomed there. Right now, it was my only hope of any contact with my father.

"Saffron!" she snapped, and I turned to leave with her.

Immediately, she seized my hand, again holding on a little too tightly. I nearly tripped, so she slowed down.

"Watch where you are going, and stop looking at people," she ordered. "When you look at people, they think they have to talk to you, and none of these people has anything to say that we want to hear."

How did she know that? Maybe one of them had met Daddy and he had told them what I looked like. Of course, without my hair, it might be almost impossible to recognize me. Everyone who ever met me or saw me commented on the color of my hair. It was very special. Daddy used to say I could be spotted in a crowd of a thousand people.

I walked more carefully so she wouldn't squeeze my hand so hard. The partly sunny sky hadn't yet done much to warm the constant wind, which had grown stronger since we had left the Umbrella Lady's house. I saw an American flag on a pole in front of a small beige and almond-brown house, flapping so hard that it looked like it was trying to fly off. Some people were holding on to their hats as they crossed the street. Now everyone was walking at least as quickly as we were and probably didn't want to stop to talk even if they knew the Umbrella Lady. I scanned people everywhere, but there was no sign of Daddy, no sign of his thinning chestnut-brown hair.

She tapped her umbrella on the sidewalk in rhythm with every step.

"Winter is marching in earlier than we were told," the Umbrella Lady muttered. "I can smell the seasons. I'll have to get out a warmer coat that will fit you and a proper hat. Now that I think of it, we had better buy some boots as well as new shoes. I have nothing your size. Shoes won't do when the snow comes, and it comes hard and fast sometimes here. Before you know it, you'll be helping me shovel out the sidewalk."

She pinched the collar of my jacket.

"We'll hang this up until next spring."

Shovel out the sidewalk? Next spring? Did she really think Daddy wouldn't come for me until next spring? It felt like my insides were twisting and tightening. I looked back and to the sides, hoping that Daddy would suddenly appear and scream out my name. I would run to him faster than I ever had.

"We have so much to do today," she said, "too much for one day, maybe for one week. But being busy keeps us alive. Those old people you see," she said, nodding at an elderly man sitting on the porch of his house, "are just waiting like you do when you go to see the doctor or the dentist. Life for them is just one great lobby now. Death will come around like the postman and tell them they have to be posted. Special delivery," she added. "They all think doing nothing is a privilege they've earned. Fools. The real privilege is still being capable of doing something to help yourself until you are too old to pee in a toilet."

That sounded terrible. Mama never talked about old people like that.

She smiled. "We don't waste a moment of our day, do we?"

She looked like she was expecting an answer, again as if we had been together all my life. I felt myself tightening up to the point of stopping and screaming. How could she make all this sound so simple and good? Why wasn't she talking more about finding Daddy? Didn't she care?

"We have to go to the police," I said, "and tell them Daddy didn't come for me."

She stopped as if I had just hit her or stomped on her foot. "Who told you to say that?"

"Nobody. I know you do when someone is missing or hurt or something terrible has happened."

"How do you know so much about missing children?" she asked, her eyes smaller.

"From television," I said.

She nodded as if I had admitted something I had kept secret until now.

"You spent more time with television than with your parents, I bet."

I didn't know what to say. She probably was right. Daddy had worked so much, and Mama had started to stay by herself more and more.

"Well, we don't have to go to the police yet. No one is missing. They'll say it's too soon. We'll look like fools, and when we really need the police, they won't come."

"Why not?"

"Why not?" She stopped again but continued to hold on to my hand tightly. "Didn't your parents ever tell you the story of the boy who cried wolf?"

I shook my head.

"That's the first lesson a parent should teach her child as soon as the child is bright enough to understand. I'm sure you are and were years ago. The story is about a shepherd boy who repeatedly tricks the people in his village into thinking a wolf is attacking his flock of sheep. When a real wolf comes and he cries for help, what do you think the people do?"

"They don't come to help because they don't believe him."

"*Exactly*. See? You understood quickly. When we really need the police, they won't believe us if we go to them now. Let's go to the shoe store and then the grocery store. We'll buy what we need and get home to start painting your room," she said. "Besides, didn't you hear what I told you earlier? You told me you have no uncles and aunts and your grandparents are dead. There's no one else.

"If the police think your father is missing, they might want to put you in an orphanage somewhere, and no will find you then. Believe me, you won't have as nice a place to live as you do with me."

Then she muttered, "But you'll soon realize that . . . Someday I expect you'll get up and say, 'Thank you, Mazy Dazy.'"

She smiled at me, but I guess I wasn't looking as happy as she wanted me to look. I saw the way her smile slowly hardened into a look of displeasure.

"I hope I have the strength," I heard her say in little more than a whisper.

We walked on, faster, the tip of the umbrella clicking sharper and louder on the sidewalk as she swung it with every step.

From what I could see when the Umbrella Lady said we were on Main Street, this village looked smaller than mine. There wasn't as much traffic or as many people walking on the sidewalks. The shoe store was just a short distance from where we had turned onto Main Street. It was in a brick building next to a hardware store. There were no other customers inside when we entered. It was a small store, with shelves for men's shoes on the right and women's and girls' on the left. In the middle were black chairs. Someone had just been here, because there still were some boxes of shoes he or she had tried on left at the foot of one of the chairs.

A short, bald man in a flannel shirt and baggy dark-gray pants came around the counter quickly. When he smiled, he showed that he was missing teeth on both sides.

"I need some substantial shoes and some fur-lined shoe boots for her," the Umbrella Lady said. She didn't say hello, nor did he. Was this the first time she had ever been in his store? Did he know her?

"Absolutely," he said. "Perfect."

She sat me on a seat, and he brought something to measure my foot.

"Granddaughter?" he asked. The Umbrella Lady didn't answer, so he went right to measuring my foot. "Let me show you some of our newest—"

"Substantial," she emphasized. "No flimsy fads."

"Yes, of course."

He hurried behind the counter, down a hall, and disappeared.

The Umbrella Lady looked at me and nodded. "You don't have to speak much," she said. "We're here to buy what we need and get moving. People waste too much time with small talk and nosy questions."

"My mother said that, too, about our neighbors."

"Um." She nodded. "I want to hear more about your mother. Not all of it today," she added quickly. "I know you don't like talking about her right now, but after a while . . . time is like a big Band-Aid. You'll be able to talk about her and not cry so much."

I didn't like her saying that. It was as if she was saying Mama could be completely forgotten.

"Why are you buying me things?" I asked.

She widened her eyes and pulled herself back as if I had spit at her. "Well, how's that for gratitude? Use that bright mind of yours and think. If I don't, you won't get them as fast, and you need them. It's getting cold. I just told you that winter is here. Do you want to sit in the house for months and wait for spring, never go out for fresh air?"

"Daddy will buy what I need before it starts to snow where we are going to live."

"Will he? I tell you what," she said, just as the bald man came back out with boxes in his arms. "When he comes for you, he'll pay me back."

"I have three new styles," the shoe man said, and began opening the boxes. "All substantial."

The Umbrella Lady inspected shoes from each, held up one of the last pair, and said, "This is the one."

He helped me put them on, and then the Umbrella Lady told me to walk around. I really didn't like them. They looked clumsy, with a square front. I thought about saying they hurt. Then I thought it didn't matter. Daddy would buy me prettier shoes, and I'd leave these in her house.

"You said substantial," the bald-headed man said. "I have others," he added, maybe because I wasn't smiling.

"We'll take those. Now, shoe boots," the Umbrella Lady said.

He nodded, quickly gathered up the other two boxes, and went down the same hallway.

The Umbrella Lady squinted. "Not pretty enough for you, huh?"

I didn't answer.

"Did your mother have pretty shoes?"

"Yes," I said. "And pretty dresses, too."

She pulled herself up and pressed her lips together for a moment. "Did she? My father thought pretty meant unnecessary. He'd have dressed me in truck drivers' clothes if he could." She nodded at my feet. "You'll get used to those substantial shoes."

"My daddy will buy me prettier shoes where our new home is," I said defiantly.

"The Daddy Dream," she said. "All little girls are born with it."

The shoe-store man hurried back out with two boxes in his arms. "I just got these in. No one else in town has them," he said, smiling at me.

"I doubt she cares what anyone else in this town has or doesn't have. I know I don't," the Umbrella Lady said.

He hurried to take out one shoe from each box. She took each and turned it around. Then she handed one back.

"This one," she said, looking at me, "is *prettier*."

The way she said *prettier* made it sound ugly. But the boots did feel comfortable and looked nice. She could see I liked them.

"All right. Pack us up," she told the shoe-store clerk. She handed him my old shoes. "Give these to charity."

She had taken away all my clothes, and now she was taking away my shoes, I thought, but I didn't say anything.

I wore my new shoes out of the store and carried the new boots in a bag. We walked around the block to another street, where the grocery store was located. When we took a cart and entered, we finally met someone who wanted to say hello to the Umbrella Lady: a tall, thin young man with dark-brown hair who was holding the hand of a little girl probably only about three years old.

"Mrs. Dutton," he said. "How are you? It's Jeffrey Polton. I didn't know you lived in Hurley now. I thought you were over in Grahamsville."

The Umbrella Lady studied him a moment before replying. "You sat in the third row, second seat," she said.

He laughed. "As sharp a memory as ever. We could never fool you. I went on to get my law degree, got married to a girl I met at college, and came home last year when a job opening occurred at Orseck, Wilson, and Stratton here. I start tomorrow, actually. This is my youngest, Kristen. Almost four. We have a boy, Josh, who's six."

He looked at me, waiting for the Umbrella Lady to tell him who I was.

"Well, it sounds like we gave you a good education," the Umbrella Lady said instead.

"Is this your—"

"Nice to see you, and I hope you don't still put your finger in your ear and shake it."

"Scrambling my brains," he added, smiling. "I remember. And I stopped doing it."

"Well, then, I was successful," she muttered.

She started us away before Jeffrey Polton could say anything else. I looked back at him and saw he was still looking after us and smiling, but smiling like someone who was a little confused.

"That's a mystery," the Umbrella Lady muttered. "I'd never have predicted he would even get into a college."

"Why did he call you Mrs. Dutton?" I asked. "I thought you said your name was Mazy Dazy."

She paused and shook her head. "You don't miss a beat, do you, Miss Marple? Dutton was my married name. When my husband died, his name, at least for me, died, too. I never liked it, anyway. There's no ring to it like there is with Mazy Dazy. Forget it. It's easy to forget a name. Even your own. You'll see."

She put her umbrella over the cart and moved us quickly

through the store, gathering different fruits and vegetables, cans of soup, bread, and milk like someone who had it all memorized. When we reached the shelf of cookies, she paused and told me to choose one. Apparently, I took too long, so she rushed forward and grabbed a box of chocolate snaps, tossing it into the cart.

"We don't have all day to pick out cookies," she snapped. "I told you there is a lot to do."

She made me want to cry. She could get angry so quickly and look so mad that most people didn't even want to glance at her.

We moved through the grocery store at a quick pace, grabbing a few more things, and headed for the checkout line. After it was all packed up, she handed me a bag that was just a little too heavy for me to carry, along with the bag holding my boots.

"You'll live," she said when I struggled to keep it all comfortably in my arms and groaned. It was too heavy to carry with the handles. With her umbrella in one hand and the bag of groceries she was carrying embraced in her other arm, at least she couldn't hold and squeeze my hand on the way back to her house.

As we walked, I held out hope that Daddy would be waiting for us on the Umbrella Lady's porch, as she said he might be. But when we approached the house and I saw he wasn't there, my heart sank again.

"Daddy didn't see your note," I said, near tears.

"Well, it's still on the station door. He'll see it later, maybe."

"Where is he now?"

"How would I know? You can't keep thinking about it. You'll

fill the jar of sad thoughts and then another with the roll of pennies I gave you." She smiled. "I'm making you an apple pie today. You like apple pie?"

It had been a long time since Mama had made a pie. "Yes," I said, partly because it was true but mostly because I knew it was what she wanted to hear.

"I'm very good at making pies. I could make them and sell them if I was desperate. I'm not. I have my teacher's pension, social security, and my dead husband's money. Lucky for you."

Nothing was lucky for me, I wanted to say. My mother had died in a fire, and my father was missing. I didn't care if she was rich or poor or if she was the best baker in the world.

Mr. Pebbles was waiting for us in the entryway. She nearly kicked him after she had hung up the umbrella and walked hurriedly to the kitchen to put her bag on the center counter. She scooped the one I was carrying out of my arms and then took a deep breath.

"Now that you're here and might be here for a long time, I will need more. It's one thing for me to buy the little I need, but to care for a child your age, a lot more groceries are required. I might just have them delivered until you're old enough to go shopping for us on your own."

"How old is that?" I asked, curious about how long she thought I would be living with her.

"We'll see," she said. "Some children don't stop being children for years after they were supposed to, and some, who are brought up properly, become mature much earlier than usual. You have a good chance of that happening to you, because you have me teaching you wonderful new things.

"Meanwhile, I'll put everything away, and then we'll address the painting of your room. Go put your new boots in the entryway under the bench. It's too early to even think of lunch, and I'll make the pie this afternoon."

She thought a moment.

"I think we'd better get you into rags for the painting. We don't want you ruining these clothes. I have some old shirts. You won't need a skirt. My shirts will fit you like a dress."

But what are we going to do about Daddy? I wondered. Maybe he was hurt. That seemed logical. He had left the train station and gotten so hurt that he couldn't tell anyone about me waiting there. The possibility filled me with strange new hope.

"We need to call the hospital," I said before she could turn to walk away.

"What? Why?"

"Maybe Daddy got hurt last night." A horrible thought occurred. "Maybe he was hit by a car and he couldn't tell anyone that I was at the train station. That's why no one knew I was there!"

She stared at me a moment. "You are a deep thinker," she said finally. "Actually, I was like you at your age. But my mother didn't appreciate it."

Then she nodded. "Okay. Let's do that."

She went to a drawer and took out the phone book. When she had opened it to a page, she traced down with her right forefinger to a number and picked up the receiver. She tapped out the number and turned to me as she waited, smiling.

"Hello," she said. "We're checking to see if a Mr. Derick Anders was admitted last night. Yes, thank you." She put her hand on the mouthpiece. "She's connecting us to admittance."

I was holding my breath. What if Daddy really was badly hurt, so badly hurt that he died or might still die? I didn't know whether to hope he was there or not.

"Yes," she said, and repeated Daddy's name. "I see," she said. "Thank you." She hung up. "No," she said. "Your father was not taken to the hospital. Satisfied? He wasn't hurt. You should be happy about that."

"But . . . why didn't he come back for me?"

"I'm sure we'll eventually find out, but for now, go on and do what I told you to do," she urged. "We have to get started. There's no time to dillydally."

I put the boots in the entryway, but I didn't return to the kitchen or go to the bedroom. I stood looking at the front door and thinking. What had she said? *Eventually we'll find out?* I wanted eventually to be now.

I was tempted to run out and return to the train station. No matter what had happened to Daddy, he would go there first to look for me, wouldn't he? If he didn't see that note and didn't see me, he might go to the police to ask if they had me waiting somewhere. If they said no, what would he do? Maybe he would never go back to the station. Then what would happen to me?

"What are you doing?" the Umbrella Lady asked. She was standing in the kitchen doorway. "Why haven't you gone to your room? I just brought you one of my old shirts to put on."

I looked at her and then at the door. "We have to keep looking for my daddy," I said.

"Oh, Lord, give me strength!" she cried, looking up at the ceiling. "Where would we look? We called the hospital. We were just in the village. You saw how small it is."

"Well, then, where is he?"

She stepped toward me slowly. Her eyes looked glassy and cold, her lips so tight that they had small white patches in the corners. She seemed to grow taller with every step, hovering over me grimly. And then, suddenly, she had a small, tight smile as she looked down at me.

"Haven't I been very nice to you? I've fed you, clothed you, bought you shoes and boots and helped you get clean and stopped your hair from stinking."

"Yes," I said. I didn't like what she had done to my hair, but she sounded nice. I was still trembling deep inside. I think I trembled even when I slept.

She nodded at the door. "I've never told you that you couldn't leave anytime you wanted to leave, have I?"

I shook my head.

"We can go looking for your father every day, if you like, but we need to be strong and keep healthy, don't we? That means we have to eat right and get good rest. I want you to be comfortable while you wait. You can't keep worrying. Doing things that need to be done will keep you from having bad thoughts. Fewer pennies in the jar. Won't it be fun painting the room?"

I nodded, feeling myself calm a little.

"And so," she said after a big sigh, "we should start and not waste our time and our strength. Eventually, your daddy will see the note telling him how to contact or find us. Okay?"

It wasn't okay, but I didn't know what else to say. She didn't seem to know anything more than I did. Why keep asking her questions about it?

She reached for my hand. *There she goes again*, I thought, *holding my hand when we walk through the house.* Nevertheless, I followed her to the room. She helped me take off my clothes and then put on her shirt, which was, as she had said, like a dress on me.

She stood back and laughed. "You are a sight. Let's get the paint ready."

I watched her open a big can and stir it with a mixing stick. Then she carefully poured some into a paint tray. She took the wrapping off a paintbrush and handed it to me before taking the wrapping off another.

"Now, watch how I do it," she said. She dipped the end of the brush into the pan slightly and began to paint up from the floor molding. "Don't put too much on the brush, or it will drip. Don't let bubbles form. Okay?"

I nodded.

"Let's see you do it."

I did, and she said, "Perfect. You have the stroke. I knew you would be good at this."

It did look nice. I kept going. She stood back to watch me.

"Just stay with it," she said. "I'm going to change into some older clothes myself. We'll work for a while. Then we'll have lunch. Remember, I'm making that pie. We'll paint until we're tired and start again the next day. We'll cover the furniture and keep going every day until the whole room is done. Of course, I'll do the difficult places, stand on the ladder, and I'll show you how we clean up every day so we don't ruin the brushes."

I worked while she talked. It was hypnotizing. And she was right. While I worked, I didn't think once about Daddy. I felt guilty about that, but it didn't last long. I didn't cry, either.

That night, we had her pie for dessert. It really was good. She told me she had taught herself because her mother wasn't much of a cook or baker. I nearly fell asleep listening to her stories about her mother, mostly stories that seemed to make her angry telling them.

Painting the room did take up much of the next day, too. She wouldn't let me rush it. We had to take long breaks because her wrist would hurt. Mr. Pebbles, as if he understood he could get in the way, lay outside in the hallway to watch us. The Umbrella Lady and I moved the furniture so we could get behind it, and we spread paper on the floor, doing everything carefully and slowly. She took down the picture of the girl in the frame so we could paint behind it, and then she looked at it and said, "We don't need this hanging there."

She took the picture out of the frame and crumpled it in her hands.

"When we get a nice picture of you, we'll put it in there instead. Okay?"

I nodded, but it seemed strange to think of it. It made it sound like I'd be here forever. She put me right back to painting. Not once did she say I wasn't doing it right or I was doing it poorly.

"I knew you would have the patience. Most kids your age just want to get things over with. They're sloppy, sloppy, and sloppy."

She complimented me constantly. She stood thinking and then nodded as if someone was talking beside her.

"We'll keep the windows open here at night so it airs out well. Until it doesn't smell too much in here, you can sleep in my bed with me," she said. "It's a very big bed."

It wasn't until then that she brought me upstairs. Her bedroom was at least twice the size of the one I was in. Her king-size four-poster dark-maple wood bed was at the center of the room, with a window on the wall on each side of the crescent-shaped headboard embossed in twirling shapes, some of which looked like fish. There were end tables on each side with lamps, the shades a pale yellow. Everything looked old, just like the furniture in the living room.

At the foot of the bed was a large brown rug. There were smaller ones on each side of the bed as well, covering part of the cold-looking grayish tiled floor. To my immediate left was a walk-in closet, the door opened enough for me to see the rack of dresses and shelves of shoes, hats, and what I thought were purses. I saw the closet drawers, too. There was a full-length mirror on the inside of the closet door. The floor in the closet was carpeted in the same shade of gray as the tiled floor.

Mr. Pebbles's white quilted pet bed was in the left corner of the room with a water dish beside it. On the immediate right was a large dresser with an attached square-framed mirror. On the left wall was a large matching wood-framed picture of a ghostlike young woman, looking like she was fleeing into the darkness, the train of her white gown floating behind her. I could see the shadowy trees in the background. Her face wasn't very clear or visible, but I thought she was probably pretty.

"Who's that?" I asked, nodding at it.

"Oh, it's no one I knew or know. I bought it because that's how I imagine my mother on her wedding day. It wasn't a good marriage," she added. "I think she knew it wouldn't be minutes after the ceremony and always wished she would be like that woman. One day, as I told you, she just became the woman in that painting, stepped on a train, and left the ghost of herself behind. When I think of her on that train, I think of an empty suitcase."

"Why empty?"

"There was nothing from her past she wanted to take with her, including me."

She pulled back the caramel-tinted comforter and the cover sheet. Then she patted the bed the way someone might pat a chair or a sofa cushion to call a dog or cat to lie there.

"It's a nearly new mattress," she said. "Like sleeping on a cloud."

I stared and didn't move.

"Come over and feel it," she ordered.

I did. It was soft. The bed had four oversize pillows.

"The bathroom," she said, "is just outside on the left. You'll find another new toothbrush in it, so you don't have to run down to get yours. Of course, you'll take a bath before you sleep in my bed. There are bath powders to use that will give you a delightful scent. Did your mother have that?"

"Yes."

"I thought so. My mother didn't. She thought taking too much pleasure in anything was a sin, especially your own body. Sometimes it is," she added pointedly. Then she crossed to the closet, went in, and came out with what was another new pair of pajamas my size, these light green with what looked like pinkish balloons.

Had she always planned for me to sleep up here? I wondered. *When did she buy all these things? When did she decide to hang them up here?*

"Whose are they?" I asked.

She smirked and shook her head. "Whose could they be but

yours? I'm afraid I'm a bit too large for them. Let's go run your bath," she said, throwing the pajamas on the bed. "If you look here"—she nodded at the floor on the left side—"you'll find another pair of new slippers."

She started out. Mr. Pebbles had come up and stood staring at me as if he wanted to ask what I was doing up here.

She called to me, "Don't dillydally."

I headed for the bathroom, glancing back at the woman in the painting, fleeing. Where was she fleeing to? And really, from what? Something terrible? Would that be me someday, too? Would I just run out and get on a train to anywhere?

I slept with her for two nights. She snored both nights, but somehow I managed to shut out the noise and sleep. She was always up ahead of me, and when I rose and dressed, she always had our breakfast ready.

On the day we completed the painting of my bedroom, taking great care with the moldings and the door, she came to the bathroom while I was cleaning up. She had gone out for her mail.

"I have a letter you'll be interested in," she said.

My heart stopped and started.

"Daddy?"

"I'll read it to you," she said, and unfolded the paper.

Dear Mrs. Dutton,

("That's how I still get my mail," she said.)

*My new arrangements for my daughter Saffron
and me have run into problems. I saw your note, and I
am aware that she is at your home and you are taking
very good care of her.*

*Would you please continue to do so until I have
comfortably set up our new home?*

*I would appreciate it. Thank you, and of course,
give her my love.*

                                        Derick Francis Anders

"So," she said. "You can breathe easier now. There is no reason to go floundering about looking for him."

"Can I call him?"

"He didn't indicate a phone number."

"He has a cell phone. I think I remember the number."

She stared.

"Why didn't he call to speak with me?" I asked. "You left the number on the note."

She changed her expression. I knew that look. She was deciding whether or not to tell me something.

"I didn't put my phone number on the note with the coloring book, just my name and address."

"Couldn't he look it up in the phone book?" I asked, shaking my head.

Suddenly, she looked ashamed. "I didn't tell you because I

didn't want you to be upset, but when I went back to get your coloring book, the note was gone."

What she was saying still didn't make sense to me. She could see the confusion in my face.

"I wasn't sure whether or not the wind blew it away. I know now that your father took it. That's how he was able to mail this letter."

I thought for a moment. That couldn't be true. Why wouldn't he have come to get me?

"So if he knows your name, he could have looked up your telephone number, right?" I said.

"I used Mazy Dazy. I don't have my phone listed as Mazy Dazy. I have nothing listed as Mazy Dazy."

"I want to call his cell phone," I said, just as firmly as she said anything.

She raised her eyebrows. "Okay. Let's see if he picks up."

We went to her phone, and she stood back to watch me. I pressed the numbers carefully and listened. A voice came on and said, *This number is no longer in service.* I turned to her, panic surely smeared all over my face. She took the receiver out of my hand and asked me the number. She waited as it rang, and then the same voice came on with the same message. She hung up the receiver and smiled.

"I wouldn't worry about that. Very often when people change where they live, they get a new phone service and a new number."

"Can't we find out the new number?"

"I'm sure there are a number of Derick Anderses in the country. We might have to call dozens, and besides, maybe he has an unlisted number."

"Well, what will I do?"

"Wait, just like he told you. You're not suffering, are you?"

Of course I'm suffering, I thought. *I'm living with someone I really don't know, and both my parents are gone.*

I pondered it a moment and then brightened with an idea. "I could write him a letter and tell him he can call me now. We'll put your name and number in the letter."

"That would be very smart, only . . . he didn't put in his current address. If you write a letter, it will just sit here."

"But why did you put the note on the station door if you thought he took the one under the coloring book?"

"I told you. I didn't know if the wind had blown it off. Besides, you wanted me to, and I didn't want you to think I didn't try. I might as well take it off the door now. Maybe tomorrow."

"But why would Daddy leave me here?"

"You heard what he wrote. He must have found out that you were in a good place and wanted to get everything ready before he came for you. Can you think of any other reason?"

She studied me. There was a dream I sometimes had that always began and ended quickly. My father was starting up the stairway. He had his hands cupped and pressed together. A small flame was coming up out of his palms. For some reason, that dream flashed. I thought about telling her, but before I could say anything else, she stepped toward me and put her hands on my shoulders.

"You have a very nice father, a man who doesn't want you to go through all the turmoil of setting up a new home. I think we should devote our energy and our time to doing the things a young girl your age should be doing, besides the chores, of course, until he has everything ready for you. It will make the time pass faster.

"That means I'll start your homeschooling. We'll pick up where your mother left off. You're very lucky, because I was a very good teacher, and I happen to have kept the books and workbooks I used and other teachers used. I was an assistant principal, really. Nothing was formal about it, but because I was there so long and was so efficient, they decided half my time would be devoted to assisting the principal. So you're luckier than most girls your age.

"Wipe your hands and follow me," she ordered.

I looked at the phone again. I had been so hoping to hear Daddy's voice.

"Saffron?"

I turned, and she led me to the stairway. We walked up, and then, instead of turning right toward her bedroom, she turned left and stopped at a closed door.

"This is supposed to be a guest bedroom, but since I never had a guest, I never furnished it as a bedroom."

She smiled and opened the door.

I stepped up and looked.

There was a classroom desk and chair, a blackboard, and two shelves of books on the left. There was nothing else in the room.

"Well?" she said. "You said you never went to school. Now you will. You'll do your lessons in here, and I will teach you everything you would be taught in a regular public school by now. You won't have to go there until I take you to do a test run by another teacher. I'm sure you'll do better than her own students."

She waited and then put her hands on her hips.

"What do you say? Isn't this wonderful? Don't you feel lucky now?"

"I won't have any friends," I said.

"Of course you will. You'll have me, and someday, when you are ready, you'll go to the public school and be ahead of everyone in the pack. Everyone will want to be your friend, many because they'll want you to help them with their homework. Don't trust those students. They're users, selfish."

I stared at her, maybe scowled. This sounded like it would take a long time.

"When will Daddy come for me?"

"Are you deaf? I read it to you. You heard it . . . when he has everything ready. I swear, the first lesson you'll learn is to appreciate what someone like me does for you."

She pulled the door closed roughly and started for the stairway.

"Well?" she said, snapping at me. "Come along. Finish cleaning up. It's almost time for dinner."

I walked toward her slowly. "Can I have Daddy's letter?" I asked.

"Of course not. I need it in case anyone asks about you."

She started down the stairs. I followed slowly, pausing only when I saw Mr. Pebbles staring up at me with the same cat-ate-the-bird smile as on the cat I had colored black with golden eyes in the book Daddy had given me.

Now that the Umbrella Lady had gotten rid of my clothes and old shoes, it was all that I had left to prove I even had a daddy.

When I reached the bottom of the stairway, she stopped being angry and smiled.

"From now on," she said, "you can call me Mazy. Just like a friend would, okay?"

Maybe I will, I thought, *but I'll always think of you as the Umbrella Lady.*

I had no idea why I should think that, or if it would always be true.

But in time, I would know.

CHAPTER FIVE

After she had read me Daddy's letter, the days were longer than any days I could remember, including the day he and I stepped on the train to go to a new home. It was probably because Mazy wouldn't let me have any time to do nothing, unless taking a nap was doing nothing. Days wove into each other. Months must have passed. She had no calendars on the wall, nor did she get newspapers from which I could keep track of dates. It was almost as if she wanted to keep time secret.

Until the moment I realized that I was going to be here in her home much longer than I had imagined, I wasn't aware that she didn't have a television set, not that during those early days she would have given me time to watch it, anyway. She had every part of my day organized, down to when I would brush my teeth. If I moaned about additional work, she claimed that she didn't want me to think too much about anything sad.

There were always kitchen chores when I wasn't in her schoolroom learning more math, reading more books, and writing to practice grammar. It wasn't long after I began that she had me start work on a science text. She said she was surprised my mother hadn't. She made me read it aloud to show her I could read it, but I think she was really trying to show me what I could do. Then she surprised me by telling me it was for seventh-grade students.

"I'll give your mother credit for how well she taught you to read and sound out words," she said. "But why stop there? It's like launching a rocket ship and immediately tying it down.

"I've seen too many good students turn lazy. Everything you do and everything you learn from now on should be a challenge. Maybe your mother had too many challenges of her own to provide you with any. But you won't grow without them. If it's too easy, it isn't worth doing."

She had what she called quotes of wisdom, new ones almost every day. She didn't want me simply to hear them and believe them but encouraged me to use them as well. "When you're older, just tell that to people," she would say. "You'll see how much more they will respect you. That's what happened to me."

I think she dreamed of turning me into a younger version of herself or maybe just to be her when she was my age. It was always "I would do this" or "I would do that." And therefore, "so should you." There was even a wisdom quote for it. "Appreciating and benefiting from my mistakes means you won't make them. You don't resent what older people tell you. It's like getting something for free, and besides, don't you want to try to be perfect?"

Sometimes I would snap back at her like a rubber band. I know it surprised her.

"No one can be perfect," I said once after she recited her own quote. "My mother told me that."

"Why doesn't that shock me to hear it coming from your lips? I'm not saying you will be perfect, but you should try to be. Otherwise, if you settle for just this or that, you'll be mediocre. That means you'll be ordinary. And any little girl I tutor will not be barely adequate. Years from now, people will ask you how you got so smart, and you will smile and say, 'Mazy Dazy.'"

She laughed, but I just stared at her and wondered what it would be like to live in her imagination, even for only a day. She could see me years from now? How could she fantasize so much and about me, too? Anyone else would be so dizzy she'd faint.

But she wasn't all wrong. As time passed and my hair grew back, I could feel myself changing. Maybe it was simply wishful thinking, but I did sense I was getting stronger, tougher, which was what she wanted, what she taught me to be.

"You have to shed the little girl in you just the way your textbook explained how and why a snake sheds its skin," she said.

I rarely cried, and my complaining didn't go over well with her. It would have the opposite effect, anyway. If there was something to do and I moaned, I had to do more of it. If there was something at dinner that I didn't like and didn't eat, she had me eat it at breakfast. It reminded me of my mother telling my father why I didn't whine like other little kids. I understood what she meant now, why it was futile. I learned to seal my lips.

But although she was quick to jump on any mistake I made, whether it involved some household chore or some math problem, she was also quick with a compliment, if I deserved it. I couldn't help but feel proud when she paused one day and said, "I've had literally hundreds of students. I can count on the fingers of one hand any who were as bright as you or had your promise."

Weeks ago, I wouldn't have understood what she meant by promise, but she was expanding my vocabulary quickly. She had me reading at least three books a week, especially since there was no television set. Some nights, I read until my eyes closed themselves. And the minute I told her I had finished a book, she peppered me with questions to be sure I was telling the truth. The lie as a tool was almost impossible to use with her. She truly seemed to know every move I made. I had this theory that because it was her house, the house would tell her any secrets I had hoped to have. She could put her ear to the wall in her room and hear whatever I might have said to myself in mine.

As she had predicted, Mr. Pebbles moved himself into my room. He was just there every morning, sleeping on the rug beside my bed. One day, she brought his bed down from her bedroom and set it next to mine on the left with his water dish.

"It's all right," she told me. "You passed a big test by winning over Mr. Pebbles. Cats like him know more about you than you can imagine. You'll feel safer with him around. He can sense a roach crawling across the floor."

"Roach?"

"Don't tell me you didn't have insects in your home," she said.

I didn't want to argue, but my mother would pounce on the hint of one. Still, it was nice knowing Mr. Pebbles was on the lookout, and hearing him purr always made me feel less nervous and afraid. I liked talking to him, liked the way he would stare back at me as if he understood every word. It became my job to feed him and clean his litter box, but I was more than happy to do it and add it to my daily routine. When I worked, I didn't think, I didn't remember, and most important, I didn't cry.

However, more chores seemingly fell out of the air after a while. When she thought I was capable of using the vacuum cleaner correctly, I was vacuuming the upstairs as well as the downstairs. It was something of a struggle to carry it up. She knew it, but she never offered to help me when it came to lifting or pushing something heavy, even when I nearly toppled and fell down the stairs.

"Straining will cause you to grow faster and stronger. Parents baby their children right up to college graduation and then some. They have no grit. You'll have grit," she predicted. "Something I'm afraid your parents were forgetting to develop in you because they had so little of it themselves."

How would she know so much about my parents? I thought, but didn't ask. I suspected she was making it up, but I was careful about my questions. Some were like lighting matches under her feet. She would leap at me with her answers, jerk herself as if she could come out of her body.

In the early days, she would take me out in the back but stand there watching me look at everything. I didn't hear the voices of any close neighbors. I asked about Daddy practically every day, and then every other, and then every other week, and then I stopped for a while after she came into my room one evening and said, "I have another letter from your father. I wasn't going to read it to you yet, but I've decided you're mature enough now to hear it and deal with it."

I put the book I was reading aside and sat up. Even Mr. Pebbles yawned and stepped out of bed to listen.

> *Dear Mrs. Dutton,*
>
> *It is taking me longer than I thought to organize my new life. One reason is I've met someone new whom I think I could marry. A new mother for Saffron would be a wonderful thing, but a young woman would*

certainly be nervous about taking on a little girl so soon.
Consequently, I haven't told her about Saffron. I beg
you to give me more time to ease her into it. I know
Saffron is in good hands, safe and well cared for.

Thank you.
And of course, give her my love.
Derick Francis Anders

This time, she handed the letter to me. It had been printed. I imagined Daddy had gotten himself a new computer. I reread it, the tears welling in my eyes.

"Do you know where he is?" I asked.

"Not exactly, no. Like the first letter, he didn't put a return address on the envelope, and the postal stamp could mean a lot of places." She nodded at the piece of paper. "You can keep that one."

I looked at it. Keep it? I wanted to rip it up.

"Why didn't he put his new address on it? Why wasn't there a new phone number?" I asked.

"It's the way he wants it. For now. Soon we'll talk more about it all," Mazy said. "Now that you're going to be with me longer, it's important that I know as much about you as possible. I'm sure you have lots to tell me about your mother and your father, how they treated each other and how they treated you. I could have asked you to tell me things immediately, but I wanted you to be comfortable and trusting first."

"What things?" I asked.

"Don't worry about that now. It's late. We won't do it all at once, anyway. Just a little at a time. Go to sleep," she said, and turned off the light as she walked out of my room.

I still sat up with the letter in my hands. Then I folded it and slipped it under my pillow. But when I laid my head back on it, I couldn't close my eyes, so I pulled it out, crumpled it in my hand, and tossed it on the floor.

Mazy Dazy was right. I had a lot to tell her, a lot to take out of the closet. Maybe I was ready to do that even more since I had read Daddy's second letter. I was so angry that I wanted to read it aloud but this time spit the words. What some new woman thought and felt was more important than what I thought and felt? How had he met her so fast and gotten to love her so fast?

I was afraid to fall asleep now. Just thinking about it threatened a storm of nightmares.

When I rose in the morning, I picked up the letter, straightened it out, and reread it before I put it under my socks in the second drawer. I could see from the way Mazy was studying me occasionally that she was waiting to see what my real reaction to my father's second letter would be. I did think about it most of the day. Another mother loomed out there. Was I supposed to forget Mama and learn to love someone who first had to get used to the idea of me? That didn't sit well in my stomach. I went from surprise and shock to anger before finally thinking about her.

How old would she be? How much different from my mother would she be? Would Daddy love her more than he had loved Mama when they had first met? Did she have a job? Were they living together already in our new house? He didn't say anything about any of that, but could she have been married before, too? Could she have children? Was he worried I wouldn't get along with her children? When would he tell me more? Every time Mazy went for her mail, I would watch and wait anxiously as she sifted through it, mumbling about bills and garbage mail. Nothing new came from Daddy. Mazy just had to take one look at me to know the disappointment I was suffering.

One night, weeks later, after the dinner dishes and the table were cleaned up, Mazy told me to go into the living room. During the past months, I had, almost more on my own than at her command, begun to clean it up the way Mama would have. I vacuumed under the chairs and the sofa, worked at taking out rug stains, straightened up magazines, polished furniture, and even began to wash the windows, especially the one in the kitchen. She said nothing, but I did catch her smiling to herself. I wasn't doing it for her; I didn't want to sit and read or do a puzzle in a pigpen. Because it was still so cold, she rarely opened a window, and I did not like the stale, dank odor.

Besides, doing things the way Mama did them helped me feel closer to her.

"I'm very proud of how you are adjusting," Mazy began after she sat down across from me.

I was on the sofa, which, despite how I had vacuumed, always seemed dusty. Whether she liked it or not, it was time to get a new one. I was working up the courage to tell her. That she could be proud of her house amazed me, but I knew she was.

"Some of the things your mother did to raise you were very good. You have some very good instincts. I hope I'm not wrong, but neither of your parents appears to have spoiled you. Since you spent more time with your mother, she would have had the most influence. Do you remember when she began to change?"

Usually, she just dropped a question about my parents while we were doing something else. Maybe she thought I would answer her questions more truthfully if they came as surprises. Perhaps because of Daddy's second letter, she thought it was time to learn more about my family. She was asking more questions than I remembered the police asking after the fire.

I thought hard about her question about Mama. It was one I had asked myself often as well. I didn't remember the exact day or anything, but I did recall when I began to sense things were different.

"I'm listening," she said when I didn't start. "Did you wake up one morning and find a different mother?"

"No. She was never a different mother. She was . . ."

"Just different?"

"Yes."

"How?"

I couldn't help feeling like a tattletale.

"It's all right. I need to know what happened to you, don't I? To do that, I need to know what happened in your home. I'm not going to publish it in a newspaper or tell anyone. You and I have to trust each other. I've told you lots of unpleasant things about my own mother. I trust you," she said, smiling.

"Mama stopped doing little things for Daddy," I said quickly.

"Like what?"

"Sometimes she didn't wash his clothes or iron anything."

"Did he yell at her?"

"No. He just began to do it himself."

She stared at me a moment, her eyes scanning my face. "She wasn't taking care of you properly, either, was she?"

I shrugged. "She didn't care if my room was messy. When I looked in at her and Daddy's room, I saw how messy it was as well."

"What did your father do about that?"

"He complained, and then he stopped, like he didn't care," I said.

"What did you do?"

"I tried to make it less messy."

"You felt more alone?"

I didn't want to say yes, but I nodded.

"People die slowly sometimes," she said, but turned away first so it looked like she was saying it to herself.

I thought that was all she would say or ask, but she turned back to me and said, "Married people have arguments, but they make up and love each other again. That didn't happen, did it?"

She waited, but I didn't want to say.

"It's better to talk about it. If you don't, it will burn you up inside."

I still didn't talk. I thought that would be the end of this uncomfortable cross-examination, but it wasn't.

"You once mentioned that you heard them arguing often recently. Do you remember what it was about?"

"No. I didn't like the sound. Once I even put my pillow over my ear."

She nodded, holding her smile like she was waiting to have her picture taken. "Did your father ever try to make your mother happy again?"

I recalled him buying flowers and candy, even jewelry. I told her how Mama stopped wearing any of it and what she had said about not wanting to be "decorated" like a Christmas tree.

For a reason I couldn't fathom, the Umbrella Lady widened her smile. She looked sincerely happy to hear what I said.

"She had a sharp tongue, did she? When she said nasty things to him, what did he say? Was he very nasty to her?"

"No. Most of the time, he would walk away and go to his office."

"Men and their offices," she said, as if she had lived with

dozens and something similar happened. "I should call them caves."

"Is that what happened with Arthur?" I asked. I thought that was fair. If she was going to ask me so many questions, why couldn't I ask her some without her jumping out of her body?

Her eyes almost exploded with surprise, looking like they were boiling. Then she seemed to simmer down and even smiled again.

"I must try to remember that your age is a lie."

"A lie? Why?"

"Life, your basic intelligence, has made you older." She sat back. "Yes, Arthur tried to be that way, but I chained him to the chair."

Now it was my eyes that nearly exploded, and she laughed. She squinted and grew serious.

"How long was it before the fire when she stopped teaching you and stopped playing with you?"

I shrugged. It was weeks, I thought, maybe months. I didn't have an exact date. Those memories seemed to float together, anyway, maybe because I so wanted to forget them.

"A while."

"This is important," she said, leaning toward me. "Did she ever go to a doctor, one of those doctors who try to help you feel better? Did your father take her? Do you remember that? Did they take you along? Did you wait in a lobby, or did the doctor come out to talk to you?"

I thought about it and shook my head. "I don't remember."

"But you said that your mother had medicine?"

I nodded.

"More than one medicine?"

I nodded, and she sat back, looking satisfied. Why did that make her happy to know?

"Did your father have to remind her to take her medicine?"

"Sometimes, especially when she said something he didn't like or just sat and stared. He'd say, 'Go take your pill, Lindsey.'"

"Lindsey," she said, and then said it again, softer, as if she was practicing how to say it.

She looked out the windows. It was late April, but it was snowing again, more like flurries. As she had predicted, we had dropped into winter like falling into a well, where it became darker earlier and colder. The winter coat she had found in a closet for me looked brand-new. It was quilted and gray, with adjustable sleeves. In the pockets was a pair of black pop-top gloves that also looked like they had never been used.

"Whose were these?" I had asked when she gave it all to me.

She had snapped her answer back at me so sharply—"They're yours. What difference does it make whose they were?"—that I stopped asking about the clothes and just took them.

The day she gave me the coat and gloves, she took me to the department store in Hurley and bought me two pairs of black waterproof pants, a sweater, and warmer socks to go with my fur-lined boots. I noticed that she didn't look at the prices. She crumpled up the receipt before putting it in her pocket. How was Daddy going to know how much he had to pay her back? I wanted to ask her, but I was afraid of the answer. She might just say, "What Daddy? Who expects to ever see him again? Stop believing in Santa Claus."

Before we had gone shopping, it had just snowed, but the roads had been cleared. The sidewalks weren't, and she had complained and muttered about the "lazy government people." She had held my hand firmly as we walked on the road and back to her house. Her walkway was always shoveled out by someone I didn't get up early enough to see doing it. She did tell me that if it snowed during the day, she and I would have to do some shoveling before we went to sleep. Usually, my job was to clean off the steps.

A man I only knew as Mr. Cauthers delivered firewood every few weeks. She kept it in the garage that had no car, but that was why she had her driveway cleared. It had soon become one of my chores to fetch a few logs for the nightly fire, and during the day, I went into the woods behind the house and gathered kindling. She had gone with me three times to be sure I knew what to bring back and what not to and how far to go into the woods.

She had a fire going right now. For a moment, she was so deeply quiet that I thought she had fallen somewhere into herself. She once told me that our bodies were like clamshells. We could close them down and snuggle up inside, safe in our own darkness.

"That's probably what your mother did," she added, and set me off thinking about the many times Mama had looked like she had done just that. She might be staring at me and not see me or hear a sound I made. In the beginning, that was frightening, but eventually it became strangely comfortable. She looked out of pain, beyond a sad word or memory. Without her knowing, I sometimes tried to imitate her, but I always got fidgety and wanted to do something.

Right now, in the silence, I stared at the flames and listened to the wood crackling in the fire. Unfortunately, it brought back the horror of our house burning. I wished we didn't have to have a fire every night, but Mazy was so pleased with her fireplace I couldn't say anything nasty about it. She knew, though; she knew what was flashing in my mind, especially when I turned away from the flames or looked down. She saw that was what I was doing now.

"When you fall off a bike, you get right back on," she said.

"What? I don't have a bike."

Was she going to get me a bike?

"That's a wisdom quote. It means you don't run off whining when you have an accident or fail at something. You face what defeated you, and you conquer it. Fear will defeat you every time. You face down your fears. Make them cower. Remember that word, *cower*, from the book about the knight and the lady?"

"Yes."

I knew what she meant for me to do. I glanced at the fire. I'd never stop fearing fire, but I nodded anyway.

"Good," she said. "I promise I won't ask you any more questions about your parents while everything is still fresh and raw in your mind."

I grimaced.

"That means it's painful to remember. Right?"

I nodded.

"We'll talk about it all again as time goes by, but whenever you remember something you think was important about your mother and your father, you tell me, okay?"

"Why?"

She looked away and shook her head. "Why didn't I expect you would ask why?" she said to the wall.

She turned back to me.

"I want to know exactly who you are, and I can't do that if I don't know the way you were nurtured. Maybe your mother eventually treated you like the magical plant in the flowerpot of marbles, planted nothing and watered nothing."

What a silly thing to say, I thought. She knew who I was.

"I told you who I am."

"A name is the least revealing thing about you, especially you. It's obvious. Saffron . . . your hair. Big deal," she said. She held up her right thumb and forefinger. "It tells me this much about you. Just like a flower, you're the result of the place your roots were first sunk. Parents mold their children with good lessons or bad habits. However, the more I get to know you, the more I think you might be one of those untouchables."

"What's that?"

"Someone so independent she can't be molded. But don't worry. We'll get to know each other lots better, and what has to change in you we'll change as time goes by. You can take that to the bank."

"What bank?"

"Oh, give me strength. That's another wisdom saying. It means it's a solid truth. Sometimes," she said, squinting at me, "sometimes, I wonder if you're playing me, girl."

What did that mean? Playing her? She saw the look on my face.

"All right. Don't worry about it. We're not going to pull out your teeth," she said, laughing. She looked at the miniature grandfather's clock on the mantel above the redbrick fireplace. Another chore I now had was cleaning out that fireplace every day. I thought now that she wanted me to do that so I'd confront the remains of a fire until it no longer triggered bad memories.

"Okay, I see we ate up quite a bit of time here. You can go to your room and read or finish the workbook assignment."

When I didn't move, she raised her eyebrows. "Well?"

"Why don't you have a television set?" I asked, my angry tone pretty clear.

"Well, listen to you, the guest who took over the house. For your information, I'd rather listen to music and read than watch the idiot box. You become a sponge."

"What's that mean?"

"Or a couch potato like my husband. From the moment he rose to the moment I would wake him to tell him to go to bed, he sat with the light flickering on his face. It didn't matter all that much what stupidity he was watching. He was just . . . hypnotized."

"But there are good things on television," I insisted. "Mama had me watch them."

She looked away, as if hearing something good my mother had done disturbed her.

"I wasn't a couch potato, hypnotized. I learned stuff. You even said I knew a lot more than a girl my age when you first met me."

She pursed her lips and thought. "I swear you could change Moses's mind. We'll see," she said.

"See what?"

"Isn't it your birthday soon? I believe you're going to be nine."

Her question shocked me. Weeks before my birthday, I would think about it, but I hadn't recently, and I wasn't thinking about it now. I never had a birthday without my parents. Maybe that was why I didn't think about it.

"Who told you when my birthday was?"

She stared at me. I was expecting her to say, *Miss Marple strikes again*, but she didn't.

"Someone put your birth certificate and the dates of your inoculations in that smelly carry-on bag you had on the train."

I know I looked dumbfounded. I hadn't done it. I didn't even know where all that had been kept in our house. Why would Mama have done it? Was she planning on going somewhere with me? Maybe running away from Daddy?

"Who?"

"Who? Who? What are you, an owl? What difference does that make? Who's not important right now. The good thing is it was there. If you continue being good, I'll see about buying a television set to put . . ." She looked around. "Maybe in here, though I once vowed never to do that. See how I'm changing just for you? Since you've been behaving and we've been doing good work, I haven't added a penny to the new jar. And you haven't, either. But we did put some nickels in the new jar. What do you have to say about that?" she asked.

"You've been keeping me too busy to think sad thoughts." I had been thinking them, but I wouldn't tell her.

She laughed harder than I had ever seen her. "I swear, I might enjoy you yet. Now, go on. Do what I told you to do, finish your book."

I rose slowly, still thinking about what had been in my carry-on bag. Had Daddy found it all before he had come to my room to get me that night? How could he have so much time to do all that and not get both me and Mama awake? My memories felt like they were under lock and key, and the safe in which they were kept was creaking open.

"I'll make you a birthday cake, too," she said as I started for the door. I looked back at her, surprised at how extra nice she was being. "It's been years since I celebrated anyone's birthday, including my own."

Normally, I would have thought that was strange, but during all the time I was here, I never saw her greet a friend or talk about a relative, talk to anyone who would celebrate a birthday with her. Maybe I should feel sorrier for her, I thought. I wondered if I could. But if I did, I thought she would be angry about it, and she would make me put a penny in the jar.

When I was back in my room, I opened the sock drawer and took out Daddy's second letter to read again. Should I wish that he'd marry his new girlfriend quickly? The quicker he did, the faster we would be together. I wanted to, but something inside me, my memory of Mama's smile especially, made it practically impossible to wish such a thing.

Perhaps when he told this new woman about me, she would be so upset she wouldn't want to be with him anymore. Surely then, I thought, he'd come hurrying back to get me.

Wish for that, Saffron, I told myself. *Wish for that.*

Three days later, a television set was delivered to the Umbrella Lady's house. As she had suggested, she had decided to put it in the living room and had the deliveryman hook it up. It took quite a bit of time to do, and while he worked, she wanted me to stay away and not be distracted. I had to remain in the classroom. After a while, she came up to tell me my birthday gift was ready.

"We'll leave it off until after dinner. For now, we'll turn it on for exactly two hours a day. You'll decide if you want those hours before dinner or after dinner. But if you watch before dinner, you'll have to stop to help in the kitchen, and you'll have to show me you've done all the work I gave you and read what I gave you first. Understood?"

Why only two hours? I wanted to ask, but I thought she would get angry and say, *Only one hour just because you asked.*

I nodded. After all, anything sounded good.

"I hope I don't regret this," she muttered, and left me.

I returned to my math workbook and the pages she had told me I had to do. Sometimes it was so easy, I could do it quickly and get it all right. When I did that, however, she added more, so I deliberately spent more time on it than I had to. She watched me suspiciously. I think she knew what I was doing. I had this fear growing. *She's playing with me*, I thought. *I've become her television set.*

The set she had bought for me was placed on the wall on the left. She had turned the sofa a little so it would face it. When we went in to watch after I had done the dinner dishes and cleaned the table, she handed me the remote.

"I imagine you know how to use it better than I do," she said.

I studied it a moment. I did.

"Well, I'm interested to see what you select," she said, and sat on the sofa, folding her hands in her lap.

There was no question in my mind that this was another test of some sort. She watched me slowly take my seat on the sofa and turn on the television. She clicked her tongue as I flipped through the stations until I found the show I knew. I never imagined she would like it as much as, if not more than, I did.

It was about a twelve-year-old girl named Laura who lost her hearing when she was ten because of a serious illness. She had to use sign language and read lips, but she still went to a regular school and had girlfriends and was getting more and more involved with a boy.

"Most kids today don't listen to their parents or other adults, anyway," Mazy muttered as she realized what the show was about. "They might as well be deaf."

Although Laura was deaf, no one was permitted to feel sorry for her. As I had when I watched the show back home, I started to practice sign language. Without thinking about it, I mimicked Laura when I knew what she was going to say.

"That's a good skill to learn," Mazy suddenly said. I looked at her, surprised, surprised I had been doing it. "Maybe you'll work with deaf people someday."

She didn't get up until the show was over and I switched to something she didn't like, a program about bees.

"Well," she said, starting out. "You can watch this show and then go to your room to read. As long as you choose good things and don't abuse it, I'll be happy I bought you this for your birthday. We'll celebrate with the cake tomorrow. I might have something else for you."

Really? I thought. Could it be the letter I was waiting to get from Daddy?

She left me wishing time would rush by.

Sometimes I wondered if a day in the Umbrella Lady's house was longer than twenty-four hours, because it seemed to take so long. I had gotten used to looking at clocks now, because so much of what I had to do was governed by time. This hour was set aside for that, and that was set aside for this. I'd move with accuracy to each assignment, afraid that if I didn't do something right, she'd only make me do it again and then add something else as punishment.

After dinner the next day, she brought out the cake she had made. During one of our meals together, I had mentioned I liked a vanilla cake with chocolate icing. Mama had made that cake for me for every birthday I could remember. It was one of Daddy's favorites, too.

Mazy had the candles ready and lit them. I blew them out, and to my surprise, she sang "Happy Birthday" to me like she really meant it. Then she opened a drawer and handed me a black velvet case. I opened it slowly and saw a pretty watch with a dark-brown leather band. The face of the watch was oval. It didn't look new.

"That's a very special gift for you," she said. "It was my mother's watch."

I looked up at her, surprised.

"I know you wished your father had saved your mother's watch. You told me a few times. Well, that's a mother's watch," she said, nodding. "You can pretend she was yours."

I took it out slowly, and she came around to help put it on my wrist. It just fit.

"You just wind it once a day, and be sure you don't overwind it. I had it checked by a jeweler a few years ago."

I touched it and looked at her. "Thank you, Mazy," I said.

"Happy birthday. You're a good girl," she said, and shocked me by leaning down to kiss my cheek. "Let's have some cake."

She cut my piece and cut one for herself.

"When is your birthday?" I asked.

"Mine was yesterday," she said.

I nearly dropped the fork. "Why didn't you tell me?"

She shook her head. "Maybe," she said, "I'll tell you next year."

CHAPTER SIX

Next year?

I was happy she had given me a watch and a kiss and made my birthday so special, but when she said "next year" so casually, saying it as if I should know I'd be here, I felt an icy surge of fear travel up my stomach and into my chest.

What made her say such a thing? Had she learned something more about Daddy? How could she even think it, imagine a whole year would go by and I would still be here, waiting for Daddy? What had he told her? Had something serious happened to him? Were there more questions for him to answer back at his new home? A year! Something had to have happened. Did he send another letter, or did he call her? If it was a letter, that letter might have been so terrible that she couldn't get herself to give it to me. But she had to. It was for me. Did she hide it, rip it up?

She had just given me a wonderful present. I didn't want to make her feel like I hated it here, but surely by now, Daddy and I were supposed to be in our new home, and I was supposed to be in a real school, where I could make friends. Next year, I hoped I'd have a real birthday party. Mama had promised me. I didn't want to believe that I was going to be here another year. When would I have friends?

"Did my daddy call you and you didn't tell me? Or did he write another letter?" I asked. "A letter you forgot to give me or read to me or maybe thought was too terrible?"

She didn't answer.

"Please, tell me."

Her face seemed to swell as it turned apple red. "Tell you? Tell you what? Wouldn't I tell you if he had called or there was a new letter? Why would I keep any of that secret? That's not a very nice thing to think about me. And after all the things I've done and am doing for you. I'll tell you what, Saffron, from now on, you be the one who goes out at two o'clock and brings in the mail every day. You can sift through it and look for a letter from your father. Snow, rain, or shine, you be the one," she said, and quickly walked out of the room and to the stairway.

She left me trembling.

The thump of her footsteps on the stairs sounded like Mama's after she had said something angrily to Daddy and had gone up to her room. Sometimes I would hurry up after her. She would pout, sit, and stare. Even though her eyes were open, she wouldn't see me. She wouldn't hear me, either. I would feel how much my body wanted to be next to hers, how much I wanted to feel her arms around me as I cuddled my head on her shoulder and fell asleep. I was afraid to touch her when she sat looking so frozen. Tears wanted to stream out of my eyes, but I would force them back. They fell inside me. Mama wouldn't see; she wouldn't know how frightened and alone she made me feel.

I felt like that now, felt as alone as I had felt when I was on that bench at the train station.

Mr. Pebbles was looking at me as if he was waiting to see what I would do about it. I was caught between feeling frightened and feeling guilty. I decided to sit in the kitchen and wait a while, hoping she would come back down and tell me everything was all right. She didn't mean to shout at me. She just lost her temper a little. I shouldn't worry. I didn't really have to get the mail every day.

But she didn't come back downstairs. The clock ticked. It seemed to be getting louder and louder every passing minute. Otherwise, the house was silent. No sounds came in from the outside. There were snow flurries rushing across the kitchen window, and since we were on a cul-de-sac, there was rarely the sound of a car. We might as well be on a street where there were no other houses or people. I had no one else but the Umbrella Lady. For a little while, when we were celebrating my birthday, that didn't seem to matter, but now that something terrible had happened, I had no one to turn to, no one to comfort me.

How could such a happy time become so sad and scary so quickly? This was like being under a cloudless sky one moment, and then, after you looked down, you looked up and saw that it was completely overcast and dark. Magically, the warm air had turned chilly, and you couldn't stop quaking inside.

Suddenly, I realized that maybe she had expected me to feel sorrier for her than I did for myself. After what she had told me, shouldn't I have stopped thinking about myself first? Who has to treat her birthday as if it was just another day? Didn't she ever celebrate it? Didn't she get nice presents from her parents before her mother had left them? Was that when she stopped having birthdays? Why didn't her father make her birthdays? There was no sister or brother calling, not even an aunt or uncle. Why didn't any of the neighbors stop by to say hello, or even call to wish her a happy birthday? She might as well be sitting on a train-station bench every day, waiting for a train that would never come.

Maybe that was why she had said next year. She was hoping that now that I was here, she could have a birthday again. Maybe I'd make her a cake. She'd let me try. She must have thought that I was acting like I didn't care, that I was concerned only about hearing from Daddy and leaving. If I did leave, she thought she'd never hear from me again, especially not on her birthday. Maybe Daddy would send her or bring her a thank-you present, but once I was used to a new home and friends, I'd forget her. Other people obviously had.

I looked at the watch she had given me and felt even guiltier. Instead of raving about how beautiful it was, I had demanded to know about Daddy, demanded to know when I'd be out of here and away from her, never returning, probably for good. Now I truly did feel terrible. I got up, glanced at Mr. Pebbles, who stood up, too, and headed for the stairway.

I walked slowly up. Maybe she was going to tell me more about the watch and more about her mother. I never let her even start. I saw that she had left the door of her bedroom open. I went to it and looked in to see her lying on the bed and staring at the ceiling. She didn't turn to me, but I could tell that she knew I was standing there.

Before I could ask anything, she began. She spoke like someone thinking aloud. I didn't move or make a sound, afraid she would stop.

"I told you my mother had left me, too. I must have told you at least a dozen times if I told you once. She didn't die like your mother did, but she might as well have died. I never heard from her again once she boarded that train. She was just like a dead person, silent in her grave, never here to hug me and give me a birthday present. The difference between you and me was, my father couldn't go looking for another wife. He wasn't a well man when my mother left us. I told you how I had to take care of him. But there is no doubt in my mind that if he could have looked for another woman, he would have done just what your father has done. He would have neglected me, practically forgotten about me. Only I wouldn't have been lucky enough to have someone like me to take care of me."

She pulled herself into a sitting position and turned to me.

"That's why I felt sorry for you from the moment I set eyes on you at the train station and then decided I would care for you. I thought of myself and how I had felt, and I was sure you were feeling the same . . . lost, with no one to care for you. I wasn't going to let you be lost. I still won't. I'm going to make you into a fine young lady who won't be dependent on a man or another woman. Someday, when you're my age, you'll think back and never stop thanking me. I know you're too young to realize it now, but you will.

"Men need a lot more than women need. They're weaker, and not just on the inside. You'll see. Your father is so desperate that some woman will have an easy time taking advantage of him. It's probably what's happening now. It's his own fault, but in the meantime, there's you. Why should you be neglected?"

Then she quickly added, "You won't," before I could utter a sound.

Maybe she thought I would still cry to find Daddy. Maybe she thought that was the real reason I had come up the stairs.

"You'll be here, safe, growing stronger and wiser. You will be happy, too. I promise you that."

She stared at me, now almost daring me to disagree.

I walked into the room, right up to the bed, and said, "I'm sorry. I'm sorry I didn't know about your birthday, Mazy. I have nothing to give you, but I would have drawn a picture for you if you had told me when it was going to be."

I wasn't sure what else I should add, but that seemed to be enough.

She smiled. "You can still do that. I'd like that. I'm sure it will be good enough for us to frame and put up in the kitchen. How nice of you to think of it. What a wonderful and strong young lady you will be." Then she looked serious again, her lips quivering as if she was going to cry. "You had some very sad thoughts before, didn't you? All sad thoughts about your daddy, right? That's why you snapped at me like that."

I didn't snap at you, I wanted to say. *I just asked a question.*

Instead, I nodded.

"What do we do?" she asked. "What do we do when we hear sad thoughts in our heads? Well?"

"I'll get my pennies," I said, and she smiled again.

"Exactly. Then you won't even think of being nasty and belligerent."

She got out of the bed and put her hand on my shoulder. We walked out together and down the stairs. I went to my room, took some pennies out of one of the rolls she had given me, and went to the kitchen, where she had the jar on the table. She watched me drop them in.

"You don't have to think about your daddy for a while now," she said. "And you don't have to go out to get the mail. That was a silly thing for me to say. Okay?"

I nodded.

"Come on. We can forget anything unpleasant now that we've put the pennies in the jar. We'll watch television together."

She took my hand and we walked to the living room. After we sat on the sofa but before I turned the television on, I took a deep breath and asked, "Did you mean it when you said I would be here another year?"

"Well, you'll certainly be here until your father comes for you, won't you? If it's another year, it's another year. I won't be throwing you out or taking you to some social service agency that will file you away."

"But my father said I would go to school when we had our new home."

"Well, you are going to school. I'm a certified teacher with years more experience than your mother had. You're in a class-room. You'll be taking the official tests. And when your father comes and you go to a public school, you'll be so far ahead of the other children your age, they won't know what to do with you. They'll have to move you ahead. I'd say you were pretty lucky I found you at the train station, wouldn't you?"

"Yes," I said, even though I didn't feel at all lucky.

"So then, let's not worry any more about school. I can tell you I'd promote you already. Come on, turn on the television. I like your programs."

She sat back and waited. I turned it on, and for a while, I didn't think about anything else or ask her any more questions.

I knew that was just what she wanted. *Silence sometimes is the best answer to everything*, I thought, and then thought she would tell me that was a wisdom quote.

Later, she did something she rarely had done. She followed me to my room, waited for me to go to the bathroom, brush my teeth, and get into my pajamas, and then she fixed the comforter around me and sat on my bed.

"Many little girls have their mothers read them a story or tell them a fairy tale when they go to bed. Did your mother do that?"

"Not for a long time," I said. I said it sadly, because I had been missing it. "But my father used to tell me a bedtime story sometimes."

"Did he?" she asked, surprised.

"He talked about Mama when she was prettier and happier and all the nice things they used to do together."

"Well, you see, some fairy tales or bedtime stories don't have a happy ending, do they? Many don't have happy beginnings, either. When I was a teacher in a public school, I liked to tell my students the truth about some fairy tales. Children who grow up believing in make-believe and fairy tales get burned by reality."

Burned? Was she talking about Mama?

"Did your mother ever tell you about Humpty Dumpty?" she asked.

"Oh, yes," I said, and recited it.

"Very good. Now, here's the truth. Humpty Dumpty was a powerful cannon used in the English Civil War. In an English town known as Colchester, the cannon was put on the roof of the church known as Saint Mary's by the Wall. The attacking soldiers fired on the roof, and the gun came tumbling down. It couldn't be fixed and brought back up there. Do you still feel like singing Humpty Dumpty now, singing about some cannon?"

I shook my head.

"That's why you have to be careful of fairy tales. See this hand?" she said, holding hers up. "Believe in what you see and touch and hear for yourself."

I stared at her hand. She closed it into a fist and looked at me. I focused on her eyes. I could almost feel what she was saying.

"Was Daddy's last letter a fairy tale?"

She smiled and sat straight. "Like Humpty Dumpty . . . we have to let time pass to see what is the truth."

"If it's a fairy tale, then it's a lie?"

"Sometimes," she said. She rose and fixed my blanket. "I've had my share of those sent my way. I'll do my best to keep your share away. Happy birthday, Saffron Faith Anders."

"And happy birthday to you, Mazy Dazy."

She laughed and went out, closing my door softly. Mr. Pebbles leaped onto my bed and curled up at my feet.

"When's your birthday?" I asked him. He stared and then lowered his head and closed his eyes.

Somewhere far-off, Daddy must have thought about me today. He must have remembered. *Oh, yes, today is her birthday.* But he didn't send a present or call me.

I'd never tell Mazy what I was really thinking.

I was really thinking Daddy was afraid I wouldn't love him anymore.

Mazy would see how sad it made me, and she would jump on me at the first signs of it. She'd whip out the jar and go into a long lecture about how hard I should try to avoid sadness. Why was she permitted to believe in a fairy tale—because that was all the jar of sadness was, a fairy tale—and I wasn't? I didn't stop thinking about these things I wished for. Did she stop thinking about all her wishes? Why was some make-believe all right but some not? I wanted to ask but was afraid to make her angry again. The jar was so important to her that she'd surely be even more enraged.

I tried not to think about Daddy for quite a while afterward. Whenever she brought in the mail, I didn't anticipate a new letter from him, nor did I ask her if there was one. I was starting to have different hopeful dreams, too. If I was really getting to be as smart as she claimed I was, she was probably right: kids my age would want to know me more when I finally did go to school.

Sometimes, when she was downstairs and I knew she wouldn't know that I was not doing the schoolwork, I would go to the window and look out on the street just to catch a glimpse of another young boy or girl. For me right now, it wasn't much different from watching television. They couldn't see me watching them, and I couldn't talk to them, nor could they talk to me, but it was still fun for me to imagine myself out there with them.

I realized there was a girl who didn't look very much older than I was, if older at all, living in the fourth house on the right, on the way toward the village and the train station. She had light-brown hair and looked to be as tall as I was. I had yet to see her when Mazy and I walked somewhere. It occurred to me, however, that we usually left the house when school would be in session. We didn't go anywhere on weekends.

Was that because she was afraid I would meet someone and make a friend too soon? Or was that because she was worried about me going to someone else's house or having someone come here to play with me? She claimed going on weekdays was easier shopping, because fewer people had the time since they were at work and school. Now that I had a watch, however, I was able to keep closer tabs on when the children on the street were out, doing things together. I tried to think of a reason for me to go out on the street, but Mazy always had something for me to do during those hours. And it was always too cold or just plain nasty to play outside, even in the spring. Why didn't the parents of those kids think the same way?

One day, when the winter came again, I even suggested that she and I build a snowman together. For a moment, I thought she would agree. Then she said, "What for? It will only melt and look terrible, and besides, why encourage these busybodies to come over here?"

It was as if she could read my thoughts and knew that my real reason was to attract the attention of the kids on our street.

She went into a long rant about why people were nosy. They either had boring lives or simply wanted to get "dirt" on you to spread and look like some sort of know-it-all.

"Gossip," she said, "is the lifeblood of the miserable, insecure failures who suck on other people's business like vampires."

The vicious and nasty way she sometimes talked about other people made me think she wouldn't mind being the last person on the earth alive. She would get so angry that her face would turn crimson, and her eyes would look like the embers in the fireplace. Her way of getting me to stop asking about going out was to increase the amount of television time I could have. The schoolwork, the constant cleaning, and the increasing household chores easily filled the day and left me tired enough to fall asleep watching television during my added hours.

And then, after I had been living with her for so long, she decided she would teach me how to cook. It was really just another class, reading from recipes and learning the techniques. For a while, it was very interesting and quite exciting for me to be the one who made our entire dinner, desserts included.

All the while, her questions about Mama and Daddy were dropped in between things we were doing and saying. Sometimes I thought that if it wasn't for her asking about them, I'd completely forget about them. I was certainly not thinking of Daddy as much as I should be. She seemed to want to know more about Mama, anyway.

I remembered her asking, what kind of clothes did she wear?

How often did she go out to shop? How often was she on the phone? Who visited her? When did all that dwindle until it was nothing? If she saw that her questions were making me sad, she stopped asking quickly. A few times, she ran for the jar and her pennies and slapped herself. It got so I was really afraid to think about Mama, at least when she could sense I was doing it.

Another spring began to whisper it was coming. We spent a lot more time cleaning the house in spring because "winter had kept us from letting it breathe fresh air." There was some new planting to do, too. As soon as the ground was ready, we refreshed all the flower beds. She took me with her to the nursery to buy the plants. Whenever we went anywhere during the school day, people in the stores always asked her why I wasn't at school.

"She is," she would always say. "She's being homeschooled. She's brilliant."

No one questioned why, but I felt funny at the way they looked at me. I had grown quite a bit. My next birthday would be my eleventh, so it didn't surprise me that they would wonder. It was as if I was something different, something very odd.

I was happiest when she permitted me to spend time in the backyard by myself and didn't stand watching every move I made.

One afternoon when I was out there, I heard voices in the woods and then laughter. I walked farther out and listened. Two young boys, probably not much more than eleven or twelve, came running from the left. They were both holding long shaved sticks they were wielding like swords, pausing every few feet to turn on each other and slap the imaginary weapons against each other's. Neither looked like he really wanted to hurt the other. They turned and continued in my direction. I didn't move a muscle, but the first boy suddenly stopped, and the second walked up slowly beside him. They both gazed at me as if I were some sort of magical figure who had just appeared out of a shadow.

The first boy was taller, with dark-brown hair. The second had reddish-brown hair. I thought I had seen them both from my home classroom window. Both were wearing jeans and black shirts with the words *Martian Soldier* printed on them. I suppose the way I stood so still confused them. I didn't think they'd be afraid of me, but neither said anything or took another step in my direction.

The first boy suddenly raised his stick and shouted, "HA!" Then they both turned and ran back in the direction from which they had come, screaming and squealing, neither turning to see if I was following. I watched them until they had disappeared behind some thicker and older oak trees.

I didn't know how the Umbrella Lady found out, but days later, Mazy just started laughing in the kitchen as we were getting everything together for dinner. I was setting the table. I stopped and looked at her, curious. She laughed often at something I had said and laughed at things we both saw on television, but I rarely heard her laugh at her own thoughts. I didn't think she would tell me why, but she turned around, still laughing.

"You didn't tell me some of the boys on the street saw you in the woods," she said.

Was I supposed to? Did this mean she wouldn't let me go out in the backyard again? I wondered.

"They didn't come onto your property," I said, thinking that might be what she would want me to tell.

"They call you the 'Tree Girl,'" she said.

"Why?"

"I imagine these boys never saw you until then, and there you were in the woods watching them. You just appeared as if you had come out of a tree."

"What does that mean?"

"It means," she practically whispered, her eyes wide and bright, "that they're afraid of you. That's good. They won't come around here bothering us. If you see them again, just stare at them, and don't answer them if they shout questions at you."

"But . . ."

"But what?"

Would these boys make all the kids on our street afraid of me? I thought. I would never have a friend.

"No one will like me here."

"Nonsense. Besides, why would you want to be around boys who made up strange things about you? When the time comes for you to have friends—"

"When's that?" I asked quickly.

"You'll know," she said. "Don't forget, I was a teacher. I saw the way other boys and girls could spoil someone who was nearly perfect like you. They're either jealous or just plain mischievous. Someone who's developing good habits like you are often gets corrupted. You could have the strongest, brightest mind, but when it comes to the false value of having the others like you, you end up belittling yourself, deliberately doing poorly in your studies, so you won't seem like you're too far above them, which you are, or . . ."

She turned back to her dinner preparations.

"Or what?"

"Or they talk you into doing bad things to yourself and others. Don't worry. I'll explain it all to you so that when the time comes, you'll be ready. Don't you see?" she asked, turning back to me. "You have a built-in fortune-teller, someone who knows from experience how other children behave and what they will become. You'll be so strong that no one will be able to ruin you.

"Just be sure," she warned, with those eyes turning beady and firm, "you do what I tell you and listen to what I say. Okay?"

For a moment, I thought only about Mama and how adamant she had been that I not go to public or private school, that I stay home with her tutoring me.

The Umbrella Lady was the same. I wondered if the reason was the same reason Daddy said Mama wanted me home. She didn't want to be alone.

But keeping me in her house until she said I was absolutely ready to go to school with other kids my age made me think of something else.

What about Daddy? He'll be coming for me someday, won't he? He'll put me in school with other kids. I'm not going to be with you forever.

Those were the words I was thinking, but I swallowed them back as quickly as they came up. They came up often, but I knew that it would make her angry that I was looking forward to a time when I wouldn't have to do what she said and listen to her orders.

"Okay?" she asked again.

"Okay," I said.

"Good." Her smile returned. She went back to our dinner and laughed. "The Tree Girl," she said. "Maybe one day, I'll paste some leaves to your arms and hands." She laughed harder.

The image frightened me, because I imagined roots growing out of my feet. I fumbled some silverware, and the forks fell to the floor.

She spun around. "What are you doing? Since when are you so clumsy?"

I picked them up quickly.

"Bring them to the sink, and get new ones. We haven't done this floor for a few days. Germs could be crawling all around us."

I did it quickly. She watched me closely.

"We'll go shopping tomorrow," she said. "I want to get you some new things. You're growing so fast now."

She thought about it.

"Tomorrow's Wednesday. It shouldn't be very busy at the department store."

Yes, Wednesday, I thought, *when none of the kids will see me in the street. They'll be at school.*

I'll be alone without friends until Daddy comes for me.

Weeks went by sometimes without me thinking about that. And when I did think about it, the thought occurred that it really was like saying *Santa Claus is coming*.

And after all, what was Santa Claus?

Just another fairy tale.

CHAPTER SEVEN

Mazy surprised me at breakfast right after she served me some scrambled eggs. She was better at making them than Mama was, although I would never say so and even felt guilty thinking it.

She paused in front of me, putting her hands on her hips, which told me something important was coming.

"I have to take you to the public school," she said.

"I'm going to school?" I asked quickly. *Finally*, I thought.

"Only to take a special test."

"What kind of test?" I asked, my voice dripping with disappointment.

"A test to see how you're doing with homeschooling. The state requires it."

"When?"

"Today," she said.

"Today?"

I thought I would need more time to prepare. I hadn't been in a school building ever. What if I failed this special test? What would happen? Would I never be able to enter public school? How angry would Mazy be?

"Don't look so worried," she said, smiling. "This is why I didn't tell you ahead of time. You would have built it up in your mind and made yourself so nervous and sick you wouldn't do well. If I didn't think you would do well, I wouldn't have arranged it yet. I would have found ways to put it off, but I don't think I'll ever have to do that with you."

She sat and sipped her coffee.

"I used to teach in this school system. Children from all the surrounding communities go there. The grade-school principal knows who I am. I had been teaching four years when she first began. She always looked up to me. I gave her good advice about her career, so she owes me. You'll be treated special."

"Doesn't a mother or a father have to be the one to take me there?"

I saw how much the question annoyed her. She pressed on her lips and dropped the corners before replying.

"Normally, yes, but that's not possible, is it? And you have to take the test. Actually, I'm looking forward to your taking it."

"Why?"

"I'll admit it has to do with my ego."

"What's that mean?"

"I was the best grade-school teacher they had." She finished her coffee and rose to take the cup to the sink but stopped and turned back to me. "Those who don't believe it will eat their skepticism and choke on it once they learn what I have accomplished with you in so short a time. Actually, they'll be jealous."

"Jealous? Of me?"

"No, silly goose, of me. I doubt any of them in all the grade-school classes has a student like you. Your talents could have gone to waste. Sometimes things happen for the best, even though we might not realize it for a long time, a lifetime, in fact."

What did she mean? What had happened was for the best? It was good that there was a fire and my mother died and that Daddy left me here? Maybe she meant only the best for her.

"I told the grade-school principal, Mrs. Elliot, that you are my granddaughter, anyway," she casually added. "You must remember to say the same thing if you're asked, just like I always told you to do. It makes everything much easier for us both. And it doesn't hurt anyone, right?"

She waited for me to nod and then smiled.

Lies as tools, I thought. *Lies as tools*.

After we cleaned up our breakfast dishes, she had me change into something nicer, something she had bought me on her own just a few days before. I was surprised, but she said she had seen it in a store window, and the saleslady assured her it was popular with girls my age. It was called a skater or fit-and-flare dress, with large flowers of pink, yellow, and green on white.

"My, you look grown-up already," she said when I put it on. I put on a light-blue jacket and my newest pink sports shoes and brushed my hair. I did like what I looked like. Maybe it was only my imagination, or maybe it was because she constantly told me, but I thought I had grown and looked years older than I was. She inspected me, smiled, and nodded.

"Let's go."

She took my hand as soon as we stepped onto the street to walk to the school. She had gotten dressed nicely, too. I had never seen her in this light-blue skirt suit. She was proud that it still fit her well.

"I wore this on my last day of class years ago," she said. "The only wrinkles are in my face."

She laughed. I was surprised at how happy a day this really was for her. I used to think she never wanted it to happen. My heart pounded with even more excitement and concern. What if I didn't pass the test? What if I disappointed her and made her look foolish? She had always taught me to keep my expectations low so that any disappointment wouldn't feel as bad. "No matter what you believe," she said, "you want there to be some surprise when something wonderful happens."

As we approached the front door of the grade school, I was sure Mazy could feel my fingers tighten around hers. She paused, nodded at me, and said, "All the necessary paperwork has been done. You're all set. There's nothing to do but take the test, Saffron. So just relax and concentrate on the questions the way I taught you."

Mrs. Elliot was waiting right inside the main entrance. She looked as old as Mazy, if not a little older, and wore what I thought was a dress suit made the same day as Mazy's.

"I should be mad at you for keeping away so long," she told Mazy. "I haven't had a good coffee klatch since you retired."

Mazy shrugged. "I'm not one to return to the scene of a crime."

"Oh, how funny," Mrs. Elliot said. She turned to me as if she had just realized Mazy had brought me along. "Why, hello there," she said, staring down at me with a broad smile on her face. She had her hands on her hips just the way Mazy kept hers when she was saying something she thought important. Was it a grade-school-teacher thing? "Posture speaks volumes," Mazy once said.

"Hello," I said.

"Your name is Saffron?"

"Yes, ma'am," I said.

"What an unusual but obviously very perfect name for you. Names have always been very important to your grandmother. Remember how we played that game with student names, Mazy?"

"Helped bring some humor to an otherwise depressing day sometimes."

"Who was our favorite? I remember," she said before Mazy could reply. "If Chris Barton married Teddy Kross, she'd be Chris Kross."

They both laughed.

Mrs. Elliot looked at Mazy seriously. "You're going to have to tell me more about all this."

"Let's get her started first."

"Yes, let's." She smiled at me. "Are you ready, Saffron?"

I glanced at Mazy, who didn't smile.

"Of course she's ready," she said. "I wouldn't be here with her if she wasn't."

"Well, let's begin, then," Mrs. Elliot said. We walked quickly through the school lobby. All the classroom doors were shut, and no one else was in the hallway. She brought me to a room in which I would be the only one sitting at a desk.

After I was seated, Mazy and Mrs. Elliot stood in the doorway and talked about me. I had been given the test to read first, but I listened keenly to what Mazy was saying. She leaned on her umbrella as she spoke. They talked first about other teachers who had come and gone and the principal who had died. I heard how Mrs. Elliot had gone on to become the principal after Mazy had retired. She said she would follow in Mazy's footsteps after another year and become the same lady of leisure. She asked Mazy if she missed being a teacher. Mazy looked at me and said, "A little, but then she came, and I was right back at it."

They were both looking at me.

"She's adorable," Mrs. Elliot said. "You devil, you, keeping it a secret for all these years."

"It was the devil who insisted," Mazy said.

"Don't say that too loud," Mrs. Elliot told her. "There are people here who would believe it. Especially about you, Mrs. Grouch."

"Suits me fine," Mazy said, and they both laughed. Then Mazy grew very serious. "Her parents died in a terrible house fire recently. If it wasn't for this heroic fireman . . ." She shook her head. Mrs. Elliot looked at me sadly, and I quickly looked at the booklet. "I know you agree with me. A little girl this fragile belongs in homeschooling."

"Well, Mazy," Mrs. Elliot said, "if anyone can get her strong enough to overcome such a tragedy and return to interaction with others her age, it's you. Look at how many others you put on the right track, whether they liked it or not."

"You mean whether their parents liked it or not."

"Yes. It's worse now, I'm afraid. If we yell too loudly, they threaten to sue us. I doubt you'd last."

They both turned to me again.

"This time, this one, will be the biggest challenge of my life," Mazy said. "And not because it's personal."

"But also she will be the biggest success, I'm sure."

Why did Mazy say both my parents had died? Only my mother had died. *Lies as tools*, I thought again. They lowered their voices and talked some more, glancing my way occasionally.

I started the exam and finished it in half the time I was given to do so. Mazy and I watched Mrs. Elliot review it. Mazy told me she was doing her a personal favor instead of assigning it to another teacher.

"It's a hundred percent," she said as soon as she had finished. She looked a little astonished. "Children under such psychological trauma don't usually do this well." She smiled at Mazy and added, "Chip off the old block."

"Old?"

They laughed.

"I'll take care of the formalities. Congratulations, Mazy," Mrs. Elliot told her.

Mazy turned to me. "Let's go home," she said, seizing my hand and moving me along as if a moment longer in the building might infect me with some incurable disease.

"Please call me if there's anything more you need, Mazy," Mrs. Elliot said.

"Thank you, Erna. I appreciate your help."

"Call me if you need any additional materials. I believe you have that updated math text."

"I do. And thank you," Mazy said. They hugged, and we started toward the entrance.

Mazy held my hand tightly, as tightly as she would if she thought I might turn and rush into a classroom. I wanted to.

I wanted to plop right down beside that girl I saw from my window sometimes, smile, and introduce myself. How many times had I dreamed of us walking home together from this very building?

I resisted Mazy's rushing us out and paused to look through a classroom door window. I could see a row of students who didn't look much older than I was. I kept looking until, although I didn't see the girl on my street, I did see some of the boys. It was clear to me that they weren't paying attention to their teacher. They were passing notes and poking each other.

Mazy stopped, too, and then she surprised me.

"Maybe it's a good idea for you to look in there," she said, and took me right up to the door so I could see the whole classroom. "Go on. Look."

I did.

"See how many students are in that room with that one teacher? It's wall to wall. She's supposed to care for each and every one of them. You know what happens? You can see how they're misbehaving."

I shook my head.

"She pays attention to a few and forgets about the others. They sink or swim on their own. That's what I had to do when I was a teacher in this building, but I don't have to do that with you. Come on," she said, tugging me away. I glanced back as if she was dragging me from somewhere I still longed to be.

Maybe the students in that room wouldn't learn as much as I did, but they had each other; they had friends.

She hurried me out of the front entrance as if the building was on fire, muttering under her breath.

"I spent years and years trying to educate children like that. Every year, they added more students to my room. One year, I didn't even have enough desks! That's right. The students had to stand until they found us more desks.

"And what do you have that those students back there don't?" she asked, as we hurried away from the building. I didn't even dare look back now as she charged forward. "You have your own classroom and your own teacher. Think I'll let you sink or swim? Absolutely not. That's why you just knocked the socks off that test and impressed Mrs. Elliot. I know she'll be telling everyone, all the other teachers, about you today. And about me! Faculty rooms are dens of gossip, but I refused to be any part of that. They always resented me for being so tight-lipped about myself. People today will tell you all their personal information in a heartbeat. There's no self-respect. But that wasn't me. That was never me."

She suddenly stopped and caught her breath. She had been ranting, and she knew it. She glanced back toward the school and then looked at me. I was actually a little frightened now. She was more the Umbrella Lady again than she was Mazy Dazy. I think she knew it.

"If I don't stop, we'll fill that jar of pennies." She took a deep breath and looked at people on the street who were looking our way. "Busybodies," she muttered. "You don't know how lucky you really are not being exposed to all this."

She looked at me and smiled.

"I'm forgetting that you deserve a reward. I know it will hurt your appetite for lunch, but we'll get you an ice-cream cone."

She turned and led me to a store with gas pumps in front of it. We had never been here, but after we entered, she knew to go to the right, where there was a freezer.

"You like chocolate the most, just like me," she said, and reached in to get the cone.

The young man at the counter was scratching on a lottery card and almost didn't notice us. Mazy slapped down the money and made him jump in his seat. "Dreamer," she called him, and led me out. She paused to unwrap the cone and hand it to me.

"As you grow older, you will find yourself surrounded by stupidity. It will be like swimming through a swamp, but you'll get through it and leave them where they belong . . . nowhere. That's what I did. Most teachers tell their students to do as they say, not as they do. I'm not most teachers. Do as I do. You'll have less grief."

Mazy could really rant and rave, I thought. It took so little to get her to explode in small speeches.

We marched on, with me trying to eat my cone and keep up with her. When we turned down our street, I paused. The girl

I had seen from my classroom window occasionally was sitting on the front porch of her house, only today she was wrapped in a blanket. The sight of her apparently reminded Mazy of something.

"We have to get you some new inoculations," she said. "I've been neglecting it because you haven't been mingling with other children."

"What inoculations?"

"We'll see what you need now. I'm a friend of a woman who is still a school nurse, Lil Miller. She'll tell us and then come to the house with them."

I was surprised to hear that Mazy had any friends. She kept so much of her life a secret, just as she had always done, apparently. But whenever she had gone out and left me at the house, I assumed it was only to shop for something we needed or go to a garage sale. She was particularly fond of buying from people who had to sell, because she'd always get a bargain.

But it suddenly occurred to me that she might be going to visit someone. Why didn't she invite whoever it was to her house? No one ever came calling on his or her own, and the phone rarely rang. When it did, she usually slammed the receiver down, moaning about "nuisance calls." Of course, I always was hoping it was Daddy.

Maybe, I suddenly thought, she doesn't want people to meet me. She would have to lie so much, just as she just had, and so would I.

We walked on, but she kept talking. She was well into an-other one of her favorite tirades.

"You see why I want to keep you from mixing with these kids as long as I can? They infect each other constantly. One gets a cold, and then they all do."

She began another story, one I had heard at least five or six times. Did she forget she had told me, or did she think I'd forgotten?

"I once had a class in which so many were sneezing and coughing I had to wear a surgical mask to keep out the germs. And I wouldn't let them come up front or touch me. I wore gloves, so when I touched their papers, I didn't contract the germs. That's what you would get if you went up and said hello to that girl back there, and if you were in her class in school, I imagine."

I turned and looked back at the girl. She was watching us. I thought she had raised her hand to wave to me, but I was afraid to wave back. Mazy rushed me through the gate and into the house as if it had started to rain icicles. When she closed the door behind me, she leaned against it and took deep breaths.

"You risk your life in one way or another every time you step out of this house or off my property. I don't want you playing out front anymore. You keep to the backyard," she said. "Those kids out there already enjoy making fun of you, calling you the Tree Girl. Who knows what else they'll make up about you? Did you hear me?" she practically screamed, because I was looking down and thinking how unhappy that made me, especially now.

I nodded, but as soon as I was able to, I went upstairs to the classroom and looked out the window toward the house where the girl had been sitting on the porch. I was disappointed to see she was gone. When I heard Mazy's steps on the stairway, I quickly went to my desk and opened the workbook she had set out yesterday.

She smiled when she entered. "That's good," she said. "You're anxious to learn. Today we start more advanced math. You'll be a high school senior by the time you are supposed to be a ninth or tenth grader. You'll see."

She handed me a new textbook.

"I gathered some new materials for you last week, including that math book Mrs. Elliot mentioned. We have new workbooks and some other books I've taken from the public library. When you're older, I'll send you there with assignments."

"How much older do I have to be? I see girls my age walking alone or with friends, not adults."

"They don't carry your baggage."

"Baggage? What baggage?"

"Your family history, Saffron. It has made you vulnerable in ways you don't yet understand. Just leave it to me to decide when you're ready to wander about on your own. It has nothing to do with how old you are. I know what awaits you out there. Assassins, all of them."

"Assassins?" I thought about the word. "How are they assassins?"

She ignored me and glanced at the window as if I had left my fingerprints on it.

"Maybe you shouldn't be spending so much time spying on them."

"I'm not spying."

"Whatever. Meanwhile, I'll arrange for my friend Mrs. Miller to come here with the shots you need. You can catch things from adults, too," she said.

She paused.

"I don't imagine your father was even thinking about that," she said.

She hadn't mentioned Daddy for some time. Did I dare ask?

"No," she said before I could. "There have been no phone calls or new letters from him. Now, let's get to work so we don't have sad thoughts and need the jar."

She didn't have to remind me. I wasn't thinking about Daddy as much as I used to. Every day, every month, every year that had passed made his voice and his face more cloudy. It hadn't occurred to me until just recently that I had no pictures of him or my mother. Daddy hadn't saved any that were in the house, and if he had any in his wallet, he didn't give them to me. Why would he? I asked myself. He wasn't supposed to leave me at the station. I wasn't supposed to need pictures to remember either of them.

Whenever I was doodling and thinking about Mama and Daddy, I tried drawing their faces, but the pictures were never good enough so I crumpled them up and threw them away. I was feeling more and more like someone who had woken up on a raft at sea. The wind and the water were driving me farther and farther away, even away from my memories. Most of the time, I was either too tired or too busy to work on my getting them back.

In the days after Mazy had found me, I would sit at the window in my room at night after Mazy had gone to sleep and thought I had, too, and look out at the stars, wondering if Daddy was thinking about me and what it was like for Mama in heaven. More than anything else, the sadness exhausted me and drove me into a deep sleep. Maybe Mazy was right about the pennies.

I rarely sat at the window in my bedroom in the evening anymore. It was as if I was afraid of the stars, afraid of imagining Mama looking down at me. As guilty as it made me feel to think it, I knew in my heart that I was deliberately avoiding ways to remember.

That night at dinner, I told Mazy about it. Maybe doing so well on the test and moving along with my life made me feel guiltier than ever. I should be suffering, curled up in a room, and refusing to breathe until my father came for me. Instead, I was thriving, growing, learning, and dreaming of doing all the fun things I saw and imagined others my age on our street were doing.

She smiled and nodded. "That's a good thing," she said. "Forgetting."

"Why? How could that be a good thing to forget my mother? And why stop hoping my father will come?"

"It's less painful. Remembering little details would only bring sad thoughts, too." She nodded toward the cabinet where the sadness jar was kept. "You have to think about nice things now. You have to think about your future and all the things you and I could do to make this a happier place to live in."

"But Daddy will come for me someday," I insisted. Even I thought that sounded so thin, as thin as words formed with bubbles.

She nodded, but I could practically feel the skepticism. It was what made the words so fragile. They practically crumbled as soon as I uttered them. Maybe to Mazy's credit, she looked for ways to get me to stop being unhappy about it.

"Yes, but in the meantime, you're growing up fast, Saffron, faster than other children your age, because you're with me, learning quicker and more. Soon you will become like me . . . skeptical of what people say, especially their promises."

"Why are you so sure of that?"

"I can tell. I can see it. You're too smart. You won't believe in fairy tales that easily," she said. "That's really what most promises are, fairy tales. That's why you're forgetting so quickly," she added, widening her smile. "You're developing a mature sense of what is true and what is not."

"I don't want to," I said. "It makes me feel like I'm setting fire to who I really am."

She stopped smiling. "You will want to," she insisted. She looked terribly confident, so confident that it made me sick inside. "You know why you will?"

I didn't answer or ask. I knew what she wanted. She had said it. Not only do as she does but become what she was. I really didn't want to know that I might very well grow up to be just like her.

"Why?" I had to ask.

"That's the only way you'll go on living and having even the smallest chance to be happy," she said, sounding just like someone who did know everything. "Let's not talk about it right now. Let's finish our meal. I have a new book for you to begin tonight, so there'll be no television," she said. "It's really a play by Shakespeare. Remember when I told you about him? I was quite the literature student, you know. That's why teaching English is my strongest subject. It'll be a little more difficult than most everything I've given you to read, but I'll be helping you more. Doesn't that excite you?"

I nodded, but I wasn't at all excited.

I saw how that annoyed her. Her purplish gray eyes glared at me, her mouth becoming a slash of pale pink again. I was sure she realized that all the schoolwork in the world, all the tests I passed, and all the promises she made for my future didn't or couldn't get me to stop thinking about Daddy.

In fact, right now I wanted, as I had wanted often, to get up and run out the front door and then continue running up the street. I imagined throwing myself into the arms of Mrs. Elliot and crying, telling her I wanted to go find my father, letting her know that everything she had been told was a lie.

Even so, I was afraid she'd say, *Oh, why? Look at how well you did on that test. You must let Mazy continue to take care of you. The lie about your parents is not important. She's right. You'll never be happy if you leave her. Go back.*

"Did you hear me?" Mazy asked me sharply, shattering my musing. "You'll start reading the play today."

"Yes."

"Then finish eating. Don't sit there staring at your food."

I forced myself to continue, each swallow harder than the previous.

"Mrs. Miller will be here tomorrow to give you your inoculations," she said. "I don't expect you to cry like some baby, either. We all have to endure some pain to be safe in this life."

She closed her eyes for a few moments, as if she was in some pain right now. Then they popped open, and she smiled.

"Don't forget we have those cupcakes we made together. Dessert, then clean up, then read what I give you, and then your bath. Sticking to a schedule," she said. "That's what makes it all bearable."

"Bearable? Makes what bearable?"

I wanted to hear her say it. *Your mother's death and your*

father's indifference, leaving you here while he created a new life for himself.

"You'll figure it out and understand. For now, take my word for it, and stick to the schedule."

Stick to the schedule? I wondered if that was what the students in the classroom were taught as the way to avoid being sad. Maybe they were told the same thing every time they had a disappointment. Was that what the girl wrapped in a blanket on her porch was taught? She looked so lonely. How different was I? The only way I would ever know was when I spoke with other kids my age, especially the girl on the porch. Somehow, I thought, I would. She waved to me, didn't she? Surely I didn't imagine it. She wanted to know me.

But what if whatever the boys in the woods had made up about me, and whatever the neighborhood children believed about Mazy, kept her from coming to Mazy's house and trying to make friends with me? I was so used to being alone in the backyard or playing with an imaginary friend that I didn't think about other kids that much until now. I used to create friends out of some of the characters in the stories Mazy had me read. I learned so much about them and their problems that I felt comfortable imagining them with me.

I especially felt like that when I read *The Diary of Anne Frank*. There weren't Nazis at our door searching for me. No one was, actually, but I still felt locked in an attic, just the way she was. Hours of make-believe conversations with her and other book characters helped me pass my free time, not that Mazy permitted me to have that much. For her, it was even more important for me to learn something new every day. It was almost as if we were in a rush, as if she had to get me educated before I did indeed leave.

In fact, we usually ended the day now with her asking me, "What new thing did you learn today?"

I had to recite whatever it was and wait for her to nod her satisfaction. "Any questions about any of it?" she'd ask, but I was usually too tired to learn another thing.

There were only two real questions I thought to ask, anyway, but rarely did: have you heard from Daddy, and when will I attend the public school?

Time, like sand falling between my fingers, flowed by, carrying along my schoolwork, my house chores, our weekly shopping for food, our nights of television and my listening to her stories about her own youth contending with parents who really didn't care about her. More often than not, I went to sleep feeling sorrier for her than for myself. I think that was very important to her.

Whenever I asked her questions about her high school and college life, she had simple, disappointing answers. She said she could count on the fingers of one hand how many parties she had gone to. It always resulted in her being critical of the immature people her age. I waited to hear some hints about a boyfriend, someone, but there apparently wasn't any back then. She did drop a hint about a college literature teacher she had liked. He was very thoughtful and considerate. According to her, he enjoyed how bright she was. But he had been nearly twelve years older and married with two children.

"I should have been born stupid," she said. "I'd be happier now."

What did that mean for me? I wondered. She never stopped telling me how bright I was. She claimed I had a photographic memory and a mind that could challenge other kids my age on computers. For now, she didn't want me using one.

"You can see how dependent children your age and older have become on their technology. Someday soon, they'll need a calculator to add one and one."

See it? How could I *see* it? I hadn't exchanged a single word with someone my age.

My twelfth birthday was coming up. Of course, the day before was hers. We had celebrated both on the same day last year—my day. Surely, I told myself, I was old enough to go out on my own now and finally make friends. Not once had Mazy suggested it. I had come to doubt she ever would. She kept me from every opportunity to do so. I never went to a single holiday celebration, not even the lighting of the village Christmas tree, which I only knew about from her own mention of it. She never let me take walks alone when I could make friends. She guarded my every moment out of this house.

But I had an idea.

After dinner one night, I didn't turn on the television right away. She was seated and waiting and then looked at me curiously.

"What?" she asked.

"I'm just trying to figure out a way to say this without spoiling it."

She sat back, looking surprised but smiling, too.

"And what could that be? I wonder."

"I want you to let me go to the village myself," I said.

She lost her smile. "And for what? You want to go from store to store asking after your father? Even after all this time and all the letters and calls proving he wasn't here?" she snapped, her lips twisting in that ugly way.

"Oh, no," I said. "I don't ever expect simply to find him wandering about the village. Of course, you're right. Why would he return to this village and not come here? He'd want to prepare me for his coming, wouldn't he? You'd get a letter or a phone call first."

She relaxed, her lips softening. "Exactly. So why do you want to go to the village? We don't need any groceries, and I have them delivered anyway."

"This is something else. I saved up the coins you gave me and the dollars for working outside planting."

"And?"

"I want to buy you a birthday present, but if you go with me, you'll know what it is, and there won't be a surprise."

Her eyes widened. *I have her*, I thought. *She can't come up with any excuse to stop me.* I'd had all the inoculations. I hadn't been disobedient. She claimed I was soaring in my schoolwork and easily qualified for junior high, if not high school.

"I tell you what," she said. "I'll go with you to the department store, and I'll wait for you outside. How's that?"

My heart sank. I couldn't even meet the girl on the porch. I had planned to stop by. She was out there so often now.

"That's okay," I said. What else could I say?

"Well, now, it looks like you deserve a better present than I gave you last time. You're a very thoughtful, unselfish young girl."

I said nothing. I turned on the television and realized as I was watching that she was looking at me instead. It made me feel a little uncomfortable. When I turned to her, she smiled and rose.

"I'm going up to bed. You turn it off and get yourself to bed on time. Lots to do tomorrow, as always," she said, and started out, pausing to look back at Mr. Pebbles, who didn't rise to follow her. "I trust you because Mr. Pebbles trusts you. He has the instincts."

She left. When Mr. Pebbles looked up at me, I could swear he was smiling, as if we had both somehow tricked her.

"I'm not trustworthy," I muttered, "so stop smiling."

Two days later, she came up to the classroom after I had been there only an hour and said, "We're taking a break so you can go to the department store. Get yourself ready." Then, as she turned to leave, she paused at the door, said, "Oh," and reached into a pocket of her housecoat to bring out a crisp ten-dollar bill. "I owe you this, and I didn't want you to be embarrassed if you chose something that was a little more expensive than what you could afford."

I took it and thanked her. I was disappointed in the time for our shopping. I was hoping that somehow our going or returning would coincide with the end of the school day, and that some of the kids on our road would see me, especially the girl on the porch.

But what choice did I have?

Once we left the house, it seemed to me that she wanted us to walk faster. The air was crisp, but it was sunny, with not a cloud in the sky. Some of the neighbors were out and around their houses. The girl on the porch was there again, wrapped in a blanket, looking small and frightened, I thought. Mazy tugged me harder when I turned back to look at her. Although I had seen her out there this time of day before and assumed she had a cold or something, I wondered why she was still there.

Thinking about her and the possibility of seeing her again on our way home, I rushed around the department store. I really had no idea what to buy Mazy for her birthday. Finally, a saleslady with what Daddy used to call a "postcard smile," because it was pasted on, stepped up to me and asked if she could help me.

"I'm looking to buy a birthday present," I said. I hesitated but realized there was no other way to explain it. "For my grand-mother."

"Oh, how sweet," she said. She had light-brown hair, close to my mother's color, and similar blue eyes. She wasn't as pretty. I wouldn't ever want to think a woman was as pretty as or prettier than my mother.

"I have this much," I said, and opened my hand to show my money. "And this," I added, digging into my coat pocket to produce the coins.

"I see." She thought a moment. "There's a sale on purses. You want to look at them?"

Mazy's purse was sort of raggedy-looking, faded, too, but what I really wanted now was to get this done fast.

"Yes, please."

She showed them to me.

"If you want something practical, this would work," she said. "It has an adjustable shoulder strap and plenty of inside pockets."

I looked at the price tag.

"I don't have enough money for this," I said.

She looked back and then smiled. "I'm adding it to our sale items today. And I'd say you have just enough. Like it wrapped?"

I nodded, and she took me to the counter. I paid her, she wrapped it, and then, when she handed it to me, she smiled and said, "Shouldn't you be in school?"

"I'm in Mrs. Dutton's class," I said.

She lifted her eyebrows. "Mrs. Dutton let you out to shop for your grandmother's birthday?"

"Of course," I said. I could see that she didn't realize I was being homeschooled or who Mrs. Dutton was. "Thank you."

She followed slowly behind me. I turned and waved to her and left. She was standing in the doorway watching as I walked up to Mazy, who took my hand quickly and started forward, tapping her umbrella ahead of us as if she was testing the sidewalk like someone blind.

When we returned, the girl was still on the porch. Mazy quickened her step so we passed by quickly. When we arrived home, she told me to go back to my schoolwork. I put her present on the desk and then realized I had no birthday card. So I made one up before doing anything else. On the outside, I drew a cake with one candle. When I signed my name under *Happy Birthday*, I stared at it as if it was the name of a stranger.

Every day, I thought, *I am drifting farther and farther away from who I am.*

Or who I was.

After lunch, Mazy usually let me out for some fresh air. Sometimes she took a nap. Today she seemed more tired than usual, and I thought she fell asleep on the sofa even before I had left.

Maybe that was what gave me the courage.

Almost as soon as I stepped away from the back door, I turned and ran through the woods on the side of the house, coming out on the street just a little before the home of the girl on the porch.

I had never been alone on this street or alone in this village since the night Mazy had found me at the train station. I had just been on this very sidewalk, but without Mazy holding my hand, it suddenly felt so forbidden. It was as if I had entered the world through a secret door. I had walked into a dream with everything hazy and then gradually becoming clearer and clearer. It frightened me at first.

Nevertheless, I turned and walked toward the girl on the porch. When I reached it, I paused and looked at her. She appeared to be asleep. In a way, I was happy about that. I wanted a very close look at her, and when people are awake and can look back, you can't truly study their faces. Her hair seemed like it hadn't been brushed for a while. Strands were curled and going in different directions. Her face had a yellowish white complexion. With a sharp nose, thin and faded orange lips, and an almost square chin, she appeared to be chiseled out of candle wax. I felt like walking up to her with my box of crayons and coloring in her lips. She was seated in a reclining chair, the blanket down to her ankles. Her arms were crossed over her stomach, so I could see the pink jacket sleeves. It wasn't so terribly cold, but she was wearing dark-blue woolen gloves.

I took a few steps toward the entrance gate to her house, but before I could reach it, the front door opened, and a tall woman, almost as tall as my father, came out so forcefully the screen door nearly flew off its hinges. She was wearing what I knew to be a nurse's uniform. Her graying copper-brown hair was severely tied behind her head, tugging on her forehead and stretching her eyes.

"What do you want?" she demanded, grimacing in anticipation of just about anything I might say.

Actually, I was too stunned to speak. The eyes of the girl under the pink blanket fluttered and then opened. She looked at me with what I thought was friendly curiosity.

"I just wanted to say hello," I said quickly.

"What is it?" I heard a second woman call from behind the nurse.

"Nothing! Under control!" the nurse shouted back. "You don't belong here," she told me. "Go home."

"She can say hello," the girl said, and struggled to get into a straighter sitting position.

I started forward.

"Stay your distance," the nurse ordered, putting her hand up like a traffic cop. "Say your hello from there."

"Let her come closer," the girl said.

The nurse turned to her. "You are vulnerable right now to any infections. We don't need to risk your health."

"What's wrong with her?" I asked.

The nurse stared at me.

"I have leukemia," the girl said.

"And the treatment she is on makes her vulnerable to infections. So *go home*," the nurse insisted.

"I'm sorry," I said. I had only a vague idea of what leukemia was, but I knew it had something to do with cancer. I wanted to ask if she would be all right, but then thought, what if she said no?

"Go home," the nurse repeated, and took another step toward me.

A pretty light-brown-haired woman in a white cotton sweater and jeans came up behind her. I knew she had to be older, but she was more like a teenage girl.

"Who is that?"

The nurse smirked and turned to her. "The witch's granddaughter," she said. "The one who came out of a tree."

I stood looking at them for a moment, stunned that a grown-up would say such a thing.

The way both women were looking at me was terrifying, mainly because they looked frightened—of *me*!

I turned and quickly ran back to Mazy's house but realized that if I went in through the front door, she'd know I had gone down the street, so I ran around back and stood at the rear door, catching my breath.

Did everyone on this street believe that Mazy was a witch? Was that why few people who lived here would say hello or smile when they saw us?

When I reached for the doorknob, I saw that my hand was trembling. If Mazy saw me, she'd know something was wrong. She might never let me out again.

I took deep breaths until I was satisfied I looked okay.

Nevertheless, I tiptoed back in, happy to see Mazy was still sleeping on the sofa. As quietly as I could, I went upstairs and to the classroom. When I went to the window, I saw that the girl wasn't on the porch anymore. Was everyone that afraid of me? Despite what those women had said, the sick girl did not look afraid. If anything, she looked disappointed that they were chasing me off.

But what about everyone else on this street? Were they going to be afraid of me and keep me from talking to their children?

I remembered Mazy once telling me that people are most afraid of what they don't know. It had been so long since Daddy had seen me. Somewhere nestled in the darkest places of my heart, I had a painful fear that he didn't know me anymore.

Maybe Daddy had left me and still didn't come to get me because he was afraid of me, too.

CHAPTER EIGHT

Mazy surprised me with far more than I had expected for my twelfth birthday. It wasn't just that she had gone out and bought me new clothes; she had bought me a whole new wardrobe. It was like Christmas when Daddy and Mama were happier and our house glittered with lights dancing on our tree, on our windows, and in our eyes. Mazy brought all the bags and packages to my room just as I awoke, just the way Mama and Daddy used to before the darkness had seeped into our lives. The Christmas presents would rain down around me back then. Ribbons seemed to float in the air.

There was so much that Mazy had to go out and come back in with the boxes and bags three times. I thought it was never going to end. Some of the blouses and dresses looked very costly. I didn't think she was rich. She didn't have very expensive things in the house. Maybe because she didn't spend money on much, she had saved a lot and had decided because of how well I was doing that she wanted to make this birthday special. Poking at the back of my mind was the fear that she knew I would never leave and I would need lots more than a simple birthday gift. I would need things for the future, a future I still fought believing would happen here.

"Girls become young ladies faster these days than they did when I was your age," she said, sounding bitter about it. "I can't keep buying you little-girl clothes. I've watched your body changing," she added. "It wouldn't surprise me if you had your first period this coming year."

When she went into some detail about it, I didn't blush out of embarrassment. I blushed out of fear. After all, it had been a chapter in one of the science textbooks she had given me and tested me on. But instinctively, I knew that becoming a young woman in a world without anyone my age to share everything with would cause me to feel even more lost and alone. There was never to be any joy in how I was maturing. Mazy was very strict about what I read, but she couldn't censor my imagination.

I had so many questions about myself, questions I didn't think I could or even wanted to ask her. Every time the word *sex* came up, she found a way to stamp on it as you would some ugly insect. Suddenly, she was referring to a world where sex rose like a bubble of air to the surface of my inner thoughts. But in the way she presented it, females were always at a disadvantage, because it was in the nature of males to pounce. Nothing had changed since the days of the caveman.

One of the items I saw she had bought me was a pair of training bras in a package, and she indicated that my breasts needed more covering.

We were never to mention my pubic hair, which had begun to grow in.

I had been informed that not only was it dangerous to touch yourself in what she called "sensitive places," but it was also sinful.

She had put it in a puzzling way: "It's like unwrapping a Christmas present in October. You wait."

Wait for what?

And yet here she was, genuinely excited about my becoming a little lady.

I hadn't even washed my face or had any breakfast. She was very excited, even more excited than I was, which made me think about that picture in the frame that was above my bed. She surely always had dreamed of having a granddaughter, or a daughter for that matter, and taking joy in watching her grow up. I was almost amused at just how much she wanted it all to be right, be wonderful and perfect. She looked sincerely worried about how things fit me and if I liked the color and the style.

But why? I wondered. Who would see me? And what if they did and wanted to know me, especially a boy? I didn't ask. I didn't want to insert a second of doubt or darkness.

"They told me these clothes are all in style for girls your age."

"Why didn't you just take me along to buy it all? Then you

wouldn't be worrying about something not fitting and having to bring it back."

"You're the one who gave me the idea the other night."

"I did?"

"Just like you, I wanted it all to be a birthday surprise. What kind of a surprise would it be if you knew what you were getting? Wasn't that what you said? Isn't most of the fun opening the boxes and not knowing what is in them?"

She laughed at the expression of shock on my face. She was listening to me, to my advice?

But that's not her real reason, I thought. She was never comfortable when someone who saw us together asked questions about me. They almost had to twist her arm to get her to say I was her granddaughter. I saw she was always concerned about how I would react. Would I do something to embarrass her, contradict her? And would the lie lead to big trouble for us both? What if I simply started to cry because it stirred up my memories of Mama? All this was surely her main reason for buying everything without me.

Amazingly, however, nothing she had bought me was too small or too large, and everything was pretty. I recognized some of the clothes from what the girls on the street wore, and there was a pretty little watch with a gold band. After I had tried on everything, she said she had one more important thing to give me at my birthday dinner. It sounded mysterious and exciting, but I didn't want to pester her for details right away. I thought it would make me sound greedy, and I didn't want to risk disrupting the good mood she was in. Because it was my birthday, she told me I didn't have to do any schoolwork all day, and I could watch as much television as I wanted. I could go out in the backyard whenever I wanted. I didn't even have to do a single household chore.

But of course, I couldn't help but wonder all day what this last thing was. She had given me a watch and practically a whole new wardrobe. There wasn't much else I needed. Was her surprise that I would finally be going to a real school? Or could it possibly be something about Daddy?

After dinner, she brought out my birthday cake, though it didn't have any candles on it. She said I was too old now to blow out candles. She placed it on the table and sat back. I was holding my breath, my imagination running wild with the wonderful possibilities about what was to come.

"Sometimes," she began, "it's good to keep something that might be very sad or disturbing secret until there is a happy time. The happy time makes the sadness of the other thing less important or painful. Happiness is stronger than sadness. Real happiness can wash sadness away. Remember that. It's one of my wisdom quotes."

This didn't sound like it was leading up to a wonderful surprise, but I couldn't take my eyes off her. My heart was still thumping in anticipation. Perhaps it wasn't marvelous to her but would be to me. Despite how much time had passed and how many hopeful expectations had come and gone, I held on to my dream: living again with Daddy in a new home and starting in a real school where I could make friends. Wasn't that what I really wanted, my ultimate dream?

"I know you keep waiting and expecting to hear from your father, especially today," she began, and then she paused.

I was right, I thought. He had called and said he finally was coming for me. That would make her sad, so I quickly warned myself to avoid exploding in happiness. It might make her feel bad or think I had hated every moment with her.

"Daddy called?" I asked as calmly as I could manage.

After all this time, he had finally called.

Her pause made flies circle in my stomach. I couldn't stand the waiting. She stared at me without saying a word. Why was she taking so long? Why didn't she simply blurt it out? Was she that upset over losing me? I'd promise to visit her, promise almost anything.

"He did," she said. When she paused again, it felt like the whole world had paused. It wasn't spinning. No cars were being driven; no people were walking. All ears were focused on what she was about to tell me.

"Unfortunately, it wasn't to wish you a happy birthday. In fact, I had to remind him what day it was. His life right now is a little overwhelming, I guess. He doesn't know up from down. Of course, that's no justification for it."

It felt like my heart was slipping down into my stomach.

"He didn't know it was my birthday?"

I shook my head. Surely she had gotten that wrong. Daddy never forgot my birthday. In fact, once, toward our final days, he had reminded my mother.

"Don't be upset. The world is topsy-turvy for him. Men are more like that than women. My father never remembered my birthday. Eventually, he even forgot his own."

All my excitement quickly retreated, pulled back into the shell inside me like a turtle pulling back its head. In fact, I was on the verge of crying, but I sucked back my tears. She was expecting me to be a little lady now and no longer a child. If she still thought I was, she would never let me go to school and meet others my age.

"So, then, why did he call?" I asked, my voice so breathy and full of fear that I wasn't sure I had spoken.

But she was taking too long to answer. I hated her long pauses, watching her think and think. Ordinarily, it meant she was searching for words that wouldn't make me frightened or hysterical.

She took a deep breath and then folded her hands in front of her on the table.

Now I was really worrying. Why was it so difficult to tell me what he had said? Fear ran up my spine like an icy-cold snake. What terrible thing had he said? Or maybe something had happened to him and he had called her from a hospital.

"He called to tell us that his girlfriend is having a baby, and because she is so delicate, apparently once having lost a baby, he's decided he can't tell her about you until after the new baby is born," Mazy said in one breath, rushing the words out and then looking happy that she didn't have to hold them in any longer.

"How did she lose a baby?"

Her familiar smirk appeared. "She didn't lose it like you lose a pen or something, Saffron. It fell out of her too soon and died. Your father is afraid that if he tells her about you, she might get so nervous that this baby might fall out too soon and die, too. She'd blame you. And that would be that . . . forever. They might not get married, either."

"Married? Isn't she his new wife by now?"

"Not yet," she said. "Young people today don't put the value on a marriage the way people used to. It's almost nothing more than a steady date. Anyway, you see he has a lot to think about."

"He should be thinking more about me," I said. I looked away. I didn't want her to see what was really in my eyes. It was far more than disappointment. Now anger rose like a snake that had been sleeping in the shadows, only for me in the shadows of every hope, every dream.

"Well, that's probably why he wants everything to be perfect this time. He is thinking about your happiness. But you don't have to worry. You can wait. You have a good life here in the meantime, don't you?"

It was like swallowing disgusting medicine to agree with her.

Yes, I had enough to eat. Yes, I had nice clothes, especially after today. And I was surely learning faster than other kids my age were learning in the public school. But I still felt like half a person. For me, the real world and the world I watched on television weren't that much different. The hesitation in my face was annoying her.

"You don't lack anything and never will while I'm alive," she pledged angrily.

Except friends, I wanted to say, but I kept the words under my tongue. There were questions that hovered like angry bees, however. I was afraid to ask most, but now, feeling more confident about myself and even angrier at Daddy, I decided to risk one.

"Did Daddy say the lost baby was his?"

"He didn't say. It could have happened before he met this woman."

She waited, watching the thoughts in my mind rush in from all directions. She looked patient, willing to take as much time as it might to get it all over with, forever.

"How does my father know everything is all right with me? How does he know you are getting me everything I need?"

She sat back, not smiling but not looking angry, either.

"Now, that's an adult question. What did your father do for a living? You mentioned it to me once, so I know you knew."

"He sold people insurance."

"Exactly, and to do that, he had to know about those people, personal things about them. He had to have ways to find out these things, information other people couldn't know or didn't care to know. People lie about themselves, and insurance agents have to be sure they know the truth. Imagine insuring someone's life and not knowing they were going to die in a few weeks."

She shrugged. "He simply must have done a routine check on me. Sometimes insurance companies go so far as to hire private detectives. He found out what he needed to know, and he is still quite satisfied and confident you're in good hands. That's not surprising. Don't forget that I was an excellent teacher, and I've never even gotten a jaywalking ticket. I'm a perfect guardian for a girl like you, and there's certainly enough room for you in this house."

"But shouldn't he call at least once to see how I sound?" I pursued. I didn't want to come out and say it, but he'd only have to hear me say a few words to detect the sadness that coated my heart.

She looked away for a moment and then nodded, as if someone had whispered something in her ear. "He and I talked about that," she said. "We decided that it would make you so depressed that you'd get sick over it, and it would keep you from growing up well. He was very unhappy that he had to not do that, but he was very intent on your well-being and wanted to do what had to be done to make sure you'd be all right."

I stared at her. There were tones in her voice when she told me things that gave me pause. When the person you're with is practically the only person you see or hear, you can tell things about her that other people cannot. She'd been the first and the last voice I heard all day for years now. Her tongue had become a tattletale, betraying what she really thought.

Lies as tools. That was why he didn't ask her any more questions about me, and why I wouldn't ask any more questions about him.

But later, thinking about what she had said, I felt like putting dozens of pennies in her jar. She appeared to realize that, and that evening she left it out on the counter. I felt a little weird, even frightened, that I wanted to do it myself, but I did it. And whether it was my imagination or not, I went to sleep that night without crying, inside or out. Did her magic jar work, or was it simply that I had no tears left, especially for Daddy?

Instead of dwelling on it, like changing the channel on the television set, I thought about the sick girl in the house on our street and fantasized ways to get to be with her. Suddenly, even though I was well and she was very sick, we were both suffering the same pains, and we were both equally lonely. Every afternoon when I had free time, I ventured a little farther in the woods in the direction of her house, always keenly aware that Mazy might see me. Sometimes I felt like someone rushing at the inside of a giant balloon, trying to break out but being bounced back instead. I'd get so nervous and frightened at how far I had gone that I'd turn and run home, nearly falling over dead wood and rocks—especially if I heard some sound coming from Mazy's house.

Months passed. As if she knew I valued my free time outside more and more, Mazy increased my work in the classroom. She made me do many things over, even though my results were nearly perfect. I barely could get outside before it began to turn dark, and she insisted I be back inside when it was dark.

"I want perfect out of you," she would tell me if I complained. "Not nearly perfect. Nearly perfect is not good enough."

"Why not?" I demanded.

"Because someday you will be competing with girls your age who come from wealthier parents or, in the eyes of those judging you, 'more normal' situations. I know how it is. Since you're being homeschooled, they'll expect you to do worse, and you'll always have to prove yourself, Saffron. Remember, I told you I can see the future for my students, and I know you're going to have a harder time. Unfairly but nevertheless harder. I want you to be prepared for it."

She didn't have to convince me I was different. I knew most girls my age had mothers and fathers and, most of all, friends their age. Reluctantly, I accepted that she was right, and I did work harder. From time to time, from my window, I'd see the sick girl on the porch, especially as the weather improved. Seeing her looking so lost and alone drove me to go farther and farther into the woods until I was right behind her house. All I would have to do was slip around the side and maybe whisper to her.

The day I decided to do it was a day Mazy wasn't feeling well. She had been complaining about aches and pains and telling me to keep my distance from her because she was convinced she had a flu. All she wanted to eat was toast and jelly with a cup of tea. She let me bring it to her, but I had to leave as soon as I put it on her bedside table. She didn't even remind me to do all my schoolwork and read the new book she had given me. Realizing she was confining herself to her room gave me the courage. Quietly but quickly, I left the house and headed into the woods. It was early in the afternoon. Other kids would still be in school.

Other than knowing when the children on the street were in school, I rarely kept track of the days of the week. They all seemed the same to me. Mazy and I didn't save weekends for something special. I had heard Mazy mention that today was a Friday, however. I thought of months and the seasons the same vague way, but today was one of those brighter days, with barely a breeze. The few clouds I saw were sliding along slowly, all looking puffy, proud, and content. The rich scent of new leaves filled me with energy and excitement. It was one of those days when I felt like running in any direction and just falling to the ground to embrace the aroma of grass and fresh dirt, one of those days when I felt hopeful but could not explain why.

I practically tiptoed up to the front porch and brought my face to the white spindles, hoping the sick girl wasn't in a deep sleep. She had her eyes closed, but the moment I touched the railing, they opened, and she turned toward me in an ever-so-slow motion. I held my breath. Did the nurse and her mother convince her I was evil? Would she scream for them?

She smiled. She looked groggy and thinner than when I had seen her last, but she had eyes so blue that they wouldn't fade under her fatigue. She wore a sort of sock hat. Her dark-blue wool blanket, which I thought was over the top for today, was tucked around her so tightly I imagined she couldn't get her arms out. It looked more like a cocoon.

"I'm Saffron," I said quickly. "And I didn't come from a tree."

Her smile widened. "I know," she said. "I'm Lucy. Sorry they chased you away. My mother and my nurse, Mrs. Randolph, are so protective. I'm lucky they let me outside. Sometimes I can see you looking out of your window." Her voice was thin, like the voice a bird would have if it could speak.

"You can see me?"

She nodded. "If you can see me, I can see you," she said. "How long have you been here living with Mrs. Dutton?" Her blue eyes grew brighter with curiosity.

"I don't remember exactly. A long time," I said. "I try not to think about it."

"You don't want to remember when you started living with her?"

"No. Years," I offered without being more specific. Sometimes I couldn't remember exactly how long myself.

She nodded, not surprised. "That's like me when people wonder how long I've been sick, and I say I don't remember. Is Mrs. Dutton your grandmother? My mother says no one knew she had a granddaughter. That's why some of the kids think you came from a tree. No one saw you move in. No one saw any of her family visiting her. She keeps to herself a lot. Where do her children live? Does she have any brothers or sisters?"

For some reason, I couldn't lie to her. Maybe it was because she looked so fragile, more like very thin glass. I could see the blue veins in her temples. I didn't need a tool with her. I couldn't even imagine being untruthful to her. I'd be afraid to touch her with dishonesty. When she found out I had lied, I was sure her disappointment would shatter her face.

"Does it hurt to be as sick as you are?" I asked, instead of answering.

"Not like a burn or a cut," she said. "It makes me tired. I sleep a lot."

I nodded, expecting that sort of answer. She wasn't crying or grimacing.

"She's not my grandmother," I said. "That's not why I'm living with her."

She looked surprised and then smiled, looking so happy that I had told her the truth.

"Why, then?"

I was silent, thinking of how to explain it all to someone else when I often had trouble explaining it to myself.

"You want the reason to be a secret?"

"Maybe. For now," I added. She had such a sweet, trusting face. I could envision myself telling her everything someday and being happy I had.

"I won't tell anything you tell me when you feel like telling me," she said, looking more excited. "Does she do magic with her umbrella? I never saw her walking without it. No one has. And it's the same umbrella for years and years, my mother says."

"No, no magic," I said, smiling and thinking that in the beginning, I'd had a similar thought. "But she thinks she always needs her umbrella. She says she's prepared for anything that falls out of the sky, and more falls out of it than rain and snow."

She nodded as if she completely understood. "If I went out into the sun, I'd have to have an opened umbrella right now. It's not good for me."

"Really?" I couldn't imagine why the sun would not be good for a sick person. "Why not?"

"I could get burned. I'm more susceptible to being burned because of the medicines I take. You know what 'susceptible' means, right?"

"Yes," I said, smiling. "Mrs. Dutton stresses vocabulary. She thinks great words in our language are dying."

"My mother says she was a very good but very strict teacher, so strict that she couldn't be a teacher now."

"She thinks so, too. What grade are you in?" I asked.

"Eighth," she said. "How old are you?"

"I'll be thirteen," I said. It sounded more adult than twelve.

"You'd be in my class if you went to our school. My brother, Stuart, says he's never seen you in the building. He's in the tenth grade."

"I don't know when I'll be going to public school yet. I go to homeschool."

"So do I. Now." She coughed and fought to stop it quickly. "Mrs. Marcus comes over twice a week to catch me up on the work I'm missing. She's a private tutor my parents hired for me. You have to work harder with tutors. There's no escape."

She laughed at what she had said, and I smiled.

"Does Mrs. Dutton make you work hard?"

"Very. I guess I'm learning a lot. I passed all the state tests I had to take with a hundred percent."

"A hundred? All of them?"

"Yes. I'm doing work tenth and eleventh graders would do."

"Really?"

"Yes. She makes me read three books a week, books much older kids are reading."

"O-M-G! You can do that? Read three books in a week?"

"Yes. I can watch only a certain amount of television, and even less if I fall behind."

"I fall asleep watching most of the time. Maybe I should have my mother get her to teach me instead of Mrs. Marcus."

"That would be wonderful," I said. "Should I ask? There's room in the classroom she created for me. And I can help you, too."

"No, no." She smiled. "I'm just wish dreaming. That's all I do now. If I asked my mother to do such a thing, she would get so upset that she would pee in her pants."

"Pee?"

She started to laugh, but it became a cough. She seemed unable to stop. I saw she was gasping, too.

"Are you all right?"

She couldn't answer. She continued coughing and gasping. I heard the screen door opening and quickly pulled back and retreated enough to be unseen even if someone looked over the railing. I could hear the nurse's voice and then her mother's. I crouched and listened and waited. They were speaking low, and I thought Lucy was crying. When it grew very silent, I inched my way back and peered through the spindles again.

She was gone.

I turned and ran as fast as I could all the way home.

All I could think was that she coughed and coughed because she was talking to me. They had to take her into the house, and they might question her. I had made her sicker. Would she tell her mother I was there?

Would they come to the house to complain to Mazy?

Once she found out, Mazy would be furious.

I stood inside, trembling and listening for the phone to ring or the sound of Mazy's footsteps on the stairway. The house was very quiet, so after a few more minutes, I tiptoed up the stairs and peered in at her. She was still fast asleep. I went to my room and looked out the window toward Lucy's front porch. She hadn't been brought out again. Despite what had happened at the end, it had been so special for me, talking to someone my age, even if she was so sick and even if it would get me in trouble.

I sat on the bed and reviewed every word we had said to each other. She was so nice, I thought. I couldn't wait to sneak back there. I would tell her the truth, tell her everything. She would get better, and we'd become the very best of friends. Mazy might not be happy about that, but why did she have to know until it had happened? Then she couldn't stop it, I thought.

Hours passed. No one came to complain, and no one called. *She's keeping me a secret*, I thought. *Surely that means that she doesn't want me to stay away. She wants to be my friend as much as I want her to be mine.*

Mazy woke, but she still didn't feel that well, so I made her some hot oatmeal and brought it to her room. Later I gave her tea and honey, and she told me she was very proud of me. I had come through a storm, whatever that meant. Her phone didn't ring, and no one came to our door to complain. I went to sleep dreaming of all the things I would do with Lucy. We would talk for hours and hours, and maybe, eventually, Mazy would let her sleep over or her mother would let me sleep there. It was certainly nice to feel good about something since Mazy had revealed my father's last call.

Two days later, I saw Lucy had been brought out again. I was sure she was looking forward to seeing me. She kept her head turned mainly in our direction. Every day, I worked hard on my assignments so Mazy would give me more free time. She wanted me to get fresh air, but she was still quite strict about how far I could wander from the house. I was tempted to tell her the truth but was too fearful she would be so angry that I would never have an opportunity to make Lucy a real friend. I had to be very careful, even about my thoughts. She had a way of looking at me, squinting, and then asking something that bounced very close to what I had been thinking.

"You can learn a great deal about nature and from nature, but you don't have to go far to do it," she told me. She was still getting over her flu and slept on and off. She said she generally didn't believe in going to a doctor because they "prescribe from the hip most of the time just to get rid of you, especially when you reach my age."

I just listened when she ranted on a subject until she was tired of it herself and urged me on to do a chore, my schoolwork, my hour of fresh air. When that time occurred, I didn't hesitate, but I was smart enough not to look too eager. I didn't want her even to suspect I had been talking to Lucy. A week later, I walked out slowly with her warnings ringing in my ear, hesitated, and pretended to be studying a wildflower in case she was watching me and then slowly meandered off to the left before charging through the woods to the rear of Lucy's house.

It was a little later in the day, but I hoped she was still out there waiting for me. When I stepped up to the porch and she saw me, she smiled so brightly that I had no doubt she had been. She looked so happy to see me that I thought today she would get well. I had mixed feelings about it. Once she was well, she would return to school and be with her friends. Maybe then she wouldn't want to talk to me anymore. When that happened, I would tell Mazy that if she didn't put me in the school, I would run away. Even though it made me feel good to think about threatening her, I knew in my heart she would just laugh. She might even say, *Go ahead. Run off. Who's stopping you? See what it's like being out there alone.*

I was sure she wouldn't tell me where my father was. Where would I go?

"Sorry I didn't come to see you sooner," I told Lucy, "but Mazy has been keeping me quite busy."

I certainly didn't want to tell her I was forbidden to see her, forbidden to go this far away from the house. She might even be frightened about Mazy coming to her house to complain to her mother, and not vice versa.

"Mazy?"

"Oh, that's the name she likes." I spelled it and told her about Dazy.

She widened her eyes and smiled. "That's funny. How does she keep you so busy?"

I rattled off all the house chores I had daily.

"You're like her housekeeper."

"When I began to live with her, she had me paint my bedroom."

"Really?"

"I've done some touch-up painting around the house from time to time, too."

"You do sound busy."

I told her how many hours I had to be in the classroom and the time set aside for my reading.

"I do some of the cooking now, too."

"You do? I never did any cooking, even before I got sick."

"It's okay. I like it. We read recipes together and experiment. She said I make the best veal Milanese."

"I don't even know what that is. So why do you live with her? Where are your parents?" she asked. "Can you tell me now?"

I wanted to tell her. I certainly trusted her, but it was as if Mazy was there, standing behind me, waiting for me to break her most important rules.

"My mother died," I began. I was going to tell her everything, but that feeling I had about someone standing behind me wasn't my imagination.

Before I could continue, I felt his hand on my shoulder and spun around to look into the angry face of a boy with dark-brown curly hair. It grew down to the nape of his neck. His hazel eyes were wide open, like the eyes of someone who had seen a ghost or something. The anger in his face was settled at the corners of his mouth, because his full, dark-pink lips whitened at the corners. He wasn't ugly, but his nose was sharp, and his cheeks bubbled as he clenched his teeth. He was tall and thin, his fisted hands pressed into his hips. He took a step back as I turned fully to him.

"Why are you talking to my sister?" he demanded. "You were told to stay away."

I thought his voice was too deep for someone his age. It seemed to echo up from a deep well. His faded yellow T-shirt looked a size too large. He was wearing torn jeans and a pair of very scuffed dark-blue running shoes.

"Leave her alone, Stuart," Lucy said. I could hear her struggle to raise her voice.

The boy narrowed his eyes. "I've seen you in the woods many times," he said. "You talk to trees. You're a nutcase and a half."

I glanced back at Lucy. Was she going to think I was weird now, too?

"Well? You do talk to trees, don't you?"

"Sometimes," I admitted.

He smiled and then looked angry again. "Do they talk to you?"

"Sometimes," I said.

His wry smile faded. His eyes widened to make room for fear beside his anger. "Did you touch my sister?"

"Touch her? No."

"Stop it, Stuart," Lucy said, garnering as much volume as she could manage.

"You'd better get out of here," he said. "And stay away, too."

"I'm not hurting anyone."

"I'll hurt you if you don't go home," he said. He took a step toward me, but when I stepped to the side and raised my hands, he quickly stepped back. "Get outta here. You're weird."

"No, she's not," Lucy said.

She sounded weaker. Now my presence was making her sicker, I thought mournfully.

"I'll see you another time, Lucy," I said. "Hope you get better."

I started off toward the woods.

"Why don't you just walk down the street?" Stuart called after me. "You going to tell the trees what happened? You really are from the woods. *You're weird!*" he shouted. "*You stay away!*"

I ran harder. When I looked back from the forest, he had gone up on the porch. I stood there watching him talk to Lucy. Then he surprised me by kneeling down and hugging her, lowering his head against her. She had her hand on his head. I was angry, but that made me sad. I wished I had an older brother or sister. Lucy was sick, but she was lucky, too. She had someone who wanted to protect her.

I started to cry, not really knowing if I was crying about her or about myself. Maybe I was crying for both of us. I remembered when my mother would embrace me like Stuart was embracing Lucy, especially if I had a cold or a stomachache. Mazy did provide anything a girl like me would need to live, but in my world now, there were no embraces, no gentle brushes of my hair or my cheeks, no real kisses, and no moments when you could feel you weren't alone, you'd never be alone.

I swallowed back all my tears before I went back into the house. If Mazy saw me crying, she would surely be suspicious enough to think I had gone off too far. I could hear her in the kitchen, and she had heard me enter.

"I'm in here," she called. "Having a cup of tea."

She was sitting at the table and looked up quickly when I entered. There were those suspicious, penetrating eyes. She was still in her nightgown. The flu had washed away anything that had disguised her age. It made me think, maybe for the first time, that she was an old lady.

"There is a nest with hummingbird eggs just off to the left," I said. She nodded. She loved to watch hummingbirds. That lie worked for me.

"I have a feeder somewhere. Maybe we'll hang it up with some sugar water for them." She sipped her tea and thought. "My mother liked hummingbirds. My father thought they were large insects."

"Do you have pictures of your mother? I mean real pictures."

"Buried somewhere." She seemed to snap out of her warm thoughts. "It's better not to dig up the dead. Why don't you make our pasta tonight? I won't tell you anything to do. You make it all up yourself and surprise me."

She rose and put her teacup in the sink. When she looked at me again, I thought she could see I wasn't telling the whole truth, but she ignored it for now and left to lie down and leave me alone in the kitchen. She did look more tired than I could remember.

I stood there staring at the stove and the counter, feeling as if I were dangling off a cliff.

The ringing of the phone spun me around. It stopped, but the little light told me Mazy had picked up the receiver.

I felt the trembling start in my legs and move up my spine.

The light went off. It was still very quiet, so I went to the refrigerator to look at what ingredients we had for a pasta sauce.

She must have come down the stairs without touching a step. I never heard her. Out of the corner of my eye, I saw Mr. Pebbles rise. When I turned around with two tomatoes in my hand, I saw Mazy standing in the doorway. She looked like her hair was on fire. Her eyes were wide open, and the grimace on her face resembled a smiling skeleton on Halloween.

"You are a liar, and you are deceitful," she said.

I didn't move; I didn't speak.

"That was Mrs. Wiley, whose daughter is dying. She was hysterical."

"I didn't do anything to her. She wanted to talk."

"You are *not* to leave this house. Don't bother with the dinner. Go to your room."

"What?"

She stared with such coldness in her eyes that I couldn't look at her. She really did frighten me. I put the tomatoes back. She stepped aside as I ran out of the kitchen. When I closed the door of my room, I didn't cry. I found the letter my father supposedly had written and read it repeatedly, as if it was a prayer, a chant.

"What did you do to me, Daddy?" I whispered. "Why don't you want me?"

I didn't need him to hear the question. I didn't need him here. I knew the answer. I always knew.

What chilled my heart even more was the thought that maybe Mazy knew the answer, too.

Maybe she always knew.

CHAPTER NINE

There was a deeper, wider silence in the house now. When I walked through the hallway and up and down the stairs, the stillness made me keenly aware of my very heartbeat, quickened with fear because of the cold storm of anger Mazy had quietly rained down over and around me. I even imagined I could hear Mr. Pebbles's paws stepping over the floor when I watched him cross a room or start down the hallway, but I didn't hear him purr the way he usually did when he was lying beside me. Could Mazy turn him against me, too?

During the days that followed, Mazy didn't confine me to my room or take away any of my small privileges. She inflicted more pain by looking through me as if I were no longer there. At times, she appeared distracted and confused herself. It was as if what had happened affected her more than it did me. It was all my fault. She repeated things she had just done, like washing a cup moments after she had just washed it. I saw her taking more pills for her aches and pains, and if she didn't think I was watching, she didn't attempt to stand straighter or avoid rubbing her hip. Maybe it was because I had seen death in someone as young as my mother and knew how fragile life was, but I suddenly saw Mazy as being older, a lot older. It wasn't until then that I realized how much I needed her. She was, after all, the only other person who was really in my life. It didn't matter whether or not I chose her. She just was.

And when I recalled that first night at the train station, I had to admit that she chose me. She could have just as easily left me there, telling herself that I was not her responsibility. I would have to admit that there were times when I wished she had left me, but there were far more times when I was grateful. We ate together, cooked together. We had even slept together in the same bed. She had treated my colds, my bruises and scratches, with the same concern any mother or grandmother would have. She bought me pretty things and raved about how smart I was. I couldn't imagine feeling closer to a real grandmother. I did expect it would be painful for her to be so angry at me, just the way it would be for a real grandmother to be furious at her granddaughter. Who better than me knew how heartbreaking it was to be fuming at someone you loved?

Even though she wasn't very affectionate, I felt Mazy had come to love me or, if not to love me, to need me. I was filling gaping holes in her life just as she was filling holes I had in mine.

Nevertheless, it took nearly two weeks before Mazy's silent treatment began to weaken, even with something as simple as the tone of her voice. She would give me my orders for the day, leave me to work, and then eat with me in relative silence. She would go to sleep before I did, after she proclaimed her usual limits on my watching television. I ended up not watching any most of the time. I had become so accustomed to her sitting with me, laughing at the things I laughed at and being just as amazed as I was at some of the shows about animals.

It was that silence, that loneliness that came as a result of her pouting, that brought me finally to break down and tell her I was sorry, even though I didn't believe I should be apologizing for talking to a neighbor, especially a girl my age. Why was she so intent on keeping me on the house grounds and not making any friends, anyway? What did she fear? Would someone take me away? Would she be arrested for all the lies?

A day after I apologized, which brought things back to the way they were, at least, I asked her those very questions. We had eaten dinner, and I had just cleared the table. She had the tea-kettle on. I tried to sound not bitter or upset but only curious.

At first, I thought she wasn't going to answer. She stirred some honey into her tea. Even before all this, she could get that far-off look sometimes and for a while seem not to know I was there.

"Mazy?"

She blinked and looked more attentive. "I've always feared

someone with authority would appear to take you away. Although you have never said it, I know that you, as well as I, have lost faith in your father ever coming for you. Even before that last phone call telling me about the expected new baby, he had sent notes from time to time, excuses for why he hadn't come for you."

"Notes? Why didn't you tell me about them?"

"Because I knew all it would do was upset you. I received another, a little longer note, yesterday."

"Yesterday? What did he say?"

"You now have a half brother and, something I never knew, a half sister about your age."

"About my age?"

"He didn't mention their names," she quickly added before I could ask. "And he finally did get married."

"But . . . how could there be a half sister about my age?"

She raised her eyebrows. "I wouldn't think you'd need to ask how. You've had your period recently, and I gave you more to read about sexual intercourse and what can result."

"Yes, but . . ."

My mind drifted.

A half brother just born and a half sister about my age, I thought. I had always wanted a sibling, but from the way Mazy was talking now, I might never see them or even know their names.

"Did he say anything more about me?"

She drank some tea. For a moment, I thought she wasn't going to answer. Then she put the cup down.

"Nothing that will please you, I'm afraid. I believe what's happened is he has settled into his new life and new family and would rather forget his past, which, I'm sorry to say, includes you. I think you've always anticipated this."

She was right. In my heart of hearts, I already knew this was very possible. I had continually smothered the little voice inside me telling me the same things, and I deliberately avoided asking questions about my father for fear of what the answers would be. But hearing Mazy say it aloud now in such a coldly matter-of-fact way sent me reeling back to that lost little girl who was truly never far away, the little girl who sat on a bench working on her coloring book and looking up occasionally, hoping to see her father hurrying back. In her dreams, she screamed for him desperately. What else could she do?

"But," Mazy continued, getting up to pour herself another cup of tea and sitting back down at the table, "I suppose there is always the possibility that his conscience will drive him to appear at our door suddenly—full of apologies, of course. He is still your father, and I certainly would understand you wanting to leave with him, regardless of what lay ahead for you in such a new home or how he has treated you up to now. Who looms higher in the mind of a little girl than her daddy?" She looked so sad I wasn't sure she'd continue. "And when that adoration is not returned, your heart doesn't break; it shatters. I'm not unfamiliar with that feeling. Unfortunately."

I saw that her sadness was not only for me but for herself as well.

"As I said, I haven't told you because I knew it would hurt you very deeply, but I think you're old enough now to deal with it. Anyway, look at all you would have to explain if you made friends here. Children your age are particularly curious about each other. They're going to ask you personal family questions, and if they should ever learn the truth about your father and how you came to live with me . . . it wouldn't be pleasant. They call it bullying now, but in my day, it was plain and simple jealousy that comes from insecurity. Three years ago, an eight-year-old girl was so upset at how her classmates were treating her that she jumped off the roof of her house and broke her neck. She lived only four blocks away from us.

"Young children can become a vicious pack of rabid wolves. Inevitably, they would talk about you behind your back and call you even worse names than they call you now. Believe me, I know how venomous young people can be toward each other, especially young girls. I saw it in my classrooms years ago. I have no doubt you would make friends quickly and even become quite popular. You're a bright, attractive young lady already, but you'd surely deliberately or even innocently threaten a best-friend relationship, and one of the girls would peck away until they all treated you like a freak because of your family history. Children are often blamed for the things their parents do. It's not fair, but it's how people often think of them.

"So you see, to answer your question, I'm simply trying to protect you from all that could come at you. Believe me, I know about this. I wasn't oblivious to what went on around me when I was teaching, like some of my associates were. They walked through the halls with their eyes shut. Cowards carrying chalk. Half the time these days, children like you are left to sink or swim. Everyone's afraid of being blamed. It's easier to pretend it's not happening, but I could never be like that. The truth is that if I hadn't left teaching, it eventually would have left me."

She sipped her tea and studied me. I was sure she saw that she had given me too much about my father to swallow. I felt I could choke to death on the rage of tears raining down inside me. Everything I had feared but had kept restrained was true. My father had literally abandoned me and gone on to have a new family. What possible misery at a public school could be more intense, more difficult to bear, than that?

Now that my fears were confirmed, anger and rage quickly overtook sorrow. *I will not wail and rage about my pain*, I thought. *I will not cry like some infant left sniveling in a corner. I didn't cry at the train station; I won't cry today.*

"I'm not afraid of any of that stuff at school," I said, eager to change the topic. "Whether you want to believe it or not, someday I will leave this house and have to depend on myself. If you keep protecting me like this, I'll be too weak, and they will torment me and trample me. But I promise you, I'll scratch and claw. They won't hurt me without my hurting them."

She widened her eyes at the fire I was sure was blazing in mine. "Will you, now?" She smiled. "You've become such a little tiger." She nodded. "Yes, I believe you might be a formidable adversary. Anyone growing up in the shadow of Mazy Dazy would be."

"I'm not afraid, especially of children my age," I emphasized.

She smiled as if she really could see something that she had never seen. "What I've enjoyed the most about you, Saffron, is how you surprise me all the time. You are a deep thinker for a girl your age. I do think you will find yourself."

"I already know myself better than anyone could, but it won't help to keep me in a cage."

"A cage, is it?"

"You restrict how far I can go out of the house. I feel like I'm on a leash whenever I do. I'm not afraid of what some children my age would say to me," I insisted. "You don't have to protect me anymore."

"Is that so?"

"Yes. I promise."

She sipped her tea. I could feel her resistance softening.

"Okay," she said. "Maybe you are ready. Let me think about all I have to do in order to enroll you in the public school."

I could feel myself nearly bursting with excitement and joy. Was this really finally going to happen? Public school? Real classrooms? Friends? Parties?

"When?"

"Give me time to do what has to be done," she said. "There are i's to dot and t's to cross before we can send you out safely."

"Safely?"

"You can't simply be a little girl I found at the railroad station, Saffron. We've told people you're my granddaughter, but we'll need some documentation to satisfy the busybodies. Be patient," she said.

"Okay," I said.

I apologized again for betraying her trust. We almost hugged, but she turned away before I could even approach her. The mixture of sad and happy feelings felt like I had a tornado going on inside me. My father might be gone forever, but I could go to school. I could have friends. I could become something more than a shadow or the Tree Girl.

I went to my room to start on the new reading she had assigned me, but I had trouble concentrating. I was too excited. Mazy never said things she didn't believe or promised anything she wouldn't do or deliver. I was confident that she wasn't simply making me feel better. Still, she could change her mind if I did something to feed any doubt she had that I could manage and survive out there in the world she sometimes made sound more like a jungle.

As soon as I rose the following morning, I was the perfect little mother's helper. What I didn't want her to believe was that the truth about my father had left me in any way helpless and full of self-pity. I went directly to my chores after breakfast, and I didn't nag about her enrolling me. As hard as it was, I kept it wrapped tightly and acted as if she had never mentioned it. I watched her fiddle about the house all morning, wondering if she had either forgotten or changed her mind. She was constantly distracted, talking to herself more. Was she debating with herself, changing her mind? It went on like this for two more days. It took all my self-control to keep from asking.

Finally, she told me she had to leave to get some important things done in order for her to proceed with signing me into the public school. She still had an old leather bag she called her teacher's luggage. In it, she would put evidence that I'd had my inoculations and of the exams I had taken, and her diary of all the work I had completed, including my reading list. Having been a teacher so long, she knew how to maintain my record and organize every moment of my homeschooling. Truthfully, I was surprised at how well she had done it. I regretted ever having doubted this was her intention from the start.

Moments after she had left the house, I was tempted to rush out and sneak over to Lucy's again. I knew her brother would be at school. I paced about, trying to decide if I should take the risk. Lucy would be so excited, I thought. Maybe she would get better faster so she could be at school with me, even go to school with me every day. But if Mazy found out . . . she could stop the process. I knew her temper.

What convinced me to do it, however, was the realization that if I was at Lucy's porch, I would have a clear view of the street and see when Mazy was on her way home. I could rush back and be there before she had entered. She'd never know, as long as Lucy's nurse and mother didn't see me. Lucy would not give me away, and I wouldn't stay long. Surely she was so sorry her mother had called Mazy. She probably thought I was gone forever.

I put a blue light cotton sweater over my blouse and slipped on my running shoes. I was very excited, but I still stepped hesitantly out the rear of the house. I hadn't realized until I was outside that the sky was completely overcast, with some of the clouds looking so bruised and angry that I thought it would surely start raining in a rage soon. I couldn't stay long at Lucy's, anyway. I shot off into the woods. I had been so anxious about telling her what Mazy was going to arrange that I hadn't even bothered to look out the classroom window to see if she was on the porch.

As carefully as I could, I cut in between trees and bushes. I had to be extra careful, because I would have no way to explain a scratch on my face or neck, and I had to avoid any mud or guck that would splash on my pants and stain my shoes. I imagined I looked like a weird ballet dancer, twisting and turning to slip past branches. When I reached Lucy's backyard, I paused to catch my breath. Then I moved quickly toward the front, hovering close to the wall as I went. I stopped and peered through the spindles, ready to whisper.

She wasn't there. The disappointment nearly brought me to

tears, but then I thought they most likely wanted to keep her out of any bad weather. I would just come back the first nice day. I had started to turn to make my way home when something caught my attention. Taking a few steps out and away from the porch so that I could see more clearly, I looked at the driveway.

If I had been stabbed through the heart with an icicle, I wouldn't have felt more chilled. There was no doubt in my mind what the vehicle parked there was. I brought my closed right fist up to stuff in my mouth, turned, and fled. I was nearly home when the tears came, and so did the rain, hard and fast, a good minute before I charged through the door. It was one of the biggest downpours I had seen.

Soaked, I stripped as soon as I entered. I went into the laundry room to get the mop and hurriedly wipe up any evidence of my having been outside. Then I grabbed all my things and rushed to my room to put on fresh clothes. Mazy could see my wet things if I put them in the washing machine, so I hid them in the closet, leaving them there until they dried. I quickly used the hair dryer.

After I caught my breath, I walked slowly up the stairs to the classroom and stood by the window watching as Lucy's family followed the paramedics carrying her to the ambulance. She was sitting upright and looking around, but clearly they had decided she had to go to the hospital. She was weak and pale when I had last seen her two weeks ago, but I never permitted myself to think she was so ill that she would end up in an ambulance with what was clearly an oxygen mask over her face.

Her brother stood beside their parents as they carefully placed her in the vehicle. I saw her mother start to crumple and her father quickly embrace her. As the ambulance backed out of the driveway, they all got quickly into their car, her father practically carrying her mother to it. The nurse was on the porch, watching them drive off to follow the ambulance. My memory of her brother, Stuart, embracing Lucy brought harder sobbing. Could I somehow find a way to visit her, maybe after I began school? If she knew, she might try harder to get better and come home.

For a few moments, I stared at the street, and then I saw Mazy walking back, her umbrella open. She was going slower, looking like it was suddenly a great effort. Was that because of the rain?

I retreated to sit and stare at the new assignments she had placed on my desk. Anger and sadness wrestled to control my heart. I lowered my head to my arms folded on the desk, but I did not sob anymore. I think I was more frightened now than anything. I was afraid that somehow people would blame me for making Lucy sicker and sicker until she had to be rushed to the hospital.

How silly, I told myself. But still, I sensed this would be a thought that would haunt me every time I left the house.

If he came, my father would surely be standing shyly at the door, hoping I would forgive him . . . for everything. Would I? Sometimes forgiveness wasn't up to us, anyway, I thought. Sometimes we had no choice but to forgive. If we didn't, we'd only suffer ourselves. I should tell Mazy that. She would add it to her list of wisdom quotes.

I raised my head when I heard her enter the house and soon after slowly start up the stairs. Mr. Pebbles had come up and sprawled out beside me. I believed he could feel when I was happy and when I wasn't, just like he could for Mazy. He raised his head to look up at me, and I touched him.

"It's all right, Mr. Pebbles three," I whispered. He began to purr again. Maybe people should purr so others would know when they were happy and content.

I opened the science text and stared down at it until Mazy appeared. I really didn't read a word and looked up quickly. She looked tired and gray.

"I'm sure you've been looking out that window," she said. "And have seen it all just now."

"I . . ."

"Don't deny it."

"Maybe they'll make her well again in the hospital," I quickly suggested instead of confessing.

"Make her well again? If you want to go out there in that rough-and-tumble world, you had better learn not to fool yourself. The worst lies are the ones you tell yourself, Saffron. That little girl's been in the hospital often. I might not seem like I know what's going on out there, even on my own street, but I do. These days at home were expected to be her last. She won't be back."

I bit down on my lower lip. I was shivering inside, but I was afraid to show her any weakness. She'd say I was still a little girl; she'd want to keep me more locked up than ever.

"The problem with living in a smaller community is you see and share tragedy more vividly. It's why I kept to myself most of my life. Hermits don't cry very much. Not even for themselves.

"Anyway, as I said, what happened today was expected. It's part of why I was so upset about you going over there and making friends with that poor girl. You probably thought me mean, but I was just trying to protect you a little more, a little longer. It's why parents, good parents, don't want their children to grow up so quickly. Well, that's going to be much harder to do now when it comes to you. I realize that."

She took a deep breath. "Tomorrow I'll have your new birth certificate, and I'll arrange for your enrollment soon after."

"Why a new one?"

"I fixed it so they'll believe you're older than you are and not put you in a class that will bore you to death. I've also legally changed your name to mine. You're now Saffron Dazy. You'll be much better off."

Maybe Mazy was right. Maybe I was better off keeping to myself and her, and spending my free time dreaming again that my father would come to get me and bring me to a fresh new world where I could forget from where I had come and what I had been doing until he arrived. All of this would be like some bad television show.

"How old am I?"

"Fourteen. Just a little bit of an exaggeration, but I think they'll put you in the ninth grade. At least, that is what I've demanded and they are seriously considering. Once they see your test scores, they might even consider putting you in the tenth."

"Tenth?"

That's the grade Lucy's brother is in, I thought. It made the prospect of school all the more frightening.

"You should be happy about that. We'll talk about it all to be sure we're on the same page," she said. "Don't worry. There's not much new to remember about yourself. If anyone pursues you with questions about your parents, the simple answer to most everything is 'I don't like to talk about it. It's too painful.' It's not entirely untrue, and half-truths are the best lies," she said.

She started to turn but paused and looked at me oddly for a moment. "Why are you wearing different clothes from this morning?"

"I felt dirty after doing the housework, and I want to always be dressed well when I go to school. Isn't that where I am?"

She stared, thinking.

Half-truths, I thought. *You just taught me.*

"You don't have to finish your assignment today. But know this about sadness, Saffron: it not only makes you sicker and older, it reminds you how fragile you are. That's a more difficult burden for young people. Whenever you have to face it, you'll feel like you've stepped out of yourself and you're in a strange place."

"I know all about facing strange places," I said.

She nodded. "Yes, I imagine you do. Well, try to think about good things, all that lies ahead." She looked down at Mr. Pebbles. "Even Mr. Pebbles is sad. I'll put pennies in the jar for us all," she said, and left.

There aren't enough pennies for this, I thought.

I closed the textbook and went to the window. Lucy's house looked smaller, almost as if it had begun to shrink since the ambulance took her away. Mazy wasn't wrong about sadness. I could feel it aging me, making places inside me darker and more bitter. The only way out was to listen to the rage, to be angry. At the moment, I despised everything that looked fresh and new, every leaf on every tree, every wildflower, and even the blue sky that was trying to peek out through the thinning clouds.

I didn't care if it rained forever. Why should anyone be happy? Why should this world continue?

Mazy spent most of the next two days lecturing me about public school, what my teachers would be looking to see in me, how I should comport myself, and how careful I should be about trusting anyone. Sometimes she really did make it seem as if I was going off to war. She saw the surprise in my face at how worried she was.

"Are you sure you're all right with all this?"

"I'll be fine," I insisted.

"Maybe you will, and maybe you won't. You have to remember, Saffron, that for your own good, I kept you well protected here. Your interaction with people your age is practically nonexistent. I don't want you to be snobby or shy, but I don't want you victimized, either. No matter how brave and tough you think you are, things will happen to you. Maybe you won't come running home crying, but I'll see it in your face. Best to always be honest with me."

I know she was being sincere, but I couldn't deny she was frightening me, too. Finally, I told her so, hoping she would stop with her continual list of warnings. She was making me regret I ever wanted to venture out into the world. I wanted her only to talk about the nice things that could come of it, but her response was, "That's good. It's good to be a little frightened. You won't make as many mistakes."

As many? Why would I make any? I thought.

Every day for the next three days, I stood at my classroom window and watched, hoping to see Lucy's parents bringing her home. I saw her brother once returning from school but not much else.

And then, one morning, when I went to the window, I saw a car pull into Lucy's driveway and a couple emerge quickly and hurry to the front door. Another car pulled up in front and parked. Then another and another. What had happened was spilling out of Lucy's house and, like a swarm of nasty hornets, was stinging friends and relatives within its reach. I imagined family was coming from far away, too.

Stuart stepped out on the porch with some of his school

friends, both boys and girls comforting him. They were surely classmates I would soon meet.

Mazy knew I was watching the house daily, but she didn't mention anything until the day of the funeral. She simply said, "The funeral is today."

Before I could comment, she added, "You'll start school on Monday."

I had been waiting to hear this for so long, but my feelings were twisted, excitement and happiness tangled in fear and uncertainty. Despite my bravado, I was sure I was feeling no more confident than a five-year-old dropped off at kindergarten. He or she was left to dangle and suddenly become totally dependent upon strangers.

I had a difficult time sleeping that Sunday night. At Mazy's insistence, I went to bed early, but that didn't help. If anything, it gave me more time to toss and turn, but excitement being what it is, I rose quickly, washed, and put on one of my newer dresses. When I looked at myself in a satin lace dress, I thought I might be over the top for a regular school day. I quickly changed into the French navy polo dress and put on my newest white slip-on sneakers. When I came out for breakfast, Mazy paused to look me over.

She smiled and nodded. "Perfect," she said. "We think alike sometimes."

She surprised me by bringing out a box and placing it on the table.

"What's this?"

"New first day of school present."

I opened it and took out a light-blue denim jacket. It fit perfectly.

"A former student of mine who has a granddaughter now directed me to that when I was shopping for you recently. I've been saving it for today."

"Oh, thank you, Mazy. I love it."

"Knew you would," she said. "Let's have a good breakfast and get you to school. I have to go with you today, but you'll come home yourself and go yourself from now on."

Further surprising me, after we had finished eating, she told me to leave everything as it was. Today was a special day—no cleanup was necessary.

Before we were about to leave, she gave me another present, a rose-gold-foil backpack.

"You don't have books yet, but there's a notebook in here, pens and pencils, some essentials like tissues, and this," she said, plucking a very thin black wallet out to show me. She opened it and carefully removed the copy of my new birth certificate.

"There'll be no better identification for you than this. A friend of mine, actually a former student who works in the government, put a rush on it for us."

I gazed at it to see my new birthday and my new name. It had the hospital I was supposedly born in and a town I never had heard of.

"Remember, if anyone asks you details about your home and parents, it's too painful to discuss. If they insist, you were too young to remember after the fire," she said. "It's all perfect," she assured me. She put it back in the wallet and returned it to the backpack. "There's a little money in there, too, although you won't need it at school. I've already paid for your lunch fee for the remainder of the year. You'll get a card today.

"If all goes well, I'll buy you a computer for your next birthday. I know young people your age abuse it, but I expect you won't. You will use it for research and to build your grades. I can envision you graduating two years early. And then . . ."

"Then what?"

"College, of course. I have the money for it set aside."

Dare I dream?

"Thank you, Mazy."

"Don't thank me yet. You have a long way to go, and there are many traps and dangers along that road."

I nodded, my excitement feeling like boiling milk about to spill out of the pot, despite her ever-fearful warnings.

She reached for my hand when we stepped out of the house but then quickly pulled it back. Maybe she could read my thoughts. What I didn't want to be or look like as we walked to the school was a little girl. I glanced only once at Lucy's front porch when we passed. I just knew that if she had recuperated, we surely would have become close friends.

As we walked, I reached back in my memory to recall how

much Daddy had wanted me to go to school. I wondered if he would have taken me to kindergarten that first day if Mama hadn't prevented it. Maybe they'd both have gone with me. Maybe I wouldn't have felt so different and so frightened as I did now.

The sight of buses arriving at the school building, some students being driven to it, and many walking to it, as I was, quickened my heartbeat. My legs felt so weak that I had to look down to see if I was still walking. I didn't want to look at anyone else yet. I was like Mazy, my eyes fixed with a stone glare on the entrance of the school. It was the best way to hide my nervousness. I might finally be attending school, but there was still a lot to learn from Mazy.

"We have to go to the principal's office first, Saffron," she said. "Someone will escort you to your first class. That's English. You'll get your whole schedule in a little while. I just want to be sure there are no hiccups, especially one in particular."

"What's that?"

"The event of your not being placed correctly," she said. "I've seen too many bright students dulled by incompetent teachers and administrators."

She had waited until we were about to enter the building before telling me she recently had insisted that I be put in all honors classes.

"I was given promises," she said, "but nothing is until it is, especially when it involves bureaucrats."

"You told me I was being put in the ninth grade."

"Yes, but not only do I want you in a class a year ahead of what you would go into normally, but also the honors classes, because they are taught work that is another year ahead."

"So I really will be doing tenth-grade work? Will I be in the tenth grade?" I couldn't stop thinking about Stuart.

"You'll be in an honors class. The classes are smaller, and you'll be with the brightest kids. Don't worry. I have no doubt you'll succeed," she said.

She smirked at the noise in the school lobby and the hallway.

"Running and screaming . . . I'd have them all whipped," she muttered.

I was expecting to see Mrs. Elliot again, but the principal was a young man named Mr. Blumberg. The school guidance counselor, a woman introduced as Mrs. Krammer, looked old enough to be the principal's mother. She had come to the school years after Mazy had retired, so neither really knew her, but both obviously had heard enough about her to treat her with more respect than they would an ordinary parent or guardian. The way they looked at me told me they were quite aware of the story Mazy had told Mrs. Elliot about me and my parents, the fire, all of it.

"I've seen the results of your work with this young lady, Mrs. Dutton," Mrs. Krammer said. "Quite impressive."

"She is quite impressive," Mazy said. "I can attest that she is not lazy. She's always worked hard and done well with any test I've given her. You know her scores. She needs to be challenged."

It was obviously very important to Mazy that I be placed in the honors classes and there be no second guesses about it.

"Well, attending public school is somewhat different," Mrs. Krammer said. She was respectful but obviously not intimidated. She turned to me. "Some children have a difficult time getting used to going to different teachers when they move from grade school to higher grades, and then someone who's been only homeschooled . . ."

"Not Saffron," Mazy insisted. "She's very independent." To emphasize the point, she added, "She's had to be."

"Yes," Mrs. Krammer said. "I'm sure."

"You're not, but you will be," Mazy hammered at her.

The guidance counselor looked at the principal. She squirmed a bit in her chair and sucked in her irritation.

"Well, Saffron," she said, waiting to turn away from Mazy to me quickly. "You have very good teachers here, but you can't expect the same individualized treatment your grandmother has provided."

"You placed her in the honors classes, didn't you?" Mazy pounced. "They're smaller, aren't they? The teachers in those classes can give their students more attention."

"Yes, but being with a dozen other students is still—"

"She doesn't need *tutoring*," Mazy snapped. "She needs challenging. I've prepared her for the classroom experience, having had well over twenty years of teaching experience. She knows what to expect and what's expected of her."

The principal nodded. "Of course, Mrs. Krammer was simply trying . . ."

Mazy gave him her best cold smile. It could chill the heart of Santa Claus.

"I do hope we spend more time encouraging young people than making excuses for them," Mazy said. "I've been told the tail wags the dog these days."

The principal blushed, his nose the only thing on his face not crimson.

"We'll make sure she's welcomed and given all the opportunities we can offer," Mrs. Krammer said. "I have your packet here, Saffron." She handed it to me. "Your schedule, teachers' names, lunch card, and a list of our rules that must be followed. It's too late to go to your homeroom. The bell for your first class will ring in a minute or so. No worries. I've informed your homeroom teacher, Mrs. Garson, that you will be joining her homeroom. Your teachers will be giving you your books in each class. Do you have any questions?"

I looked at the packet. "I haven't time to read the rules and go to class," I said.

Mazy actually laughed. Mr. Blumberg started to smile but stopped.

"I doubt you'll break a rule so quickly," Mrs. Krammer said. "But do take time to read the rules sometime today, if not at home."

"Any other questions?" Mr. Blumberg asked, looking from Mazy to me and then back to Mazy.

Mazy looked at me, and I shook my head. The bell rang anyway.

"Shall we start your education?" Mrs. Krammer said, standing.

"Oh, she's done that long ago," Mazy said.

Mrs. Krammer forced a smile.

I rose.

"Good luck," Mr. Blumberg said. I thanked him and followed Mrs. Krammer to my first class.

"Your English teacher is Mr. Madeo," she said. "He's been teaching here as long as your grandmother taught."

Mrs. Krammer described the building, where everything was located—the cafeteria, the gym, bathrooms, and my other classrooms—as we walked. I was afraid to show how excited I was moving among all these kids. There was an energy I had only dreamed of feeling. I smiled at the way no one seemed to be paying attention to where he or she was going. The noise of conversations was loud. Somehow the students around us avoided bumping into Mrs. Krammer and therefore me, but I did see some pause to look at me. Did they know who I was? No one had smiled at me.

We turned a corner. Another bell rang, and most everyone walked into a classroom. We paused to wait as the last few rushed into mine.

"Okay," Mrs. Krammer said, and we entered.

There were no more than a dozen students, mostly girls.

Everyone was at his or her desk. We paused just after entering. Mr. Madeo looked up from his desk.

"Mr. Madeo, I have a new student for you today," she said. "This is Saffron Dazy."

"Welcome," he said, and pointed to the first desk in the first row. I wondered why it was available, but I could see the eight girls were together and the four boys were scattered. Mr. Madeo had my textbook in hand as I started forward. Until then, I hadn't looked at anyone.

"She's dropping daisies all over the floor," I heard, and turned to see one of the boys I had seen at Lucy's house after the funeral seated at the last desk in the row by the windows.

The whole class laughed.

I paused as Mr. Madeo rapped on his desk and called for quiet.

I continued to stare at the boy. He looked so gleeful, proud of having everyone immediately laugh at my expense.

"Well, I'm sorry flowers frighten you so much. Stay out of my garden."

These was a pause, and then the whole class laughed. They were looking at the boy, whose face reddened.

I couldn't be sure, but I thought there was a small smile on Mr. Madeo's lips as I continued to my desk and thanked him for the textbook. He nodded at Mrs. Krammer, who then left.

"Page forty-eight," he told me. "We're reading Stephen Crane's 'The Open Boat.' Have you ever heard of it, Saffron?"

"I read it last year," I said.

He looked quite surprised. I wasn't about to tell him Mazy had gotten the reading list for all the classes more than a year ago.

"Really? Do you know what Crane was trying to say in the story?"

"The universe doesn't care about us," I said. "Shocker. We're on our own."

Mazy didn't want me simply to read important stories and books. She wanted me to read *about* them, and I remembered this one very well, because what it taught was something I had keenly felt but didn't know how to express.

His eyes brightened. "Well, let's see how Miss Dazy came to that conclusion, class," he said. "Welcome to ninth-grade honors English, Miss Dazy. You can drop all the flowers you want."

I gazed back at the boy, who was now staring out the window.

The pretty dark-brown-haired girl on my right was smiling at me. She had a button nose and sweet hazel eyes. Her lips were full and perfect, which made her look older. Of course, everyone was probably older than I was.

I smiled back at her and opened the text to the short story.

"Nice," the girl behind me whispered.

I glanced at her. She had short light-brown hair and kelly green eyes, but she wasn't that pretty, I thought, definitely not as pretty as poor Lucy.

Mr. Madeo began to read a paragraph aloud. I sat up. Mazy was always after me to have good posture. It was silly to think it, but I couldn't help feeling she was in the room with me, sitting in the rear, smiling proudly.

Maybe a normal life was beginning for me after all.

CHAPTER TEN

The pretty girl who had smiled at me and two of her friends surrounded me instantly after the bell rang to end the class. All the other students glanced at me curiously but moved around us, as if they were afraid to make any contact with me, even eye contact.

"I'm Karla Matthews," she said. "This is Trudy Samuels and Missy Brooks."

"Hi," I said. We all kept walking, me a little more hesitant and unsure of where I was going.

The corridor, with coffee-white walls and shiny grayish black floor tiles, was lit by narrow light fixtures and an occasional window. There were posters prohibiting everything from loitering in the bathrooms to acts of vandalism, as well as posters announcing upcoming school events. Although no one ran, everyone was walking fast and talking. Peals of laughter came in waves from every direction. Excitement and, I hoped, well-smothered nervousness swirled up from my stomach. This was school; this was where I had dreamed of being for so long. Was everyone looking at me? Would I make a fool of myself in my next class?

"Your name really is Saffron?" Karla asked.

"Yes."

"I thought that was something to eat. I think my mother uses it in recipes."

"Ingredients are often used as names," I said. "Ginger, for example."

I tried not to look at them, but out of the corner of my eye, I could see they were laughing.

"You live with your grandmother, Mrs. Dutton, but your last name is Dazy?" Karla asked.

"That is correct," I said.

"That is correct?" Trudy said. I glanced at her and kept walking. "Sounds like you're taking a test, Karla, and Saffron just gave you a passing grade."

"So Mrs. Dutton is your mother's mother?" Karla pursued, ignoring her.

I just nodded. To explain that my grandmother took back her maiden name would take too long and only raise dozens of new questions, especially why I had taken on her name, too. Was this normal? Was this how you made friends? By cross-examining them?

"You have algebra next, correct?" Karla said, imitating my *correct*.

"Yes." I looked at her clever little smirk. She was fishing for a laugh at my expense. "Don't you like being correct?"

"What?" Her smile started to fade.

"Forget that, Karla. I loved how you put down Donald Nickels," Trudy said, stepping forward to move closer to me. She was the tallest of the three, with straight licorice-black hair sharply cut at the base of her long neck. Her ebony eyes pulsed with glee. "He's so puffed up with himself that he can't fit in a selfie."

All the girls laughed. The tension I felt among us dwindled, and I smiled.

"However, we all hafta admit that he is good-looking," Karla practically sang. She leaned in to me to emphasize. "He's hands down probably the best-looking boy in our class, maybe the whole school."

"Trouble is, he knows it," Trudy responded, and looked to me for some confirmation. "Wouldn't you agree, Saffron Dazy?"

"I don't know anything about him."

Trudy stopped walking, making us all pause. "You don't have to know his biography. You can tell just by looking at him. If his nose got any higher, he'd have to be on oxygen."

"I'll let you know if and when I meet him," I said.

Trudy lost her smile. "But you know what he meant with his joke about flowers. You are the Tree Girl, aren't you?" she asked.

"No. I just told you, I'm Saffron Dazy," I said sharply, and kept walking, just a little faster than they were.

They caught up at the door of math class.

"How long have you lived here?" Trudy asked. Before I could enter the room, she quickly added, "Where's the rest of your family?"

"In the forest. Where else?" I said, and entered the classroom to introduce myself to my teacher, who was already waiting with a textbook in hand.

Until I smiled at them, the three girls didn't look happy when they entered and took their seats. Trudy laughed and whispered something to the two others. Then Karla smiled back at me, nodding her head. Missy grinned. From the way they were all grinning at me now, I thought I might have passed some test they had designed for new students.

Apparently, I had. They never stopped talking to me, walking with me to every class and insisting I sit with them at lunch. Maybe they had briefly discussed it first, but when they sat with me at the table, none of them asked any more particularly personal questions, even though I could see how much they were dying to do so. Instead, they competed to tell me things about the school, the other girls, and the boys, each rushing to get me more interested in what she had to say than what the others had said, sometimes talking over the one speaking.

Karla, especially, didn't like the attention I was giving to Trudy, who did speak louder and faster than the other two.

Mazy's warning about coming between best friends echoed in my mind. The temptation to favor one of the three was like bait leading me into an early trap. Other kids from our small classes came around to say hello. Karla took the lead in introducing me, but I caught some of the glances between my three guides and the other students. Their eyes were jammed with the same question: *What have you learned about her?* I was sure every text among them tonight would have my name. What golden nugget would I provide? Which one of them would claim it first?

Would it help me or hurt me to continue to be mysterious? I wondered. The danger was that they'd get tired of trying to learn things about me or simply make things up, unattractive things. But despite how much I wanted to confide in someone and share my feelings and especially my history, I kept that urge tightly reined in. My dead silence and expressionless face at times didn't stop their fishing.

"I don't know anyone homeschooled," Karla said, "but having someone who taught as long as Mrs. Dutton did surely helped."

"We saw that already," Missy reminded her. She turned to me and, almost suggesting I had somehow cheated, said, or more like whined, "You had the algebra problem solved practically before Mr. Wasserman had finished putting it on the blackboard. No one else in class had a chance."

"It's a common equation," I said.

"Common?"

She looked at the other two, who shrugged. She had reddish-brown hair neatly cut. Her face was explosive—her crystal-blue eyes brightening, her nose twitching, and the dimples in her cheeks bubbling when she tugged in the sides of her mouth. Despite the jealous way she described my work in class, I felt she was the least threatening to me. She was small, a good two inches shorter than I was, with doll-like features, and insecure. She wanted so to be liked, I thought, even more than I did. It was too obvious.

Mazy had warned me about that: "The more you want someone to like you, the harder she'll make it for you, dishing out her favor like spoonfuls of gold."

I imagined that Missy was one of those who was always close to bursting into tears. Mazy would say she had been babied too long. "She'll need a caretaker, not a husband."

Like my mother, I thought, but never said.

"Still, even if it was a common equation, Missy's right. You wouldn't have become so smart in homeschool if you didn't have a teacher like Mrs. Dutton," Trudy said. "How did she teach you so much so quickly?"

"That's not a big mystery," I said.

They all stared, waiting for more.

"First, she created a classroom for me in her house."

"A real classroom?" Karla asked. "You mean with a blackboard and desks?"

"Only one desk," I said. "And don't forget the chalk."

"Did you have to raise your hand to ask her a question?" Trudy asked, smiling. She thought she was so clever.

I didn't smile. "Sometimes," I said, and they all looked quite surprised.

"You're kidding," Karla said.

"Why would you have to raise your hand if there was no one else there?" Missy asked.

I decided that teasing them was fun. "Training for coming here," I said. "It was a simulation."

"A what?" Trudy asked.

"An imitation of something, like when an astronaut goes into a machine that makes it seem like he's really in outer space so he can practice."

I could hear Mazy calling *simulation* another example of a dying word.

"So going to school is like outer space for you?" Karla asked, with a smile that was really closer to a smirk.

"In a way, it is."

"Really?" Missy asked. "So you're telling us you were being trained to go to public school?"

I nodded. "She had a bell she'd ring between subjects, and there were announcements over a speaker in the house describing rules of the day. I had to walk on the right in the hallway and never run."

They all stared at me. I couldn't help myself. I was having too much fun.

"There was a bathroom pass and a list of rules and a school uniform. She had a room with the word *Principal* on the door, and there was a detention room, too, with no furniture and no windows. Is there a detention room here?"

Their mouths were slightly open now.

"I had to sit on my hands in the detention room. Anyone ever have to do that for an hour?"

Missy gasped.

"You're making all this up," Trudy cautiously concluded.

"Well . . ." I said, looking around before turning back to them. "Maybe a little."

Missy laughed, relieved. "You're funny," she said.

"She's hysterical," Trudy said dryly.

"You deserved it," Karla told her. "You made her feel odd."

"Me? What about you two? 'Saffron is something you eat?'" she mimicked.

"Well, it is, isn't it, stupid?" She turned to me. "You weren't upset, were you?"

Now they were going to fight over me, I thought. Should I take one's side over the other's? Mazy had frightened me enough with the warnings about being too friendly too soon. The night before, she had come to my bedroom after I had gotten into bed and said, "Remember, your friendship is very precious. You don't give away precious things quickly. Be a good listener and not a good talker. Roll everything around in your mouth first, and then give your tongue permission to perform."

When she finally left, I thought that was another one of her wisdom quotes.

But I wasn't following her advice. Would that hurt my chances of being just another student here?

The girls were waiting for my response.

"Maybe a little," I said. "Nobody likes to be cross-examined."

The three looked equally defensive.

"We're just interested," Trudy said. "It's not a cross-examination. You should appreciate our attention. Most new students have to scratch and claw to get into the real action around here. And believe me, we're the real action."

"I was just interested. Honest," Missy said.

"Okay," I said. "The real answer about me is simply that education is and always was the most important thing in my grandmother's life. I guess I'm just lucky she was in charge of it until now."

"Why didn't she put you into school immediately?" Trudy pursued.

I shrugged. "She thought she would do a better job. From the looks of it, she might have been right."

"Meaning?" Karla asked sharply. Did I mean they were all dumber?

I shrugged again. "I think I'm doing better than most do their first day. What do you think?"

They were all quiet for a moment, pondering. I kept eating my lunch.

"So then, why now?" Karla asked. "What took so long?"

"She thought I was ready, I guess. There was just so much she could do herself. She wanted to . . . expand my horizons," I said. "You all know what that means, right?"

"Of course we do," Trudy said. "We're in the honors classes, too, you know, even though we weren't specially tutored."

When she was being sarcastic, she spoke out of the side of her mouth.

"That's good," I said. "I'm happy for you," I added, tapping my lips gently with my napkin. "The food's not as good as I hoped it would be, but I guess I'll get used to it."

"It's a simulation of food," Karla said. The other two laughed. "Did your grandmother ring a bell for lunch?" she asked. They laughed again.

"Actually, she did. I'd get too involved in my work."

"When I'm hungry, I couldn't care less about good grades," Trudy said.

"You always ate with just your grandmother?" Missy asked.

"No. There is a cat, too. The third Mr. Pebbles. My grandmother had two identical ones previously. There's a picture of the first Mr. Pebbles on our kitchen wall. Anyone have a pet?" I asked, tired of talking about myself.

"We have a German shepherd," Missy said. "Just two years old."

"My grandmother is not crazy about dogs. Cats are independent, but they can be devoted," I said.

"Whoopty-do," Karla said. "Your best friend was a cat."

I glared at her. When would they put their knives away?

"I once saw you walking with your grandmother," Trudy said, sitting back. "But that was years ago. I never knew you were still here until the boys talked about you. We used to plan sighting expeditions in the woods."

"What does that mean? Sighting expeditions?"

"Thought you were such a good student. Don't you know that's what explorers do? We were exploring. We'd venture close to your grandmother's house to see if we could catch a glimpse of you," Karla said. "They said you had branches instead of arms and leaves where your hands should be."

"So is that what you saw?"

"Of course not," Trudy said. "We accused the boys of lying about you, but they claimed you could go back and forth from human to tree. It got to be boring, actually, and we stopped spying on you."

"I forgot all about you," Missy said, smiling. "Until you showed up at school."

I nearly laughed, because she sounded like she was bragging about it.

"Actually, most everyone did. Most of us thought you had left Hurley some time ago," Karla said. "Until recently. I don't know how you put up with homeschool so long. It almost sounds like solitary confinement."

She leaned toward me, her eyes smaller, more intense.

"Tell the truth, for once. Weren't you bored to death living with your grandmother? I'm bored after spending ten minutes with either of mine."

"The truth is . . . she made sure that I very rarely had time to be bored."

They all stared at me as if I had said the most fantastic thing they had ever heard. I suspected they were often bored, despite the freedom they had compared to me and all the things they were able to do that I couldn't.

"I'd still be bored," Trudy said. "Suicidal, maybe."

"You all make boredom sound like a disease," I said. "My grandmother would say, 'If you're bored, start a new book. Try to write a poem or draw a picture.'"

"I read only what I have to read," Trudy said. "And that's too much as it is."

"I do sketch things sometimes," Missy admitted. She looked down quickly.

"It always looks childish," Karla told her.

Missy's cheeks quickly turned pink.

"I'd like to see your drawings sometime," I offered, and she brightened.

"Show her. Maybe her grandmother taught her how to be an art critic, too," Karla said.

I nearly bit down on my lower lip. Taking sides too soon, I told myself. There was too much temptation to do so.

Karla leaned forward. The other two did as well.

"We haven't told you the whole truth," she said.

"Oh?"

"Stuart Wiley was the one who brought you back to our attention. He told us how he had to chase you away from Lucy."

They were all keenly waiting for my self-defense.

"That was a mean thing for him to do—mean to his sister, too. I hope he feels sorry. If he tries to make me into some sort of scapegoat, lies about me . . ."

"Then what?" Karla asked.

I glared at them, feeling the anger in me rise like mercury in a thermometer. They all looked a little frightened now, and it suddenly struck me that they thought I might be threatening to do something to Stuart, something I might be able to do to them, too.

"I didn't realize how sick she was," I said in a more apologetic tone. "I was only trying to be friendly. She looked lonely sitting by herself every day on her porch."

No one spoke for a moment, but I could clearly see now that there was some other reason for their interest in me besides normal curiosity. Suddenly, none of the three had the courage to speak.

"What?" I demanded of their silence.

"You didn't do anything weird like touch her with a branch or something?" Trudy asked.

"What? Is that what Stuart said? Did he tell people that?"

"Forget about it," Karla said.

"I'm just asking," Trudy said.

"You're frightening her and getting her upset on her first day of school," Karla said sharply.

"She's not frightening me, but if he said that, it was a lie. Is he back in school?" I glanced around.

"Tomorrow," Karla said. "But don't worry. He's not in the honors classes."

"Oh." Despite how hard I tried not to, I sounded relieved.

"He's another one who wishes he could be Karla's boyfriend," Trudy said. "And he's good friends with Donald Nickels, who Karla likes more."

"Shut up," Karla protested. "You don't know who I like more."

Trudy leaned toward me to reveal a secret. "I tease Stuart to death sometimes, walking behind him and singing 'Jessie's Girl.'"

"What's that?" I asked.

She pulled back as if I had struck at her like a snake. "You never heard 'Jessie's Girl'?"

"Don't start singing it to her," Karla warned. She looked at me. "I don't give Stuart any reason to believe he could be my boyfriend. And I didn't spread any stupid thing he told me about you."

"A lot of boys wish they could be Karla's boyfriend," Missy offered enviously.

That seemed to calm Karla. I thought she and Trudy were friends with Missy because she seemed to idolize both of them.

"That's true," Karla said, returning quickly to her more con-

fident self. "But the boys in our class especially are very immature. I have an older brother who's in his first year of college at
NYU. There's a friend of his I wouldn't mind dating." She gave
a little smile before adding, "I just might, one of these days."

Trudy smirked. "Sure you will."

"He's bringing him home at the end of the month for a long
weekend," Karla bragged. She looked at me. "If you're as smart
as you seem to be, it won't take you long to see what I mean
about the boys in our class."

I smiled. Right now, I couldn't even imagine a boyfriend.
How would Mazy react if some boy at school came to see me, especially an older boy? When would I be able to see him? Would
she let me go anywhere with him?

"Karla's not all wrong about that. Just watch out for some of
the boys in our classes," Trudy warned. "They'll be asking you
to help them with their schoolwork."

"Which means . . ." Karla began.

"Means what?"

"Then *you'll* become their schoolwork," Trudy said.

"Especially female anatomy," Karla added.

Missy's cheeks turned pink again, but she joined them in
laughing.

"Anyone makes a pass at you, you check with me," Karla said.

"Yeah, Karla would know which one to trust," Trudy said
dryly. "The rest of us are boy-stupid."

"Poor you," Karla told her. "What was that line Mr. Madeo

quoted from the play we're going to read next month? The Shakespeare play? 'Beware of jealousy,'" Karla said, and paused, not recalling the rest of the quote.

"'It is the green-eyed monster which doth mock the meat it feeds on,'" I said.

Their eyes nearly popped.

"Maybe she doesn't need your help, Karla," Trudy said.

"Maybe you need *hers*," Missy said, laughing.

Karla didn't change expression, but her eyes looked inflamed. The bell rang.

"Just like it does at home, huh?" she said. "Grandma's coming. Better move, girls," Karla said, smiling coolly.

They looked at me for some sort of comeback, but I ignored it. *Sometimes*, Mazy had told me, *it's better to let a fire burn out.*

My afternoon classes went as well as the morning ones. Trudy had asked for my phone number and said she'd share it with the other two. As we parted and headed toward the exits, Donald Nickels caught up with me, and I heard him say, "You might have some of the girls fooled, but don't think you have me fooled. I know what you are."

I stopped and looked at him. He was with another two boys, all smiling.

"That's good," I said. "Maybe you'll be more careful now."

I made a circle in the air with my right hand. His smile drifted as mine widened. Then, although I was battling with fear, I walked toward the exit confidently, believing Mazy would be proud of me. There was an explosion of screams and laughter as all the students around me burst out of the building as if they were escaping from a house on fire.

I had all my texts and notes in my new backpack and walked down the sidewalk the way Mazy and I had walked to the school, my face forward, quite satisfied with my first day. I hadn't merely survived it. I had excelled. I had done well in class and certainly did better than hold my own when it came to chatting with the other girls.

When I reached our street, I slowed my pace as I came to Lucy's house. There was still a gray shadow around it despite its being a bright day, with puffy clouds looking more like God had dabbed them onto the blue as an afterthought. I once suggested to Mazy that we should think of God that way, think of him as more of an artist. Every day, as if he was bored, he changed something in our world. He was trying to change this horrible moment, perhaps.

"Maybe the Bible is wrong," I had told Mazy. I was only nine at the time. "Maybe he's never rested."

I recalled how she had stared at me for a moment and then had nodded and said, "You're going to be quite a lot to handle when you're older."

I didn't know exactly what that meant, but I thought it didn't sound like she was offering me praise. If anything, she was predicting disaster. When I really thought about it, all her warnings and instructions seemed more like what I would need to survive in some great battle, as if there was something about me that would make me a target for hate and evil. Maybe she didn't mean it, but she did frighten me and make me wish I would grow porcupine quills.

I was in deep thought about all this, my first school day, and poor Lucy. As if he had been waiting for me to appear, Stuart stepped out of his house, folded his arms, and stood at the edge of the porch. He just glared at me.

I didn't look away.

"Lucy should be sitting in the seat you're in at school," he said, almost too low to hear.

"I'd gladly give it up for her."

He came down the steps and paused, his hands on his hips. It was as if he was afraid to get too close to me. "That's a lie," he said.

"I don't know why you're blaming me and making up silly stories about me. I did nothing to hurt her. I wanted to be her friend. That's all. She wanted a friend. I bet all her so-called friends stayed away from her when she became very sick."

"Is that what you want everyone to believe?"

"I want them to believe the truth."

He looked toward Mazy's house and then smiled. "My friends already called me and told me what a snob you are, showing off in class and all."

"That's a lie."

"They say you already act like a little old lady and know

things you shouldn't for someone your age. No one's ever going to trust you."

"Who told you that? Donald Nickels?"

I shook my head and then stepped toward him, intending to explain how Mazy had been tutoring me and why there was really nothing terribly special about it. Maybe I could get him to be my friend. But he put his hand up and stepped back. The look of fear on his face actually shocked me. I froze.

"Don't come any closer. You're not putting any curses on me," he said.

"What?"

He knelt down and picked up a rock. "Keep walking," he ordered.

I saw it would do no good to keep talking to him, and I believed he would throw that rock at me if I took another step toward him, so I turned and continued on.

"You shouldn't have been let in the school!" he shouted. "No one's going to be your friend. The girls think you're weird. You'll see."

I kept walking. Despite everything I had done, how well I believed I had handled my first day at school, I felt the tears welling in my eyes. I was hoping to step through the door and blast Mazy with all the good news, how all my teachers had complimented me and how well she had done preparing me for public school. I would even brag about how I had handled the girls in my class and followed her instructions to a T, even though it wasn't completely true. But the moment I stepped in and she looked at me, she threw the dish towel at the counter and asked the question I had so hoped to never hear from her lips.

"What did they do to you? I want to hear it all, every detail."

She followed me into the living room. I took off my backpack and began to describe the day from the moment I had left her in the principal's office. She sat and continued to listen, not interrupting or asking any questions. I even summarized my lunchtime talk with Missy, Trudy, and Karla, before I concluded with the accusations Stuart was making and our confrontation just now on our street.

"He was going to throw a rock at you?"

"I know you'll tell me all this is a result of my going over there without your permission, but how am I going to make friends at school if he spreads these stories? Everyone's going to be afraid of me."

"Maybe that's good," she muttered.

"*No*," I said sharply. "No, Mazy. It'll make everything harder for me."

"It won't help you if I go to see the principal about it," she said. "Those boys will be called in and bawled out, but that will just antagonize them more. They'll double up on their behavior, but just more subtle, perhaps. No. You have to solve this yourself, Saffron."

"How?"

"You get the ones you like to see the lies others are telling about you. Just, as I told you, be careful of whom you trust, maybe even more so now. After a little time passes, I'll have a talk with Stuart's mother. Eventually, I'm sure you'll become yesterday's news, especially if you don't give them any satisfaction. Ignore, ignore, and ignore. Stick to your schoolwork, and feel out the ones you can trust."

She smiled and stood.

"The main thing is, you are fulfilling my scholastic expectations for you. Teachers will respect you, and eventually other students will as well. I've prepared one of your favorite dinners tonight, just the way we've learned how to make it together, chicken piccata with couscous. And then a chocolate cake. Go wash up and change. Remember what I told you about bringing home germs from school. A good hot shower every day as soon as you're home. Go on," she urged. "I'll look at your homework with you later."

Maybe she's right, I thought. I decided I was lucky to have her. Without even having met them, I was sure the parents of the girls I had met couldn't come up to Mazy's knees. Her dinner cheered me up. Afterward, I went to our classroom to do my homework. I decided that even though I wasn't going to use it anymore to learn and study what Mazy taught, it still felt more like being in school to work there. I had no distractions, of course, and no need to look out at the street. I'd be on it tomorrow.

Less than a half hour later, Mazy came knocking on the door, a strange look on her face. There was no anger, just a lot of surprise mixed with some concern.

"Someone is on the telephone for you," she said. "I was going to tell her you were doing homework but decided you would know not to stay on too long, and I know you want to make friends."

"Who is it?"

"I didn't ask. She asked for you, and I said 'Just a moment.' You can use the phone in my bedroom. It's the closest."

She stepped back, and I rose quickly. I had never had a phone call from anyone. My life was quickly being filled with firsts. This was exciting. Mazy's phone was on the table at the right side of her bed. I lifted the receiver but remained standing.

"Hello."

"It's Trudy. I don't suppose you heard the news," she said.

"What news?"

"We're at Karla's house. She's been quite hysterical."

"What news? Why is Karla hysterical?"

"Donald Nickels was in a bad car accident a few hours ago. He wasn't wearing his seat belt. Mitchel Franklin lost control and went off the road at Jackson's Bend. Mitchel's all right. He's actually out of the hospital. Donald is in critical condition."

"Oh." I felt my heart do flip-flops, and for a moment, I couldn't catch my breath.

"Did you put a curse on him?"

"What?"

"His friends say you did when you were leaving the building today."

I could hear Karla crying in the background.

"Are you serious? A curse?"

"Did you?"

"I was just teasing him. I can't put a curse on someone."

She was quiet.

"I can't. That's ridiculous," I said firmly.

"Stuart said you came at him today on the way home, and he kept you from putting a curse on him by scaring you off with a rock. Everyone's talking about you."

"That's crazy," I said. "I didn't do anything."

"No one knows where you came from; no one knows anything about your parents."

I was silent.

"Donald might die," she said. "We just thought you should know."

She hung up.

"Trudy?"

I stood there holding the receiver.

"What is it? Who is it?" Mazy asked. She had been standing just outside her bedroom listening.

For a moment, I couldn't speak. She stepped closer. Trudy's words echoed in my ears: *No one knows where you came from; no one knows anything about your parents.*

"Saffron?"

I knew I was crying. I trembled and suddenly felt terribly hot.

I felt like I was back at my house when I was little. Daddy had scooped me up.

And the flames were snapping and growing all around me. I reached back, expecting Mama's hand.

But it wasn't there.

It never would be.

CHAPTER ELEVEN

Despite my protests, Mazy decided she had to accompany me to school the following day. The wind was a bit snappy and cool. She muttered to herself as we walked, sharply stabbing the end of her umbrella into the road and walkway with each step she took, practically creating sparks. Obviously, something more than Trudy's phone call was bothering her. The phone had rung twice more before I had gone to sleep. Each time, I had anticipated her calling me to it, but she never did, and when I had asked her about it in the morning, she'd said, "Wrong number."

Her shifting eyes told me that wasn't true. Whatever it was, it was still disturbing her. Her cheeks were splattered with patchy red dots, and she walked more bent over. She looked like she was lunging forward, the umbrella suddenly a real cane.

"I'm going to get rid of that phone," she muttered. She was breathing hard, probably from the rage ravaging her insides. "I'll get a mobile phone and not give the number out to anyone. In fact, I'll get it today."

But Daddy won't be able to call us if he decides to do so, I thought.

"What if someone wants to call me?"

"We'll cross that bridge when we come to it," she said. "First things first. You just do your work. Just do your work," she chanted. "You ignore any nasty remarks. They'll peck at you like vicious chickens. Don't pay attention. Look away. Avoid eye contact. Walk away. After a while, they'll get bored. They have the attention span of pigeons."

The way she was warning me told me she knew more.

When the school came into view, we saw groups of students mingling. Some of the girls were crying, and others were trying to comfort them. My heart felt like a yo-yo whose string had snapped on the way down. *Oh, no* formed on my lips. Almost without my being aware of it, Mazy seized my hand and steered us a little more to the left.

"Mazy. Something terrible must have happened. The accident."

"Just do your work, do your work, and come directly home. No. I think I'll be out here waiting for you. Just do your work, and don't get into any arguments," she said.

We paused at the entrance. I could feel we were being watched, but I kept my head down.

"Maybe we should go home," she said.

"What? Why?"

She looked at me and then, after a deep breath, said, "Okay. Go on. Go on. Do as I say, and you'll be fine."

She let go of my hand, opened the door, and waited for me to step into the school. I thought she was going to follow me right to my homeroom, which would have embarrassed me. Fortunately, she held back and just watched me walking through the lobby. I was clutching my schedule in my hand, hoping no one could see how much I was suddenly trembling. This morning, I was to go directly to homeroom.

I did what she said, walked without looking at anyone. There were four girls talking softly right in the doorway, one wiping away tears. They were blocking my entrance, but when they saw me coming, they stepped aside so quickly that anyone would think I was carrying an infection.

When I entered, I recognized a few from my honors classes, but I didn't say a word to any of them or anyone in particular in the room. I could feel their eyes practically glued to me. I looked for Karla, Trudy, or Missy, but none of them was here.

Mrs. Garson came around to the front of her desk. She was a tall, very thin woman with thin almond-brown hair that looked like it was the last thing she cared about before she left her house. Some strands were curled, and her bangs were in desperate need of trimming. She wore no makeup, and the freckles splattered unchallenged over her cheeks and forehead. She even had some on her chin.

"Saffron Dazy?" she asked, like someone who was hoping I might say no. I nodded. "Please take the last seat in the row by the window. I take attendance in five minutes. We'll hear the day's announcements and leave in an orderly fashion for our first classes. You can't sit with your backpack on," she said, as if she had expected I would.

I made my way across the room to my desk and set my backpack beside me. The boy next to me glanced at me and then turned away. No one moved; no one said a word to anyone. Mrs. Garson sat behind her desk and looked up at the ceiling. I could feel the funeral atmosphere thickening. The warning bell rang, and the students from my homeroom who were in the hallway rushed in. Everyone was quite subdued. Some looked at me, and some, when they did, quickly turned away, as if my looking back might burn them. Mrs. Garson stood at her podium and began to take attendance. When my name was called, most turned to me. Almost all had said, "Here," but I said, "Present." It was how Mazy had taught me to respond.

Mrs. Garson sat and stared at the ceiling again, her hands lying on her small bosom. We heard the PA system buzz, and then the principal, Mr. Blumberg, began by saying, "This is Mr. Blumberg." At least half the homeroom immediately lowered their heads, anticipating the words, "We will begin with a silent prayer for Donald Nickels."

Surely it wasn't that long ago when all these students were lowering their heads for Lucy Wiley, I thought. This wasn't any less sad, but I couldn't help thinking how much sadder it was for me first to have known Lucy and then to have had only a mean-spirited contact with Donald. I wanted to feel more terrible, more like the others were obviously feeling. Trudy's phone call made it more uncomfortable for me, but it was clearly very disturbing for everyone in the school, some looking absolutely terrified.

Mr. Blumberg talked about counselors being available for anyone who needed to talk. They were told to go to the guidance counselors' office. I wished that Mazy had decided to enroll me three or so days later, maybe even the following week. But I also believed that Stuart Wiley would have caused trouble for me no matter when I had entered the public school.

The bell rang, and I reached for my bag and left homeroom to head for my English class. No one said a word to me as we all left. Most who spoke kept their voices low. They moved ahead of and around me quickly, as if they were afraid to touch me. I wondered if I would confront my three short-lived friends before I entered the classroom. Were they waiting to ambush me with accusations and threats and their predictions of disaster? I surprised myself by suddenly laughing, maybe to ease the tension I was feeling. They had become something else in my mind, thanks to the Shakespearean reading list Mazy had set out for me this year; maybe they were churning up frogs in a cauldron.

"'Fair is foul and foul is fair,'" I whispered. I turned the corner. Would I find the three witches from *Macbeth* waiting for me?

It was worse. Stuart and another boy I had not yet met were

standing with the three of them near the entrance to the English classroom. They all turned to watch me approach. None of the three girls smiled at me. They looked shocked that I was smiling, but the little joke I had told myself had given me more courage.

I didn't look away. I headed directly at them.

The girls did take a step back, but Stuart stepped forward. He had his arms folded across his chest, trying to look immovable.

He's showing off, I thought.

"What, no rocks?" I said. For a moment, my aggressiveness did shock him.

"You'd better not curse us," Karla said.

"Stop that. It's stupid. For someone in an honors class, especially," I added. I knew Mazy wanted me to avoid any conflicts, but they weren't going to make me cower, not now, not ever.

She stepped back again. I thought that would end it. I'd get through the day, and just as Mazy predicted, they would all get bored with it. Eventually, I'd find new friends.

But Stuart continued to come toward me. That seemed to give the others new courage. They stayed close to each other. Moving in a clump obviously helped them feel safer. Despite the lies Stuart was telling about me, it was still difficult to imagine that anyone would believe I was really dangerous.

"We heard the truth about you," he said. He looked so self-satisfied that it made me feel a little sick to my stomach.

I paused and looked at them, not flinching. Missy quickly looked down, but Trudy and Karla stared at me so hard that they would surely have gone through a steel wall if they could send daggers out of their eyes.

"And what did you hear, rock man? That I could turn you into a toad by touching you with a branch? Maybe I have a leaf in my pocket."

I was hoping to embarrass him and not vice versa. He would certainly not look like he was courageous if they knew how afraid of me he was.

His face did redden.

But Karla poked him. "Tell her," she ordered.

"Right," he said, and widened his smile again. "The elementary school principal's secretary is a gossip, especially since her boss retired and she doesn't have to worry about keeping secrets," he said mysteriously. He folded his arms again, pulled back his shoulders, and broadened his smile. The other boys were smiling, too.

"What secrets?"

He looked at the others and then at me. "The secrets your grandmother told."

"There aren't any secrets," I said, unable to keep my voice from sounding a bit shaky. "You're making something up."

"No, I'm not. Your parents died in a house fire. You set it, accidentally or not, and went a little nuts. That's why you're so weird. That's why your grandmother had to keep you practically locked away until now. She was told you were dangerous to yourself and others. She couldn't let you out with other kids until you passed some psychiatric exam."

He looked at Karla to be sure he had said it right. I saw her nod.

I didn't move. Students rushed around us. I wanted to lunge at him and rip the smile off his face.

"Stay away from us," Karla said. "I thought you were weird yesterday, and I still think it."

The warning bell rang.

"Let's go in," Trudy said. "We don't want to get detention because of her."

"Maybe she'll set her house on fire and burn up her grand-mother, too," Stuart said.

His friends laughed as they started moving down the hall.

The three witches of *Macbeth* went into the classroom, but I couldn't move. The halls emptied and grew quiet. Visions of flames and the crackling sound of wood crumbling crossed my mind. I really couldn't move. Someone closed the door. A moment later, Mr. Madeo looked out at me and then came out, closing the door behind him.

"What is it, Saffron?" he asked. "Why don't you come into the classroom?"

"It's on fire," I said.

"What?"

"You had better get everyone out."

He just stared at me. I shook my head and then turned and ran all the way to the exit. I didn't stop running after I burst out, either. I ran and ran . . .

But I didn't run to Mazy's house. I turned and ran up the small hill to the railroad station. A train had just left. People who had arrived were walking quickly toward the village. I stopped to wait for them to go by, and then I walked slowly to the bench I had sat on years ago. It hadn't been moved or changed. Before I sat, I slipped off my backpack and put it beside the bench and just stared ahead.

Somewhere in the back of my mind, rising like a bubble from the deepest place, the thought emerged, and I recited it.

"Daddy's coming back for me for sure now. I'll just wait."

I don't know how much time passed. Another train arrived. People boarded it, and it left. The platform emptied, and it grew strangely quiet. I didn't hear a bird or a car horn. It was as if the world beyond was drifting away. It saddened me. It was a pretty day, with clouds here and there just the way I liked them, looking puffy and clean white. I didn't feel any breeze, nor did the leaves move on the trees. I so wanted to be part of the warm calmness, but I couldn't.

And then, as if nothing had happened since Daddy and I stepped off the train, Mazy appeared as she had that night. Only she did look a lot older, leaning forward even more as she walked. Shadows darkened under her eyes and made the wrinkles in her forehead look deeper. She wore a dark-blue sweater over her housecoat, and her black socks were gathered just above her ankles where they had slipped down her legs. She was wearing those same heavy black shoes with the big heels I recalled from that first night.

Her umbrella had really become her cane. She leaned on it as she stepped onto the platform. When she reached me, she put both hands on the handle and took deep breaths. She had obviously come quickly. Her bosom rose and fell. The strands of her gray hair rebelliously curled in every direction. There were beads of sweat on her forehead.

"Not as tough as you thought you were, huh?" She wasn't smiling, but she looked self-satisfied.

"Why do they hate me so much?"

"They don't hate you. They're afraid of you."

"Why?"

"You're different. You're unexpected. That frightens people, but especially children."

She looked around, as if she was surprised to be here herself.

"How did you find me?"

"I didn't have to go looking for you, Saffron. If you didn't come home, you'd go only to one other place. What better place to hope for an escape? You're still dreaming of that train."

She looked harder at me. I didn't even try to deny it.

"What did they exactly say that upset you so much?"

"They knew about the fire that killed my mother. Mrs. Elliot's secretary told people what you told Mrs. Elliot, that both my parents were killed and that I may or may not have started the fire."

"People love to elaborate when they spread gossip," she said. "A woman like that needs to have her tongue cut out."

"Are you going to complain about her?"

She shook her head. "That just keeps the chatter going. She'll deny it, anyway. Lying comes easy to busybodies. Who said all this to you?"

"Stuart Wiley."

"Ah. He's in pain, so he wants everyone else to be."

"He made it sound like you told Mrs. Elliot that because I felt responsible, I needed to be raised the way you raised me, homeschooled."

She nodded. The rush of blood and breath that had come into her cheeks faded. She looked more white with anger than flushed with red rage.

"I warned you they could be vicious and make up terrible stories."

"Did Daddy tell you that? Is that why he's never come for me?"

"Of course not. I told you to ignore them. Now your mind is filled with wild ideas."

I gazed down the tracks. "What if the train didn't stop here? What if it had stopped at a different station? What would have happened to me?"

"It didn't. Things occur for a reason we cannot first see or understand," she said. "Sometimes it takes a lifetime."

I looked up at her. Her eyes seemed more puffy, swollen.

"My instincts were right. I should have turned you away from that entrance and spared us both. I knew I should have waited before enrolling you."

"What? Why? I didn't do anything to make them afraid of me or hate me. And my teachers like me. I could see that."

"Why shouldn't they? Let's go home. We'll sleep on it."

"Maybe they don't hate me. Maybe you're right and they're afraid of me. But I hate them."

She nodded, looking pleased. "If that makes you stronger, then good," she said. "Come on."

She reached for my hand. For a moment, she looked like she didn't think I would take it.

"Maybe I'll go back tomorrow," I said. I was really talking more to myself than her now. "I shouldn't have run away. They're so happy I did, I'm sure."

She returned her hand to her umbrella. "If that's what you want, more pain, go back."

I rose. "I might. Don't try to stop me. I'm not afraid of more pain."

She raised her heavy, now mostly gray eyebrows. "I won't stop you if you're determined."

I thought about how they would all look at me if I went back, those wry, smug smiles. They'd try to make me feel like I was hiding behind my teachers, using them as shields. Couldn't I still beat them?

"I'll go back," I said, nodding.

She shrugged. "Yes, maybe you will. We'll see. C'mon. Let's go home."

We walked off the train platform. I did pause when it came time to make the turn to home, but only for a second. I could return now, I thought. I would simply walk into my next class and enjoy the look of shock on the faces of the three witches.

"Saffron?"

"They called you from school?"

"Of course."

"What did they say?" I asked as we continued.

"That you were upset and ran out. Your English teacher had gone to Mrs. Krammer. He was worried. You said something about his classroom being on fire."

"No, I didn't. Did I?"

"She didn't know much more, but she did go out to look for you. I promised to call her after I found you."

"I'm sure they're making fun of me right now because I ran away. I can almost hear the laughter."

"Stop thinking about it, Saffron."

"I'm just ashamed of myself. I should have told them off."

"That's good. Maybe you will," she said. She paused to catch her breath again. "Unfortunately, meanness comes with the territory."

"What territory?"

"Humanity," she muttered. She groaned. "I get so tired of it."

Vaguely, I thought as we walked along, Mazy was not as spry as usual. Did all this sicken her as much as it sickened me, or was it something else? She did tell me that anger and unhappiness give the pains in your body permission to sound off. The way she was walking looked like hers were screaming.

It did take us longer to get home, but when we did, she went right to the phone to call Mrs. Krammer.

"I found her," I heard her say. "She's fine. We'll see," she added after listening. I didn't have to ask her what she meant by that.

I went to my room. I was so upset with myself that I didn't even want Mr. Pebbles with me and shut the door. Mazy didn't come to get me for lunch. The excitement and tension had made me tired, and I fell asleep. When I awoke, I was confused for a few moments and then looked at my watch, saw how late it was, and got up. I washed my face with cold water and went to the kitchen. I was surprised Mazy wasn't there. A covered dish was on the table. She had left me some cold chicken and salad, but I wasn't very hungry.

She was not in the living room, so I walked up to her bedroom. The door was open. She was on her back, and there were no lights on, but she wasn't asleep. Mr. Pebbles was on her bed, curled up.

"Are you sick?" I asked.

"A little tired," she said. "I left you some lunch."

"I saw. Thank you."

Somehow this was all my fault, I thought.

"I'm sorry," I said.

She lifted her head a little and then lay back again.

"You have nothing to be sorry about. That's what they do. They always manage to get you to blame yourself."

I stood there looking at her. "Can I bring you anything? Tea?"

"No. You eat. I just need some rest. I'm not going to tell you what to do. If you want to go back tomorrow, go back. If not, we'll keep going and ignore them. You decide."

"Okay," I said. I left and returned to the kitchen, where I sat nibbling on my lunch. After I ate what I wanted, I started to clean up and then stopped and stared at the doorway.

Mr. Pebbles was standing there looking at me. I poured some cat food into his dish. I was surprised Mazy had forgotten. He walked to it cautiously, suspiciously, and sniffed. I watched him eat, and then I went out back and sat on one of the wooden lawn chairs in the yard. The forest looked deeper, darker, and suddenly not very enticing. I had wanted it to be my refuge, that escape Mazy had referred to at the train station. In it, I had hoped I could find another world for me, a magical place for new memories.

But suddenly, not now. Now it was just the forest.

I had never felt this lost and alone, even when Mazy first brought me here. She had been right, of course. Although I never wanted to admit it, even to myself, I knew Daddy wasn't ever going to come for me. Mazy never prevented me from leaving, and maybe because of that, I never tried to leave. What she did was provide a home for me, get me everything I needed, including a private education. She kept me protected for as long as she could, and when I felt the need to be with others my age, to have friends and maybe someday to love someone, she made that possible, too.

And yet somehow I felt as if by doing all this she had only locked me up more tightly. When she had found me at the train station, she had said, "If you didn't come home, you'd go only to one other place. What better place to hope for an escape?"

The key word was *hope*. She was right. I wasn't getting on any train. I didn't know where I would go. I could only come back here. There was no escape, not even in the woods now. Maybe if I returned to school tomorrow and faced down the ugliness and the threats, I would eventually find an escape. I'd break through, overwhelm them with my determination. Surely I would win over my teachers. I had a good start on that. Thinking this gave me some confidence, but was it enough? I'd know in the morning, I thought. I'd either get up and get dressed and go or go up to our private classroom.

Darkness was creeping in from the woods. It was cooler, too. I embraced myself and almost instantly remembered doing that at the train station just before Mazy had found me. It had been so long since I had thought about it, envisioned Daddy walking quickly away, his collar up, disappearing around the corner.

Odd, but it wasn't until this very moment, recalling that moment, that I remembered a feeling I never wanted to acknowledge. It was relief. Was it possible that I was glad he was gone?

I shuddered.

Did Mazy always know that?

I had brought a secret with me to this house, a secret I had even kept from myself.

But it belonged here.

It was coming home.

Why? What made this its home?

I would get on that train someday, but not until I had that answer.

Surely I would. Secrets can't keep secret. They don't exist unless someone else knows them.

I rose and went inside, half-expecting Mazy had come down. It wasn't long until dinner. Maybe helping to prepare it would take my mind off the decision I had to make. We would watch television and both go to bed unsure. What should we have? Should I put up some pasta?

I started upstairs and paused, realizing it was dark. Mazy hadn't turned on a light. Was she still asleep? I continued up slowly, quietly, and paused in her doorway. She was exactly as before, lying in bed, faceup. All this must have exhausted her as much as it did me, I thought. I'd just make dinner and come up when it was ready.

Getting everything prepared, doing our salad the way she liked, and working on a marinara sauce just the way she had taught me, kept me from thinking about what had happened. She would be proud of how well I had blended the tomatoes, tomato paste, chopped parsley, minced garlic, and oregano, with just enough salt and pepper. Every once in a while, I anticipated her standing there in the doorway, happily surprised.

I set the table and got the water ready for the pasta. I couldn't put it in until she came down, of course. Meanwhile, I stirred the sauce, let it simmer, and then prepared the garlic bread just the way she enjoyed it.

Suddenly, I stopped. I was so determined to have everything ready that I didn't realize something. Mr. Pebbles had not come down or come out of my room the way he always had when Mazy and I began dinner. She thought he liked to watch us work and smell the scent of good food.

I turned down the water and went to the doorway to listen. It was still dark upstairs. She would want me to wake her, I thought, and started up. When I was more than halfway, I paused, because an old dream image flashed across my mind. It was Daddy walking up the stairs, his hands cupped together, the small flame emerging from his palms. I felt a chill and hurried up the remainder of the stairway, this time practically bursting into Mazy's room.

Nothing was different.

"Mazy?" I said. She never slept this long in the daytime. I started toward her bed and then stopped. "Mazy?"

Her eyes were wide open. How could she sleep with her eyes wide open?

I inched forward and reached for her arm. It was cold, stiff. My heart was skipping beats.

"Mazy, wake up!" I cried, and I shook her. Her lips were slightly apart.

Before touching her again or saying anything, I turned on the lamp at her bedside. Her cheeks looked swollen, and her eyes were like the marbles I remembered circling Mama's flowerpot. I reached out to take her hand. The fingers were stiff and cold. It was only then that I saw Mr. Pebbles lying at her feet. He raised his head to look at her and then me and lowered his head again.

The cold that was in her hand and her arm seemed to travel quickly through my body as well. Then my heart felt like it was sizzling. Absolute fear overcame any feeling of sadness, but I was crying. I was finally crying the way that little girl should have been crying on the train-station bench years ago. It was almost the same fear, only this time there was no hope. Mazy would not be coming around the corner swinging her black umbrella.

More to drive home reality than anything else, I turned on the bedroom ceiling light. Mr. Pebbles took that as some sort of signal and leaped off the bed. He stood there looking up at me, and then he walked out the doorway. I drew close to the bed again. I was actually afraid to touch her face. I didn't want to feel death. For me, it was something that had gone up in smoke.

Thankfully, I didn't have to or couldn't look at Mama. I wasn't able to look at Lucy or even the first and second Mr. Pebbles.

"What am I supposed to do?" I asked Mazy. Mr. Pebbles knew what to do. He went down to the kitchen. Of course, that was what he would do. "Everything is ready for dinner," I said. "I'll just put in the pasta. I'll stir and wait between two and three minutes, just as you showed me."

It seemed so odd, maybe so wrong, to turn away, leave the lights on, and go down to finish the dinner, but I did. And as I had expected, Mr. Pebbles was there waiting and watching.

"Maybe she'll wake up," I told him. "Maybe the aroma of the sauce will drive death away, Mr. Pebbles."

He sat so patiently. Was he wise or totally empty of any thought and feeling, sort of how Mazy was right now?

I continued, and when it was ready, I put it all in the bowl, brought it to the table, and then brought the bread and the jug of cold water. I sat and looked across the table. It was easy to imagine Mazy there; she was always there.

"I hope you like it," I said, starting on my salad. "It's doing what you always like, still cooking in the dish."

I served myself some.

Eating and pretending kept fear down at my feet.

"Yes, I know," I said, as if I had just heard her say it. "Do it right, and you don't need to hope. It tastes good to me."

It did taste good.

"I think this is the best I ever made," I said. I looked down at

Mr. Pebbles. "Okay, you get a taste," I said, and put some in his dish. He went right at it and then, smacking his lips, looked up at me. "It's good, I know."

I continued eating.

And then suddenly, as if reality came rushing in from all directions, I stopped and vomited just about everything I had eaten. I sat there, catching my breath, and then rose and walked back to the stairway, battling back the pain in my stomach. It was as if I had been rehearsing this for as long as I had been here. I walked up the stairs, went into Mazy's room, avoided looking at her, and went right to the drawer in the nightstand on the left side of her bed. I sifted through it until I saw the ring of three keys I had seen in her hands many times and plucked them out quickly. Still, without looking at her, I went to the closet and found the key that would unlock the top drawer.

There was a dark cherry wood box in it. A second key on the ring unlocked it. I carried it out without glancing at Mazy and went directly to the classroom, turned on the lights, and sat at my desk.

I unfolded the first paper on top.

It was a letter. My eyes went right to the bottom, where it was signed *Derick*. I took a deep breath and began to read.

> *Dear Mazy,*
> *Over the years I occasionally joked that there would be a time when I would ask a favor of you. That time might come soon.*

From the first time when you contacted me, I was quite obliging. I kept our correspondence secret as you had requested. My and Lindsey's parents never knew a thing about this.

I vividly remember the day Lindsey learned she had been adopted. Our parents had waited until she was twelve. I think it was more my mother's idea than my father's to do it then. She was more involved with her, of course, and thought when she was approaching adolescence it would be wise to reveal it all.

Lindsey had many questions about you, but my parents, my mother especially, wanted you to be more of a shadow. Maybe she was afraid of losing Lindsey's love. Whatever her reasons, my father went along with them, and Lindsey only knew that you had to give her up for adoption. The story was that even you didn't know who her father was. I never told her anything I knew from the papers I had discovered and read.

It was quite shocking and traumatic for her. That was when she and I grew even closer, probably. It seemed to free us of so many restrictions and inhibitions, and as I told you in a previous letter, we did make love when she was seventeen. To be honest, I didn't think we'd go on like that. When I graduated and went into the army, we certainly drifted farther apart. I thought she'd find a boyfriend in college, too.

As you know, when I was discharged and started working, Lindsey was in her last year. When our parents were killed shortly before she graduated, we lived together for a while, and then finally, when she became pregnant, married and moved on.

If you look back at some of my correspondence, you will see my concerns over her stability and our relationship, so this shouldn't come as a total shock. I have found someone else who keeps me sane through all this, and when the time is right, if I think it's something that could last, I will let Lindsey know my intentions. Maybe then it would be good for her to have this sort of contact with you, at least.

For now, let's just wait to see. Saffron seems quite enough for her at the moment.

I'll call soon with something of an update.

Hope you are well,

Derick

I folded the letter and sat trying to digest what I had just read.

Mazy really was my grandmother. My father and mother were once brother and sister, although not related by blood. Everything I had been told about my grandparents wasn't true. When I thought about it now, I realized how many ways and times Mazy had tried to tell me who she really was. The lie that I had thought was just another tool was the truth.

As I sat there thinking about her in the next room, I realized that knowing this didn't make much difference. In my heart and mind, she was my grandmother. I couldn't love her more.

I started to sift through the remaining pages and stopped as soon as I saw the special delivery envelope. Very carefully, I plucked out the letter. It was quite wrinkled, suggesting Mazy had taken it out and read it many times before refolding it and putting it back in the envelope.

> *Dear Mazy,*
>
> *Tragedy has struck us in a most terrible way. Things had reached the point where Lindsey and I were practically strangers sharing the same house and child. I am guilty of avoiding the truth, becoming that famous ostrich who buries his head in the sand. There was probably more I could have done, but I was simply overwhelmed. I believe the one who has suffered the most from all this is not me, not Lindsey, but Saffron.*
>
> *I stopped being her father, really. I let what happened happen. As a result, Saffron is at quite a disadvantage when compared to other children her age. A great deal of remedial work has to be done, and I'm*

simply not capable of it now. Maybe I never was. It's quite heart-crushing. Once she really was Daddy's Little Girl. At least I have the memory.

To come right to the point of this special delivery letter, Lindsey caused a fire to start last night. I was sleeping in a separate room by now. I heard Saffron's scream and leaped out of bed. Lindsey, who was on serious anxiety medication, was dead to the world. I rushed out, scooped up some of Saffron's things, and managed to get us both out of a burning building that was already far gone. There was no way to go back for Lindsey. I'm sorry.

The truth is, I'm too distraught to continue here. I've decided I have to start anew, and I'd like now for you to return that favor.

Saffron and I will be on the three o'clock train that will stop in Hurley about eight. You will find her on a bench at the station, waiting for me to return so we can take another train. There is no other train, and I will not return.

You've always been so interested in your grand-daughter. You will have her now, and I'm sure you will be able to give her the home and education she will need to compete in the future.

I will, from time to time, be in touch, but for now,
and perhaps for some time, it's better that I remain a
man still traveling on a train.

> *Thank you,*
> *Derick*

I folded the letter and put it back in the box.

I thought I really didn't have to read it. I knew it. But there was a sentence in it that drove the cold, sharp pain even deeper.

I did not scream.

EPILOGUE

There were more letters, all much shorter. I sifted through them and read the things Mazy had told me. She hadn't lied about it. My father had kept her dangling on his promises just the way she had first described. The only thing she had hidden from me was his address. It wasn't on many of the envelopes, but it was on two. Maybe he hadn't realized it. Maybe he thought it no longer mattered.

Under it all, there were two neatly stacked piles of money wrapped in rubber bands. One stack was all twenties, and the other was all fifties. There was a thick envelope that contained Mazy's will. It had been relatively recently rewritten, with me the sole beneficiary. Thanks to how hard Mazy had pushed me on reading and vocabulary, I understood it all. I was sure most of the kids I had met at school would not.

There was one more envelope I wanted to open. On the outside was written *Photos*.

There were at least three dozen of them, capturing my mother from when she wasn't much older than I was now until she first married my father. In all the pictures, she looked happy. It was a smile I barely remembered, but it was easy to see the resemblances between her and me. The very last picture was of her holding me when I was probably no more than six months or so. I thought her smile in that one was her brightest and happiest.

For a few moments, I sat back and thought about what it was like for Mazy to see these pictures. There was nothing written that would tell me how or why she gave up my mother for adoption. She had once told me she had been pregnant. I remembered asking her if she had ever had someone inside her.

"Yes," she had said. "But it was sad." I thought she meant her baby had died. I imagined that was the way she liked to think of her in the beginning. It was clear from my father's letters and the pictures that she wanted to know more and more about the baby she had given away.

Did my father do a good thing by being in touch with her and telling her about my mother?

There was no question what he wanted from her in return.

I returned to Mazy's room and her closet, barely looking at her. At the back of the closet were some luggage bags. I took the smallest one and went out and down to my room. Poor Mr. Pebbles followed me and watched as I chose clothes and shoes and neatly packed them all in the bag. I went to the bathroom and gathered the toiletries I wanted. I moved quietly, slowly, carefully, but like one in a hypnotic spell. Occasionally, I paused to fight back tears.

When I thought I had everything I wanted and needed, I went into the kitchen to search through some notes Mazy had jotted for her own memory and found the telephone number I wanted. I stuck it in my jacket pocket. I had put on the new jacket Mazy had bought me for school. I stood there thinking about the dishes and the mess on the table.

Can't leave it like this, I thought, and quickly went about cleaning up, putting dishes in the dishwasher, and bundling the garbage. I took it out to the garbage can the way I always did and then returned to inspect the kitchen once more. Mr. Pebbles, who had heard the commotion, had returned and was lying by my seat at the table.

"Someone will look after you," I said, and started up the stairs.

As I went up, I imagined that I had overreacted, imagined it all. When I looked in Mazy's room now, I thought, she would be sitting up, grinding the sleep out of her eyes with her small, age-spotted hands, and then she would look at me with an expression of complete surprise.

"What on earth? Where do you think you're going?" she would ask. "You have homework to do, and besides, I don't recall our eating dinner."

She'd gaze to her right and look at me angrily.

"Why is the drawer in my closet unlocked and open? What have you done?"

"Exactly what you would have done," I would say.

She would laugh. She'd know I was right.

I imagined it all before I entered her bedroom. She wasn't sitting up, of course. I sat with my back to her. Then, although I knew how it would feel, I reached for her hand and held it.

"Sometimes I hated you," I said. I wasn't looking at her. "I'd go to sleep dreaming of running away, especially during the early days. I often fantasized about returning to the train station and finding Daddy there, of course. I knew how much that irritated you when I said it.

"I don't think I ever left the house, with you or without you, without expecting to see my father appear. He'd be walking up the street, wearing the same coat he wore when he left me, even in midsummer.

"'Sorry,' he'd say. I wouldn't care about the reason or reasons. I'd just take his hand and walk off with him.

"Funny how after a while, that dream made me feel guilty. After all, you were the one left behind, sometimes just standing there in the front of the house shaking your head. I didn't even say good-bye.

"And the truth is, you didn't even say good-bye."

I turned to look at her.

"I wonder how often you looked at me and saw something of yourself. You did a good job of keeping that secret. I think the reason you took me places and eventually enrolled me in school was so you could claim to be who you really were, my grandmother.

"I wish we could have talked about all this now. I wish you had told me everything and I could ask you about your pain and suffering. Maybe you would have soon."

I saw that Mr. Pebbles had come up and was standing in the bedroom doorway.

"Everyone thinks the real sadness is dying, but the real sadness is carried by those you leave. Poor Mr. Pebbles," I said.

I let go of her hand.

"You know what you never said to me and I never said to you, Mazy? I love you. Is there enough of you left to hear me say it?

"He shouldn't have left me at the station, but if he hadn't, I never would have known you. Do all bad things have something good in them? Maybe I'll find out for the both of us."

I didn't want to look at her glassy eyes. I kept my back to her all the way out the door. Mr. Pebbles stayed behind, as if he knew he should. I hurried down the stairs, grabbed my bag the way Daddy had grabbed his case on the way out of our burning house. This house was burning in a way, too.

It was as dark as it had become the first night Mazy had led me to her home. The same lights were dim, the same shadows thickening. I hurried along, glancing at Lucy's house. Stuart was probably enjoying a phone call at my expense. Maybe a real Tree Girl would come along and touch him with a branch.

I laughed—giggled, actually—and picked up my pace. Minutes later, I turned up the hill to the station. It was still open, so I knew I was right. I showed the ticket teller the address.

"Well, your train is in only ten minutes or so. You get off there. It's bigger than Hurley, but I don't think you'll have too much trouble finding it or getting a taxi."

"Thank you," I said, and gave him the money. Then I got change for the phone. He told me it was an antique.

"Who uses a pay phone these days?" he asked, laughing.

"Mazy and I do," I said. I unfolded the note from the kitchen drawer and called the number. I said, "Hello, Mrs. Miller," as soon as she answered. "I'm calling to tell you Mazy Dazy needs you."

"What's that?"

"Please check in on her. And take care of Mr. Pebbles. I left the front door unlocked," I said.

"Is this—"

"Thank you," I said quickly, and hung up.

Then I went out and sat on the bench. I reached into my bag. There was something I had taken and shoved in it, something Mazy had kept in her closet and never told me about, reminded me of, or anything.

It was my coloring book. The crayons were there, too. And there were still some pictures to complete.

Follow Saffron's journey in

OUT OF THE RAIN

By V.C. Andrews®

Available from Gallery and Pocket Books!

Keep reading for a sneak peek . . .

CHAPTER ONE

There were a little more than a dozen or so people on the last train leaving Hurley when I boarded that night my grandmother died. Only two other people had gotten on with me, both strangers. We had two stops along the way before I would reach the town in which my father now lived a new life with a new family. By the time I stepped off the train, there was only one other passenger left, a young woman with light-brown hair. My imagination played tricks on me because sometimes she resembled my mother. I imagined her turning and smiling at me, telling me I was doing the right thing.

Although I had never revealed it to Mazy, I had memorized the entire train schedule, even where I could make connections to continue north, south, or west, because I didn't know what my exact destination eventually would be until I had found the secret letters my father had sent to her. However, this trip was always out there like a promise dangling. Maybe it was a fantasy most of the time, but I believed that someday, just as my father had done, I would continue the journey to a new home and a new life.

After I had boarded and sat, no one gave me more than a passing glance before returning to his or her reading, texting, or sleeping. To everyone else, there was probably nothing unusual about my appearance, even though I felt like I was exploding with anticipation. My face felt on fire. I imagined that the excitement in my eyes had turned them into hot coals brightening and fading, brightening and fading, with every breath and every heartbeat. Why didn't anyone else see it? Or did the sight of me upset them so much that they had to look away?

Although there was central lighting and anyone who wanted it had a light above his or her seat, darkness soon seemed to be seeping in like water in a sinking ship as the train continued on its route, every bolt, screw, and wheel locked in its predestined journey, just like me. It could never leave the tracks, it could never turn around before its final station, and it could never simply stop before a set location. I had to go where it would lead me and do what I had to do. Mazy had died; my mysterious grandmother had died. The train whistle had sounded. The future was out there, hovering like a hawk, waiting to pounce on me and take me to my fate. Meanwhile, as the car rocked gently, soothingly, I could feel myself drifting back through time.

The moment I closed my eyes, it was as if everything that

had happened between my original train ride with my father and my ride now was truly imaginary. As long as I kept my eyes tightly shut, I could feel him sitting beside me, even smell the fragrance of his aftershave, despite how long ago that was. There are scents that are embedded forever in your memory. For me, his aftershave was one of them, but no odor was stronger in my mind than the painful, bitter smell of smoke coming from our house fire.

Despite all the years I had taken care of Mazy's fireplace and sat with her in front of those dancing flames, it really never became comfortable, nor did the sharp pain in my lungs and heart diminish. Flames, no matter where I saw them, would always be frolicking in glee, even a tiny one on a birthday candle.

Daddy and I had said so little to each other on the train that day. He had fallen asleep first. I could hear his soft inhales and exhales. That rhythmic sound was enough to help me fall asleep, too. I felt safe again. Until we had left, every day, almost every moment of every day, I had lived below bruised, angry clouds that rumbled long after the night of our tragedy. However, no one, not even Daddy, seemed to hear them. The rumbling was there only for me, even if there wasn't a cloud in the sky. I was trapped in the surrounding flames and deafened by the high-pitched scream constantly in my ears. The moment I began to stand still, no matter where we were, I started to tremble. My lips felt like they were bubbling. I was living in a shell with spidery thin cracks that was threatening to shatter and fall at my feet, leaving me as naked and alone as a baby born and left in the cold, dark night.

Despite how calm I might have appeared to a stranger back then, inside, the real me was crying hysterically for my mother. When I looked at other people, I was surprised they didn't hear me. They smiled at me, held my hand, and couched their words carefully in expressions of compassion and hope. Their assurances fell into distant echoes. How could everything ever again be all right? After a while, I didn't hear them at all. I might as well have been deaf.

When Daddy had told me we were leaving to start a new life, I unashamedly felt joy. We were escaping from the darkness, maybe from those flames in my memory, too. Because I was so young, I had believed we would just go a little ways and every terrible thing that had occurred would disappear. I recall even thinking that maybe Mama would be waiting for us. That her survival of the house fire had been kept secret. After we had stepped off the train, no matter where we were, she would be standing there waiting. The smile I remembered would be back where it belonged, nestled on her face, brightening her eyes and filling her lips. I'd rush into her arms, and the three of us would walk off into a scene as happy as the last scene of *The Wizard of Oz*. We'd be holding hands and laughing as if everything horrible that had occurred was now only a bad dream. Everyone has bad dreams. Why couldn't that be true for me? Couldn't someone say, "You're safely back in Kansas, Saffron"?

When Daddy had left me at the Hurley train station, filling out figures in my new coloring book with new crayons, I never doubted that he would come back for me after he had bought some of our necessities, and then we would take the next train to our new home. The speed with which he walked off, practically ran off, convinced me that he didn't want to leave me alone for too long. I actually was proud at the start, delighted that he would consider me old enough to be by myself in a strange place, even though I knew in my heart that my mother would be furious at him for doing so.

Thinking back to it now, I suspect that Mazy, the elderly lady who had suddenly appeared and turned out to be my real grandmother, deliberately had waited until the train station was deserted and I was alone. If she had appeared earlier, while trains and people were still going to and fro, I would never have taken her hand and permitted her, a total stranger at the time, to lead me away to her home and her lonely life. Time, the realization that Daddy wasn't returning for me, and the chill of darkness had to embrace me first.

After Mazy had taken me in and after days and then weeks had passed, I grew more skeptical of her true intentions, but she was very methodical, cleverly answering every one of my questions and seemingly honest about her efforts to reunite me with my father. She drove back my doubts almost as soon as they had occurred.

Now when I recall those early days, I realize that her experience and training as a grade-school teacher had enabled her to ease me into a new reality, with the main realization being that my father really had deserted me. She'd had to lower me into the truth the way a parent would lower her child into a very warm bath. Even so, what child could live with that revelation? Where could he or she ever find self-respect after having been discarded with maybe not so much as an afterthought?

Daddy's one saving grace was that everything had been pre-arranged, even as heartbreaking as that was to realize. At least, I eventually learned that he didn't out-and-out desert me and just leave me dangling in the unwelcoming night. Mazy had lost her daughter, my mother, when she had given her up for adoption practically the same moment she had been born—and my father's parents had brought him and my mother up in the same home—but Mazy could and would enjoy her granddaughter. My father had seen to that with his secret correspondence with her.

As the train carried me farther and farther away from Mazy and the life she had tried to make for me, I felt deep sadness for her and the pain she had kept hidden in her heart most of her life. Despite the way she had encouraged me to keep hoping my father would return for me, especially in the very begin-ning, I bore her no resentment and, in the end, blamed her for nothing. In her own way, everything she had done to keep me isolated and protected was born out of her own guilt over giv-ing up her daughter, despite how difficult it would have been for an unmarried woman to raise a child with no visible means of supporting herself at the time. That night when she led me to her house from the train station, she finally was doing it. I was to be her redeeming light. How could I fault her for that?

Mazy was possessive and domineering, for sure, but her intense need to weave her love and her worldly knowledge into me drove her to hover over me, spreading her wings like an angel, to be sure no one would harm me. She wanted to be certain that I'd be well prepared to do battle in this world, for that was how she saw it . . . filled with a constant series of challenges and conflicts. It had made her quite bitter. Countless times she told me that if I listened to her, I would be strong enough to survive and happily so. It got so I feared stepping out of the door on my own, even if simply to play in the backyard.

The proof that she had prepared me well lay just ahead in a whirlwind of what I expected would be major challenges even for someone twice my age. Both mentally and physically exhausted from my stream of memories and all I had just done to effectuate a good and safe escape after Mazy had died, I welcomed the deep sleep during the trip. Just as on that first train ride years ago, this train's slowing and coming to a stop at the station I wanted was what woke me. When I sat up and looked out the window, I felt like an astronaut gazing out at a new planet.

The young woman I imagined resembling my mother did not disembark, and when I walked by her and she looked at me, I saw she was nowhere as pretty as my mother was. There were no passengers waiting to board. The train lingered like a great beast catching its breath. Being alone on the train platform when I stepped off made it all seem more like a recurring dream. Was I really here?

This train station was cleaner and more up-to-date than mine at Hurley. I was both happy and angry that I didn't have to travel too far, just a little over two and a half hours. I wondered whether my father had taken this exact trip in the opposite direction from time to time to catch sight of me. Was he ever on our street waiting for a glimpse of the little girl he had left behind? Did Mazy alert him ahead of time when we would be in the village so he could stand in some storefront and look at us passing by? I wanted to believe that. I wanted to imagine that he still harbored some love, some curiosity, and still possessed something of any father's need to know his own child.

But I wasn't completely convinced he would welcome me now with open arms. Before I had left, I had read all his secret letters to Mazy and looked at the pictures of my mother as a child and then as a woman, a mother herself, pictures he had sent to my grandmother. Even as a very young girl, I had spent hours and hours trying to understand why he would have deserted me in the first place. The letters explained so much, but most of what he had written had stunned me and left me cold. Now I suspected that he had been planning to transfer me into Mazy's care for a long time, perhaps even before the fire. He had kept his intentions hidden that well. But even if there were clues, why would I have noticed and read into them back then?

Whom can you trust more than your own father and

mother? Who did you least expect would betray you? There wasn't a hint in his eyes or in his voice to warn me he was going to do just that when we had started out on the train that fateful day. For so long, I would wonder why he didn't want me with him. Buried deeply in my heart and mind was the realization that leaving me behind couldn't only have been for the reason he had given to Mazy in his letters, his desire to repair her loss. But why would he make such a sacrifice for someone he barely had known? He had to have had other reasons. And besides, why ignore my losses and what the desertion would do to me? I read no lines of regret about that in those letters. There were no apologies to be given to me, and no expressions of any worries for my emotional well-being.

That only reinforced the dark places in my heart and the ugly answers hanging like bats in a cave, answers to questions that I had always fought against exploring. Wasn't it Mazy who told me, "You never ask a question for which you don't want an answer. There is much truth to the adage 'Ignorance is bliss'"?

None of this denied that my early life had its moments of sunshine, but mainly before my father and mother had become more like strangers to each other and my mother had fallen into a deep depression. Images and parts of sentences between them lingered in the air filled with static, all of it threatening to connect and then eventually force me to realize the truth, a truth a little girl my age was unable to face or admit at the time. It meant that the bond between my mother and father, the bond that keeps a child feeling safe, was already shattered. Much of who and what they had become to each other had really gone up in smoke with that fire.

What was left of love and tenderness before the first spark leaped out? Where did the wind carry the ashes of all the anger and unhappiness? What greater horror lay in waiting out there? What monster, uglier than any I could imagine, sneered and clawed the ground, anticipating its opportunity to seize me and destroy what little remained of faith and love? I would soon know.

Nightmares had become more like movie trailers, snippets of the terrifying reality that had my name across its forehead. But I had little choice. I had to head toward it like someone driving on a road that she knew would end at a cliff. How long would the fall take? Would there be anything left, any reason to continue? Perhaps that was the biggest, most pressing question of all. Even if I found a hint of love, it would pale in the presence of what had happened, what had been real and not imagined. Could I live with it? The simple questions that followed me off the train were: Did any of what I was hoping to find matter? Did family matter? Did everything Mazy had done for me matter under the shadow of all that?

Did knowing who you really were matter?

Was I in a different shell, and should I bother to emerge?

I almost turned around and crossed the platform to take a train going in the opposite direction. If I didn't continue to go forward, I would never have to confront those answers. "Ignorance is bliss," Mazy had told me, but could I really live on without knowing these answers? I feared the questions would haunt me forever.

I stood there, indecisive. The train that had brought me started away. There was another choice. I was tempted to rush back on and continue into the unknown, go on and on. I felt like a deepsea diver who, after she had jumped from the edge of a cliff, wondered in midair if she should have. But I didn't return to the train.

No, I told myself. *It's far too late to change your mind, Saffron. Let yourself keep falling.*

In the end, what kept me going wasn't a young girl's need for love or truth or justice. My motives weren't that noble. Truthfully, where else could I go now? There were no family friends, no living relatives. I had a fake birth certificate, but what kind of a life could I have alone?

What had brought me here was just a brutal need to survive first and a hope for restoration of any family, any love, second. In no sense was I coming home, no matter how I wished and pretended I was. Living with Mazy had made it more difficult to lie to myself. Because she wouldn't tolerate deception in any form, I found it distasteful, too.

I walked slowly off the train platform to a taxi parked nearby. The driver had his bushy, gray-haired head back and his mouth wide open, looking more like someone who had just died. He did resemble who I imagined to be someone's grandpa driving a cab. Mazy once told me that older people show their age the most when they sleep. I thought about Shakespeare's line in his sonnet about getting older, "Death's second self." Mazy had been amazed when I ruminated about it, and I asked, "Isn't every sleep a taste of what's to come?"

That day, she had stared at me hard before she said the strangest thing. "I'm sorry you're so intelligent, Saffron. You'll suffer more."

"Should I stop reading?" I asked, terrified.

She laughed. "Not for an instant," she said, smiling.

I tapped on the window, and the driver stirred, realized where he was and what was happening, and jumped up instantly. He rolled his window down and said, "Hey. Sorry, missy."

I gave him the address and got into the back of the taxi. The moment I did, he started to talk, beginning with why he had fallen asleep. I smiled to myself listening to how guilty he felt. If he had only known the forest of guilt through which I had come, he would laugh at his meager shame.

"This is the last train stoppin' at Sandburg Creek," he said. "Most of the time, no one gets off, or if they do, someone is waitin' for 'em, but I can't afford to miss a possible fare. Still, ya'd think a girl as young as you would have someone waitin' for her. I tell ya, the risks parents take with their children in this day and age are astoundin'."

I'm really not that young, I wanted to tell him. *Your real age is inside you because of what life has done to you.* But I didn't want to get into any deep discussions. I was still trembling.

"I have the last shift, so I see what goes on. Kids no older than you, and girls especially, are wanderin' the streets in the early mornin' hours. Who knows where they came from or where they're goin'? Who's checkin' ta see if they ever came home? For a lot of 'em, I bet no one.

"I'm not married and don't have no children, but it doesn't take much ta realize that's bad. So where ya been, missy?"

"Away," I said, looking anxiously at the houses we were passing. They were bigger than the ones in Hurley, with more elaborate landscaping. The streets were wider, too. There were pruned medians and modernized, stronger lights, making the macadam glitter as if there was a thin layer of ice over them. Here and there were wooden benches.

It was still early enough in the evening for windows in all the homes to be well lit. Traffic was light in both directions. I saw people walking dogs and talking in the early evening. The taxi driver was right. Girls as young as I, if not younger, walked with older kids who poked and teased each other playfully. Others about my age were walking with their parents. It looked like a dream world, the idyllic community Mazy would describe as a Norman Rockwell painting. He was her favorite artist. People were laughing and looked friendly in many of his pictures that captured rural scenes. Was this that world? Could there really be one? Was I too desperate to believe a place like this existed? I was afraid of hope. I knew too much disappointment.

"Ya live here in Sandburg Creek, right?" the driver asked. "Or are ya visitin' someone?"

"I'm coming home," I said. It was noncommittal enough for him to look at me in his rearview mirror.

"How long have ya been away?"

Was he writing a book? This was my first taxi ride. Were all taxi drivers this talkative and nosy? The silence in my hesitation was uncomfortable, even for me.

"A while," I said. "I am in a private school," I added to hopefully shut him up. In a true sense, I had been in a private school with Mazy, not that it mattered too much to me that I might lie to a taxi driver.

"Oh. Well, welcome home," he said, turning onto a new block.

I caught the house numbers. This was my father's neighborhood. All the homes had good-sized plots of land, so they weren't on top of each other. They weren't modern in style. Most of them were Queen Anne, more reason to believe I was in a Norman Rockwell painting. It felt as if I had dropped through time to a place where people might still leave their houses and cars unlocked. Strangers were people to be curious about and not to be suspected of some evil intention. Lights that looked like candles flickered in windows. Maybe mothers and fathers were with their children watching television, the way Mazy and I had done. Perhaps that was what my father was doing right at this moment, never dreaming he would be seeing me in his doorway.

Now that I was really going to ring his doorbell, what made me tremble inside was the idea of not only confronting him but of meeting his new wife and his new children. I finally faced the thought, the frightening thought, that I had a new family. What would they see when they looked at me? How much did they know? I wasn't just carrying some of my clothes in a small bag; I was bringing along a horrific past. The flames would be snapping and crackling right beside me. Maybe he had told them that I had died in the fire, too. When he and his family saw me, they might all chant it together: "You can't come here; you don't belong here. You're dead; you're gone, forgotten." They would probably be more frightened of me than I of them.

If so, where did I belong now? Would I join the homeless whom Mazy and I had seen on television news? Would I live in shadows, covered in the filth of the street? Would I die in some alley like a scrawny cat, scratching at the approaching image of death with its smile full of sharp, yellow teeth and its eyes swimming in cold glee? In a few more minutes, my whole life would be decided. Dare I breathe?

As the taxi began slowing down, I wondered if I ever could be more terrified and my body ever more frozen in fear than it was at this moment.

We stopped in front of one of the larger houses. It was a brick three-story with a veranda and an octagonal extension on the right and a three-story octagonal tower on the left. A half dozen matching brick steps led up to the front entrance at the center of the house's wide veranda. My father's home was easily almost three times the size of Mazy's house. Even though there was no one on the veranda, it was well lit. The lawn looked more like a rich, dark pool of green soaking in the light. Well-pruned roses grew close to the veranda, hugging its shadows. On the right was a dark-pewter fountain with a sculptured little boy and girl under an umbrella, off which the water flowed back into the bowl.

An umbrella, I thought, remembering the first time I had seen Mazy with hers and how she wouldn't walk out of the house without it, rain or shine. I would never look at one, even in a picture, without thinking of her immediately.

"Wow. Nice house," the driver said. "Yer family live here long? What's yer father do? Is he a doctor or somethin'?"

"How much?" I replied, as if I hadn't heard a word.

"Nine-fifty will do it."

I gave him a ten and opened the door slowly.

"Say," he said. "Really. How come nobody met ya at the station?"

"I'm not supposed to be here yet," I said, smiling. *Lies as tools*, I thought, remembering how Daddy once had explained why sometimes a lie was okay. "It's a surprise."

"Oh. Gotcha."

I closed the door before he could ask anything else. He watched me in his rearview mirror until I walked around and started down the cobblestone walkway to the stairs. He didn't drive off until I was nearly there. I could hear the television in the house, some comedy show with its usual canned laughter. Visions of Mazy smiling when she and I had sat together to watch television gave me some courage.

You're his daughter, I thought. *You're his daughter*, I chanted. *He can't turn you away.*

But what would he do? a little voice inside whispered. *He turned you away once, didn't he?*

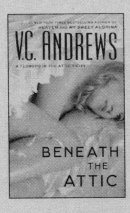
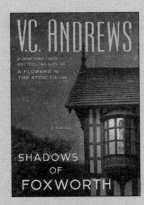
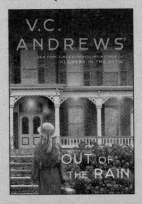

Learn more about the woman who took us to the heights of a secluded attic and the depths of our own dark psyches in

The Woman Beyond the Attic

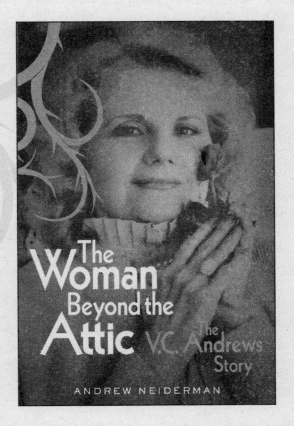

Available wherever books are sold or at SimonandSchuster.com